SHE WAS WRAPPED IN A WHITE HOTEL TOWEL, FRESH FROM THE SHOWER, HER FACE RADIANT, HER BODY EAGER, WAITING . . .

Joe hung up the phone. "I'm sorry, Karen. I have to go."

Her eyes registered shock, then she struggled to hold back her tears.

"Your wife's a psychologist," she choked. "Ask her something for me. What does it mean when you ache all through your childhood because your father's never there? Then you grow up and have a husband who's never there, so you take one lover after another who's also never there. Is there a name for it? Besides stupid?"

He was already half dressed, but he reached out to take her in his arms. "Look, he said softly, I'll stay."

"No! Go!" she cried, thrusting him away, running toward the bathroom door. "Go! Your goddamned country is calling."

The Seduction of Joe Tynan

RICHARD COHEN

A DELL BOOK

Published by
Dell Publishing Co., Inc.
1 Dag Hammarskjold Plaza
New York, New York 10017

Dell ® TM 681510, Dell Publishing Co., Inc.

ISBN: 0-440-17610-7

Printed in the United States of America
Published simultaneously in Canada
First printing—August 1979

CHAPTER 1

From around the corner of the hallway the sound of heels echoed off the polished marble floors of the Dirksen Senate Office Building. It sounded like a small army moving fast. In the middle of the group, heading for the floor of the United States Senate and what might be a real pasting, was the junior senator from the State of New York, Joseph Tynan—politician, husband, father, Rotarian, and Odd-Fellow by virtue of honorary inductions, and author of the public works bill which, momentarily, was going to go right down the tubes.

"What are we here for gentlemen?" Tynan said to himself, practicing his speech as the group moved down the hall. "Are we here for the six million unemployed? No. That's not right is it, Ken? How many million unemployed are there, Ken?"

"Six million, give or take," said Ken Rothenberg, Tynan's legislative assistant.

"Give or take what?"

"Give or take another million."

As usual the senator was dressed in a dark, three-piece suit and as usual his hair was cut so that he looked just one day short of needing a haircut and as usual his face was glowing with good health—"Not much improvement needed here," the makeup lady for *Meet the Press* had recently told him. He was six feet four inches tall, well-built, in a lean way, attractive, but not pretty—saved from that fate by a nose that bulbed a bit at the end. That bulb, someone had said, was worth fifty thousand votes.

Tynan continued to work his speech. "Are we here for the four million children who go without lunch each day? Four million? Ken. Is that right?"

"Right!"

In his hand, Joe Tynan held a deck of large index cards. It was his speech. He almost never wrote out a speech. He believed that written speeches sounded stilted in the age of television—that they had gone out, as he once said, with "the Cross of Gold and the rest of that shit." Instead, Joe outlined his speeches on index cards. Sometimes he began in what had been the middle and sometimes he turned the speech on its head and began with the ending. It always sounded like a new speech. He learned the technique, he said, from Ronald Reagan. "Ronald Reagan almost became President with one speech," Joe was fond of saying. "If he had another speech he probably could have gone all the way."

The group stopped before an elevator marked SEN-ATORS ONLY. They were on the second floor of the Dirksen Senate Office Building. Along with the Richard Brevard Russell Office Building, it was where the nation's one hundred senators maintained their public Washington offices—the offices where tourists and constituents alike flocked.

The elevator arrived and they all piled in. With Tynan was his administrative assistant, Francis O'Connor, a lawyer out of St. John's in New York, half Irish and half Italian, with the Italian showing in his complexion. He was thirty-three years old and what he did was run Tynan's senate office and just maybe his life as well. Also in the elevator was Ken Rothenberg, the senator's legislative aide—short, paunchy, balding before his time, twenty-nine years of age but the sort of fellow who looked like he had never been a kid. He was brilliant but dull, dressed always in the same gray suit, white button-down shirt, and maroon tie. There was a joke in the office that he had seven of the same suits; in fact, he had only three. He spoke as the elevator plunged to the basement.

"We're down six, maybe seven," he said. Joe nodded. "I thought we were down two, the most three, but *The Washington Post* this morning says the bill is an easy loser. It said that we'd miss by six or seven votes. It quotes knowledgeable sources. My guess it's the leader, maybe the whip. It could be we're in bad trouble."

Joe nodded and smiled at Francis as if the two of them were sharing a joke. They both suffered Rothenberg for his intelligence (but politics was not his forte). He was always telling them what they already knew. He had just done exactly that: Joe's bill was in trouble.

"You got the new stuff?" Francis asked Ken.

Ken patted a large manila folder. "Right here," he said, turning to Joe. "We have the stuff from Ludenberg at Michigan. He says a million jobs and I think it's a good figure. I think you can use it without fear of contradiction, although someone will come back at you with the stuff from the boys at Stanford. There is no reconciling the two. Just say that you disagree and Ludenberg disagrees and that the only way to find out for sure which one is right is to pass the bill. Ludenberg—I'm impressed with the man. Now I know why Humphrey used him."

"Humphrey used this guy?" Joe said, showing real interest for the first time.

"Yes."

"Jeez," Joe said, "I'm going to take a pasting on this. I didn't expect this. I mean, I thought it would be a lot closer—one or two either way. But not this. What the hell are they trying to tell me, Francis? What's the message?"

The elevator arrived in the basement of the Dirksen Building. The group turned left and walked to the subway platform. The train was waiting when they arrived, and they all climbed into the middle car. The operator, a woman, pulled back on a lever, closing the doors. In the rushing noise of the subway, no one said a word. Joe's face was tight, his jaw working away, grinding his teeth. His dentist had told him that ten more years in Washington and he would have no teeth left. His dentist had told him that he could tell by looking into a man's mouth how long he had been in Washington and whether he occupied a high-level job. His dentist had told him that Pentagon people wore down their teeth the fastest and that he had one undersecretary as a patient who ruined his teeth during the Bay of Pigs crisis. His dentist . . . his dentist, Joe concluded, was a pain in the ass.

The subway sped under the Capitol Park and arrived at the basement portal of the Capitol, where an escalator took them half a flight up to the elevator level. Little groups of tourists stopped and stared at Joe, some of them venturing close and then backing away. One man, dressed in a hat decorated with beer-can labels, came up to Joe.

"Pardon me, but I've always been an admirer. I wonder . . ." he shoved a piece of paper at Joe who reached behind him out of habit. Francis put a pen in his hand. Joe signed his name to the paper, feeling good about being recognized.

"Thank you very much," the man said. "I was a great admirer of your brothers also." Everyone laughed. The man looked at the signature, flushed, started to say something but turned on his heels and walked quickly away.

The group entered an elevator marked Senators Only, which was manned by a young man with a bad case of acne. He had pasted the pictures of the newer senators in his cab so that he could recognize them when they came in. He spotted Joe right off.

"Good morning, Senator," he said.

"Good morning."

"Good luck in there today."

"Gonna need it," Joe said. "Thanks".

The elevator braked at the first floor. The group made a left and then a right and stopped in the Senate reception room, a high-ceilinged affair with portraits of great and dead senators hanging on the walls. It was

9

the place where lobbyists gathered for one last crack at a senator about to enter the chamber. There were other ways to get to the Senate floor—entrances used by senators not wishing a last-minute encounter with some hostile lobbyist. Joe, however, had chosen this way of going in. He had been told that some New York constituents would be there. As he stood and shook hands with various people, Rothenberg drifted off to get the pass that would entitle him to be admitted to the Senate floor.

Joe shook the last hand and went to the door. He paused, gave the staff the thumbs up sign, and started in. He was stopped by two men, one on either side of the door, both dressed in brown suits, white shirts, both with closely cropped hair. They were FBI agents, posted to make security checks. As Joe was about to enter, one FBI man stepped forward.

"Do you know Aaron Bobinsky?"

"Yes," Joe said with a smile. "I know him very well. We were in the party together back in the old days. He was a whiz at microfilm and all his shoes had hollowed out heels. Sneakers, at that. Quite something that Bobinsky."

"Just doing a job," the FBI agent said in a hurt fashion.

"Okay," Joe said. "I know Bobinsky. He's a super-American. Very patriotic. Salutes in his sleep. Hums "America the Beautiful" while . . ." He checked himself. "Better not say that."

"Anything negative? Detrimental?"

"No, nothing."

"Thanks, Senator."

Joe started into the chamber and then backed out.

He had forgotten Angela. He turned and saw her, an anxious expression on her face, standing on her tiptoes, searching the room for Joe. She was a dark-haired woman, about twenty-eight years old, who had come to Washington from the hills of West Virginia. She had worked for a short time at the Pentagon and then switched to the Hill.

All in all, she had been working for congressmen or senators for more than ten years, and if she had one fault it was a tendency to fall in love with whoever was her boss. Joe backed out and came over to her. She looked grateful.

"Not much after your bill," she told him, referring to a clipboard she held. "There's the monetary fund amendments and the debt authorization which is also an easy yes. You voted for it last time around but I don't think they'll get to it today anyway. You are having lunch with David Broder. Don't forget. You can either eat here or in the office. Let me know and I'll have something sent in. *The Star* says that the President will announce the appointment of someone named Anderson to the Supreme Court. I have you on the eight forty American to LaGuardia. If you miss that, you can still make the nine o'clock shuttle. If you miss that, Senator, you are out of luck and your wife will be furious. I've already talked to her and told her you'll be on the eight forty." She paused as if trying to remember something. She checked her clipboard.

"Oh yeah. Your wife said, 'Knock 'em dead.' " Angie read the words from the clipboard and Joe laughed. "That's it," she said, looking up. Francis, who had joined them again, shook his head no.

"Bimm Twins," he said.

"Bimm Twins?" Joe asked.

"They're the toothpicks heirs," Francis explained. "We're going to try to get them in before Broder and after this, right, Angie?"

She nodded her head. "Your son Paul has a rabbit," she said. "He got on the phone to tell me to tell you. You have been told."

Joe laughed. "Anything else?"

Francis and Angie shook their heads no.

"See ya later," Joe said. He turned and went through the doors into the Senate chamber. His desk was on the left, in the Democratic section, and in the last row where freshmen were traditionally seated but where Joe was determined to stay. Teddy Kennedy had killed the old tradition of moving up toward the front with seniority, preferring to remain at his brother Jack's old desk. Joe Tynan had done the same, and over the years the back row had become populated with the most glamorous of the young liberals—"the discotheque," some of the old hands called it.

Ken Rothenberg was waiting for Joe when he arrived at his desk. He was wearing a tag on his lapel identifying him as a Senate aide. His lap held the material that would be used in the debate over the public works bill. Joe sat down.

"Aaron Bobinsky?" Ken asked. "Aaron Bobinsky of the Brookings Institute?"

"No, Aaron Bobinsky of Bobinsky and Bobinsky, Caterers. Yes, yes, Aaron Bobinsky of Brookings. He's going to join the staff of the subcommittee. I've slotted him there and maybe later I'll move him over to the personal staff. I finally got him. It's a feather in our cap. The guy's class."

12

Rothenberg looked as if he had been kicked in the teeth.

"C'mon, Ken, Bobinsky is *foreign* policy; you're *domestic* policy. You know you can't do everything. You've been stretched too thin."

"I could have used an assistant."

"You got one. You got one with a Ph.D and a Brookings pedigree. I know we'll be just one big happy family. Right, Ken?"

"Right. Right. Right." He mumbled the word "right" until Joe could hardly tell what he was saying. "And it's also right that your little ole public works bill, as Birney would call it, is in a load of trouble," he said suddenly. "We are short six or seven votes and we don't know which ones, do we? Maybe Francis knows. No, not maybe. I'm *sure* Francis knows." He looked at Joe who was getting sick and tired of Ken's little games, his constant and patently obvious attempts to play office politics.

"Francis said you'd know," Joe said, flashing his aide a huge drop-dead smile. They both laughed.

The Senate moved into its routine morning business. A clergyman, intoned the prayer and then a temporary president or presiding officer was chosen. The majority leader, speaking from the first desk on the Democratic side of the chamber, announced the order of business. He, in turn, yielded the floor to Senator William Proxmire of Wisconsin, a senator renown for his jogging and his hair transplants, but not for his one-man crusade to have the Senate ratify a treaty outlawing genocide. He rose nearly every day on the issue. Proxmire's desk was towards the back. He looked up to the chair for recognition.

"Mister President, I recently received a letter from Archbishop Iakovos of the Greek Orthodox Church of North and South America," Proxmire began. "He enclosed an essay entitled 'Human Rights' by Professor Constantine Tsatsos, a Greek legal scholar and philosopher. In his treatise, Professor Tsatsos critically explores several philosophical questions concerning human rights. He begins his essay with a definition of human rights. I quote . . ."

As Proxmire was talking Ken and Joe gathered up their papers and moved down to the desk recently vacated by the majority leader. From there they would manage the public works bill.

Copies of Joe's speech were already in the hands of the reporters in the various press galleries. Additional copies were dispatched by messenger to the Washington bureaus of all the New York newspapers and other important newspapers from around the country. Key editors had received hand-delivered copies of the speech with notes from Joe saying, "I thought you would be interested in this." A machine had signed Joe's name to the notes. The jist of the speech was summarized in a newsletter that was already in the mail to every voter in New York State, and Joe's staff had prepared a one-minute tape of Joe reciting a part of the speech. Radio stations could use it by simply calling a number in Joe's office.

This was all part of the Washington game, and while it had disgusted Joe when he first came to town, he had since become very adept at that sort of thing—an "All Star Player," a columnist had called him. Joe, more than most, was one of those senators who had flags run up and down the Capitol flagpole and then

14

mailed to constituents with a letter saying the banner had flown over the capitol. He never missed a birth, if he knew about it, or a Bar Mitzvah or a similar event. His staff scoured New York newspapers for announcements and then sent out congratulatory letters. He had a file of every constituent in the armed services, and he had the Pentagon notify his office of every transfer and promotion. He was mute, however, about court martials, divorces, and paternity suits, although he once joked about making up a bad luck newsletter—"Dear Clyde, Sorry to hear about your———."

Proxmire was preparing to wind up. He would yield to Joe, that was already determined, and then Joe would begin his speech. He reached for the microphone on the side of his desk, lifting it from its hook and activating it. He clipped it to his breast pocket. A light went on on the sound engineer's console on the gallery level. He stood by to adjust the volume to suit Joe's voice. In the visitors' galleries, tourists watched Joe. They pointed to him when he stood, a face they knew from television and from the cover of *People* magazine. They hushed when he stood and reached for his mike.

"Mister President," he boomed. "Will the gentleman yield?"

"I yield," said Proxmire.

"Mister President," Joe began, "today we take up the public works bill and we take it up in the face of what everyone concedes is unparalleled inflation." Joe paused and looked around. Proxmire rose and left the chamber. So did Javits. One by one, most of the dozen senators on the floor ambled out of the chamber. Ted Kennedy came in, looked at Joe speaking, and walked out. Three members of the Senate remained in their seats. Two sat toward the back, chatting in a conspiratorial fashion, and the third, the very old and very venerable Hayes Goodwin of Florida, was either reading or asleep. It was hard to tell.

"I realize the expense involved," Joe went on. "Mister President, this is going to be expensive. Fourteen billion dollars is expensive. It is not, of course, an aircraft carrier and it is not a missile program and it is not a water program of dubious value for the West. It is fourteen billion dollars for jobs and for public works. It is fourteen billion dollars to put men to work and to keep families together and to get children off the dole. It is money to break the vicious cycle of welfare—mothers raising children on welfare and they, in turn, raising their own children on welfare. It is fourteen billion dollars, and when you look at it as a chance to break the welfare cycle, it is nothing short of a bargain. A bargain at twice the price, as my mother used to say.

"But, Mister President, I concede the initial start-up expense. I concede that we'll never be able to count the lives saved, the hopes salvaged, the families kept intact, the men who retain their pride, the fathers who can come home at the end of the day with the satisfaction that they have earned their own bread. No hand out for them, thank you. Instead, Mister President, it is all too easy to count the bucks, to add them up and take in some breath with a low whistle at the enormity of the expense and say that we cannot afford it all. So on the one hand you have this payoff you can't measure, and on the other hand you have this expense you can measure, and what you're left with, Mister President, is a sense that we must have come here for something other than keeping an eye on the books, for looking men in the eye and saying, 'Sorry, we cannot afford to put you to work.' We are here, Mister President, to do exactly what this bill intends to do. If we are not here for that and for reasons like it, Mister President, then what, I ask you, are we here for? What are we here for gentlemen?

"Ten million people are not able to put bread on their tables. Are we here for them? Four million children have never seen a doctor. Are we here for them? Six million mothers have not the faintest idea about birth control. Are we here for them? Six million men are out of work. Six million! Are we here for them?"

Joe spoke and watched himself at the same time—both participant and observer. He liked what he saw. He had a good cadence, a fine rhythm. Years ago, he had patterned his public speaking after John F. Kennedy. He liked to point and give the air rabbit punches and he liked, also, to invert his sentences—"ask not what your country can do for you." He glanced up to the press gallery to see if he was still holding his real audience. He cared little about the senators on the floor and not at all for the tourists in the galleries: his real audience was the press. He not only wanted it to carry his message to the people, but he wanted to impress it with his arguments and with his style. It was an exaggeration, he was sure, that the press chose the candidates. They merely chose the group from which the candidates were chosen in the end, and what Joe knew was that at that very moment there were men and women in the press gallery who were sizing him up—sizing him up for the presidential sweepstakes. Joe's measure was being taken this day, and it had nothing at all to do with the issue or even, for that matter, the eventual outcome. He could lose, but he better lose well.

"This bill is not a cure-all," Joe continued. "At best it will create only a million jobs." He stopped and looked around. "Only a million. But the question has been raised, can we afford to subsidize that many jobs? That question, in fact, was raised in committee by the distinguished Senator from Arizona. Well, let me ask my distinguished colleague from Arizona, how many children can the nation afford to let go hungry?"

"Will the Senator yield?"

Joe looked behind him. It was Birch Bayh of Indiana, an ally. A Senate page, a young man dressed in the traditional navy blue pants and white shirt, came bounding down the aisle. He handed Joe a slip of paper. "I yield to my esteemed colleague from Indiana," Joe said. He looked at the note. It said, "Quorum call—Birney." He looked back at Bayh.

"How does the Senator arrive at the figure of one million jobs?" asked Bayh, serving up one to Joe underhand.

"I'm glad the distinguished Senator from Indiana asked me that. That figure is supplied by Professor Paul Lundberg in the economics department at the University of Michigan. Professor Lundberg, as you know, is the author of the classic study proving that unemployment decreases in direct proportion to public works spending by the federal government. It was his work that resulted in the tax bill of 1967; the public works provisions of which proved him exactly right. His full analysis of the effect of this particular

18

public works bill is part of the committee record." He looked down at Ken Rothenberg. "We have a copy of it available here for anyone who wants to see it." Rothenberg nodded to Joe that he was correct.

"Thank you," Bayh said. "Your answer was most informative." He sat down, smiling slyly.

"Mister President," Joe said, turning back to face the dais. "I suggest the absence of a quorum."

"The clerk will call the roll," boomed the acting president, the junior senator from Montana.

The second assistant legislative clerk, sitting at the far end of the dais, leaned forward in his chair and pressed a button. It activated a tape and the names of the senators boomed through the chamber. The clerk hit the button about once every ninety seconds, the request for a quorum call being a mere formality—a stall for time. It would soon be rescinded since no senator in his right mind truly would require his colleagues to sit through a speech, dragging them from committee meetings and other business, important or unimportant. Joe took off his microphone and walked briskly to the back of the chamber. He pushed aside two cream-colored and etched glass doors and walked into the Democratic cloakroom.

The room was long and ell-shaped, narrow with couches lining the walls. At the foot of the ell was a huge desk manned by clerks who worked for the Democratic majority. A right turn at the desk brought you to the telephones. There were ten of them, all equipped with government-financed WATTS lines, enabling a senator to call anywhere in the country for free. At the far end, past the last telephone booth and lodged in the corner, was a cooler that contained two kinds of bottled water—Mountain Valley and Poland Water. The joke was that Poland Water was there at the insistence of Edmund Muskie of Maine, the Senate's foremost member of Polish origin. It was, but not because Muskie was Polish, but because the water came from the state of Maine. At the other end of the room, an enormous RCA color television hung from the ceiling.

Joe craned his head first one way and then the other, looking for Senator Samuel Birney, chairman of the Judiciary Committee, the man who put his name on the most famous program of government fellowships for study abroad, a most senior member of the Senate, a conservative Democrat from Louisiana, a cantankerous old man who had years ago taken a liking to Joe, awarding him his first subcommittee chairmanship and showing him the ropes to boot. What staff Joe had over and above his personal staff he owed to Birney, and what sagacity he had been able to show on the floor of the Senate, especially in his early days, he also owed to Birney. Right now he was holding Birney's cryptic note and wondering, as most senators did sooner or later, what else he might owe to Birney—and what the price might be.

Joe spotted Birney in the corner, sitting under the television set reading a newspaper. He started for him but was stopped by Senator Edward Pardew, the Michigan Democrat. He extended a hand to Joe and then seized him by the elbow. Pardew was another of the Senate's physical education nuts and his grip was like a vise. It hurt.

"Joe, I'll do everything I can," Pardew said.

"Thanks Ed," Joe said, thinking to himself, "A lot

of good that will do." The trouble with Pardew was that he was the Senate's straight arrow, insufferable, unwilling to cut a deal with anyone on anything. When Pardew said he would help, he would, but he was worth his one vote, nothing more, and there was always the chance that his one vote could cost you some. You could always count on Pardew to have recently offended someone. Joe hoped for the best and moved on to Birney.

The old senator sat heavy and unforgiving on the couch. He was dressed as always in a dark suit with a little American flag pin stuck in the lapel. His hair, white and thinning, ran back until it curled a bit at his neck. It had not receded much over the years and the mustache had managed to retain a hint of its former color. The glasses were dark-framed and heavy. They rested on a nose that bumped twice on the way down to the nostrils and then flaired suddenly, giving Birney an air of surprise. At seventy-seven he was still one tough politician, pure southern aristocracy, a living amalgam of the great families of the South—especially the cotton South. The Birneys were originally from Maryland, high church with a history going back to the Norman invasion of England, while the LeDroix, which was his mother's family, went back even further—all the way to Charlemagne, his mother had told him. He was French on one side and English on the other and pure southern all the way through. Once there had been slaves and a home in New Orleans and another upriver. The slaves were gone and there was no home in New Orleans, but the plantation remained. It was called Harmoney and it ran for sixteen miles along the river—a huge, white-pillared affair that stood as a monument to the old South. It was located three miles outside the town of Birney, Louisiana.

To some, Senators Birney and Kittner seemed alike—both being southern and all. They alone knew the difference, and the difference was substantial. Kittner was what Birney once called trash, and while he had learned to work with his colleague over the years, and from time to time even had lunch with him, he never once had him to his home. "It would upset Mrs. Birney too much," he once explained. Samuel LeDroix Birney was a man of awesome pride.

He looked up at Joe, patted the cushion next to him, and said, "Sit down." Joe handed Birney the note delivered by the page. "You rang?" he asked.

Birney glanced around the room as Joe sat down. "You're just going to squander the voters' money, aren't you?" Birney bellowed. Conversation in the cloakroom stopped. Heads turned to look at Birney and Joe on the couch. Joe laughed.

"Well, I'm sure going to try," he said.

"You amaze me. No matter what we debate in there you have the absolute talent for being on the wrong side." Birney was also smiling now. The conversation in the cloakroom picked up in volume. After a minute or so, the two men in the corner were largely ignored.

"What's your count?" Birney asked Joe, dropping his voice.

"I'm still shy a few. Six, maybe seven, my guy tells me."

Birney looked at Joe with surprise. "We'll get back to that directly," he said. "Look, you know I can't vote for this bill. Number one, I don't much approve

22

of it." Joe started to say something but Birney held up his hand like a traffic cop. "Don't want no arguments. Just don't like it. That's one. Two is more to the point. Two is that my people don't like it. You understand that, don't ya?"

"I understand that, Senator."

"Now the fact of the matter is that I *could* go for that bill of yours. If I had to, I could. If you really needed me, I could do it. I would make you pay for it, but I could do it and live with it. I'd explain it somehow. But you don't need me. You don't need no seven votes or whatever the hell number you just gave me. Sometimes I think none of you young fellas can count votes. You need two, most three. If you can get those three, the rest will come. They're lined up out there like dominoes. Topple one and the rest will come. If you get Kittner, Anhalt will come, and if Anhalt comes Dreiser comes. My good friend Kittner is the key. My good friend is holding three votes—his and two others. I have been delegated to tell you that you have those three votes. Now you say, 'In exchange for what?'"

"In exchange for what?"

"Damn good question, Senator Tynan. I admire your probing mind."

"Some kinds of deals I can't make."

"I know, Joe, I know. I'm not asking for too much here. Kittner's got his good points, too, y'know. Don't ever forget that. The man is not the raving fool he pretends to be. He knows exactly what his national allegiance bill is. All he wants is to bring it up. Get some ink. Make a splash back at the legion posts. He wants you to hold a hearing or two on it down home. That's all. You bring it up, Joe, and I'll kill it. I promise you that. You give it life, Joe. I'll take care of the rest." He drew his hand across his throat in a slitting gesture.

"Now here's the way I see it," Birney went on. "You can tell me to tell Kittner no deal, in which case you will lose your little ole bill. That I also promise you. I don't know if that matters to you or not. It will make the papers anyway—maybe even the Walter Cronkite show. Thing is, of course, the smart thing to have done from the start was to tack on the public works feature to another bill so that you wouldn't give guys like me such a good target. Things we can vote for if you don't call them certain things. That's what I would have done if I wanted those million jobs real bad. There's one trouble with that approach, though. No speech."

"Listen, Senator," Joe started to say.

Birney put his fingers to his lips. "Shoosh," he said. "Don't take it personally. How many times I got to tell you that? Nothing personal in what I said. Nothing wrong either and nothing that isn't the truth. I know what you want. You want both. Nothing wrong with that. I can get you both. You want to deal or you want to sit and stew?"

Joe stood. He looked down at the old man, giving himself some time to think.

"You don't have much time," Birney said, reading his mind.

"You got yourself a deal, Senator," Joe said coldly.

"Me? I have got myself nothing. I got myself no deal at all. I got myself a deal between you and Kittner. And now you go over there where my esteemed colleague is standing and just whisper one word to him. Keep it down to one word and even he will under-

24

stand." Birney stopped and looked up at Joe as if Joe was to supply the word.

"The word?" Joe asked. "The word I'm supposed to say?"

"Oh," Birney said, appearing to snap out of a trance. "Subcommittee. Yeah, subcommittee. Go whisper that in his ear. Subcommittee. God, I almost forgot."

"Subcommittee?"

"Right. Subcommittee."

"Just one thing, Senator, if I may. What is in this for you?"

Birney's face crinkled into a smile. "The everlasting thanks of a grateful nation," he said. "And maybe a future draft choice."

Hugh Kittner was standing over by the clerk's desk, pretending to be leafing through some telephone messages. He was fifty-eight years old, dark-haired, and powerful-looking. The years had not shown on him. His face was still firm, just a touch of gray had crept into his hair. On television and on the stump he appeared distinguished, but in person he was quite a different matter. The joke was that Kittner bathed once every four years and then only if the Democrats won. The one good thing you could say about his personal habits was that the bourbon on his breath usually cut the smell coming from his body. Joe went over and tapped Kittner on the shoulder.

"Well, hi, Joe," Kittner said, friendly and warm. "Howyoo?"

Joe ignored the question. "I have a message for you, Senator: subcommittee. The message is subcommittee."

"Music to these old ears, Joe. Pure, unadulterated

music." He stuck out his hand. "Congratulations on the passage of your bill. I think I can safely say that. In fact, I think I can personally guarantee it. All those men working. It makes me feel so proud." Joe was forced to smile.

He walked back into the chamber where the quorum call had progressed to the letter S. He went to his desk and picked up his mike. "Mister President."

"The Senator from New York."

"Mister President. I ask unanimous consent that the order for the quorum is rescinded."

"Without objection, so ordered."

Joseph Tynan completed his speech and asked for a vote on the bill. One hundred senators voted and seven more than a majority voted for his bill. He got the three he had been promised plus four more, and he never knew if he always had enough votes all along or if they, too, had come with the others. Birney, as promised, voted no and so, at the last minute, did Kittner. He had come up to Joe as the roll call had started and whispered his about-face. "You don't need me," he explained. "I got you more than enough." Joe nodded.

Up in the gallery, tourists watched the vote. They saw senators file in, announce their votes, and file out. The group's guide walked down to the lowest aisle and motioned that it was time to go. When the tourists got outside, a man holding a beer-can hat announced that he had met Joe earlier and that that was far more exciting than what he had just witnessed. He turned to the guide. "What are we here for?" he asked her.

The group laughed and moved off.

CHAPTER 2

In his eighth year as Senator from the State of New York, Joseph Tynan was presented with a key. The key was handed to him by the sergeant at arms, a fat man with a wide grin, but it actually came at the orders of the Senate Rules Committee. The committee had done two things for Joe that year. It had moved him out of a small suite of offices in the Russell Building to a larger suite in the Dirksen Building, and it had also provided him with a private office in the Capitol building itself. That was what the mysterious key was for.

There are, it is rumored, something like fifty of these offices in the Capitol building itself, and they are awarded on the basis of seniority to the senators who have been in the Senate the longest. They provide these senators with an office close to the Senate floor—the sort of place that comes in handy during a filibuster when the roll calls are fast and frequent. But they are essentially places designed for utmost privacy, places to go when a senator wants to have a very private chat with someone, when he wants to have a pop of his favorite booze, when he needs a place for a quickie of any kind. Secrecy is the rule and if you go to the architect of the Senate and ask for a floor plan of the Capitol building, you will get something called **GPO** (Government Printing Office) :1974 0-45-295, which lists every room on the four floors of the Capitol building, everything including the kitchens and the cafeterias and the plumber shops and laborer rooms, and even something called the flag department of the architect of the Capitol itself, but you will find no mention of these private offices. They are secret and even the staffs of the various senators do not know of them or what their room number may be or even what the telephone number is. It was in this office that Joe chose to meet with the storied and fabulously wealthy Bimm Twins. He was expecting the worst.

The Bimm Twins were twenty-two years old, both six feet six inches tall, both skinny as could be, both weak in the body and weak in the eyes, and both wore granny glasses. They attempted beards, but they could manage no more than mossy growths. Each had dirty blond hair worn long and tied back in a ponytail. For this, their first and they hoped their last visit to Washington, they had compromised to the extent of putting on jackets, buttoning their workshirts all the way to the top, and wearing what passed for ties. Dressed like that and armed with gallery passes supplied by Joe's office, they had watched the entire debate and had been bored silly by it. They had also been kicked out of the gallery for smoking.

It was Francis who had discovered the Bimm Twins. They were his project, so to speak, and he guarded them jealously. They had first come into his life after *Newsweek* did one of those cover stories on potential presidential candidates. Joe had been named. Twelve other men had been named, but the important thing was that Joe had been named. The story had pointed out, quite accurately in fact, that Joe had an informal planning group to map strategy for his eventual run for the presidency, and it also pointed out that he was attempting to raise more money than he could possibly use for yet another Senate race. Joe had poo-pooed the importance of the fund raising, but the Bimms had telephoned anyway.

They called collect. The call was refused. They called a moment later and again the call was refused. They called a third time and still the call was refused. By this time there was a bit of a titter in the office. Francis noticed.

"Ask them to call right back," he yelled. "Tell them to give us five minutes."

Francis ran back into his office and called a friend at the Library of Congress. Then he called someone he knew at the Foundation Library on Connecticut Avenue, and then he called an old girl friend of his who worked as a professional fund raiser. "B-I-M-M," he told her. "Bimm. Rings a bell with me, too. Something. Don't know. Right. I'll be waiting." He hung up the phone and paced his small office. Every once in a while he ducked his head out into the reception area to ask if the Bimms had called back yet.

"Nothing yet," Gail, the receptionist, said.

He paced. "It happens," he thought to himself.

"These things happen. They just do. Jerks like that call collect. They think everyone's got money. Idiots. If I'm right . . . If only I'm right . . ." But he *knew* he was right. He was always in the ball park. You could play games with Francis; throw a name at him and he would just recite information like a computer: "Johnson: Governor of North Dakota. Born Pierre, South Dakota. Married to, I think, the daughter of former Senator Mundt. Was state attorney general, then lieutenant governor and has been governor for two terms. Very popular but had to introduce income tax two years ago. Some think he's vulnerable. I don't. He's the next senator." The phone rang and Francis jumped for it. It was the fund raiser. Francis reached for a pencil and made some notes. He hung up the phone and then took another call from the person at the Library of Congress. Again he took notes. He strolled out to the reception area, a look of triumph on his face.

"Accept the charges," he told Gail.

He invited the Bimms to Washington.

Now the three of them, Francis, Ronald Bimm, and Richard Bimm, were in the Senate subway, heading toward the Capitol and Joe's private office.

The door was unmarked. Francis gave it a pro forma knock and went right in. Joe was on the phone. He waved them all in, motioning with his hand for the Bimms to take the two chairs nearest his desk. The room was a large one, dominated by a picture window view of the Washington Mall, the Washington Monument in the foreground. A nice, but not terribly impressive chandelier hung from the ceiling and along the wall was a couch and two end tables. Glass-enclosed bookcases lined the far walls, the bookcases nearly empty. The room had a cozy touch to it and none of the studied informality of the Dirksen Building office with its family pictures and crayoned drawings done by the children. It was Joe Tynan, after all, who had once suggested to a reporter that he check and see if the Government Printing Office supplied members of Congress with crayoned pictures. Joe hung up the phone.

"Senator," Francis said, still standing, "this is Richard and Ronald Bimm." He waved his arm from one to the other and then a look of panic came over his face. "Did I get that right?" he asked. The Bimms smiled.

"Yes," they both said simultaneously.

Joe rose and walked around to the front of the desk, his hand extended. The Bimms started to rise.

"Sit, sit," Joe said. He leaned against the back of the desk and Francis, with nowhere else to go, faded to the couch against the wall.

"You mind if we smoke?" asked Richard Bimm.

"Of course not," Joe said. "Francis, hand me that ashtray." Joe took the heavy ashtray with the senatorial seal on it and placed it on his desk, ignoring the strange look on Francis's face. The Bimms reached into their shirt pockets and took out little leather pouches. They opened the string with their teeth and then reached into their jacket pockets for paper. They tapped some of the tobacco into the paper, licking the end, and then rolled the cigarette nicely. Then they pulled the pouch closed with their teeth and returned it to their shirt pockets.

"Roll your own?" Joe asked.

Francis put his head in his hands.

"Francis has told me about your kind offer," Joe said. "I can't thank you enough."

The two young men simply nodded their heads. One of them was fishing for a match.

"In fact, I was flabbergasted. I mean, fifty thousand dollars is a lot of money. In two senatorial campaigns, I never received a contribution as large as that and, as Francis has probably told you, I never will. That kind of money is now illegal. I voted for that bill. I know you mean well by it, nothing but good, I'm sure, but imagine what that kind of money could buy if you were, say, a corporation." Joe looked at the twins, waiting for some sort of response.

They looked up. "Yeah, we can dig it," Richard said.

Jesus Christ, what freaks, Joe thought. Kids like these always made him think of his own children, always made him vow to spend more time with them to make sure they did not wind up like this. He imagined his son, Paulie, looking eight years old but six feet, four inches tall, coming home one day in a saffron robe and saying, "Hari Krishna, daddy." A chill went up Joe's back. He looked at the twins. He didn't even know how to talk to them, to relate to them, whether to descend into jive talk or to come on like Dean Acheson. He decided to be frank.

"I would be lying if I told you that I had no interest in the presidency. I do. But it's too early to do anything. We have an incumbent Democratic president who will seek and get the nomination in two years. I, myself, have to face reelection in New York. There's a lot of water to come under the bridge yet, but we're planning. We're working on it and what I tell reporters is what I'll tell you: all I want to be is the best senator I can be.

"Now what that means is simple. By being a good senator, I serve the people who elect me. I also serve me in the sense that the better I am at my job, the more attention I get and the more qualified I appear to be. There's one further thing. The more often I get mentioned as a presidential candidate, the more attention gets paid to me. I can make or break an issue. What I say gets reported, and the more ways I can think of increasing my clout, the better off I am and, I suppose, you are. Now we get to you and your money. I want it."

Joe turned his back on them for effect and walked around his desk to his chair. He stood in front of it rather than sitting.

"We have an election year coming up. There are lots of good people running for office out there who could use money. Many of these people are friends of mine—people who I think will support me. A lot of them back the causes I do—poverty, ecology, nonproliferation. That sort of thing. What I propose is that we sort of set up a fund. I can count on your fifty thousand dollars, and in your name I can make donations to candidates of my choice. Are you willing to do that?"

The twins looked at each other and then nodded yes.

"Are you willing to leave the decisions to me?"

Again they nodded yes.

"Okay, terrific," said Joe, smiling broadly and reaching behind him for a matchbook. He handed it to the twins. "I have to ask you something. I mean, it's awkward, but what is it that has prompted you to make this money available to me? You said something to Francis about my positions—my stands. Any in particular?"

Richard Bimm struck the match and lit his cigarette. His brother leaned over and while Richard held the match, Ronald took his light also. The two of them inhaled deeply. Francis looked pale. Richard Bimm held up his cigarette.

"This, man," he said.

"The cigarette?" Joe asked, puzzled.

"You're for decriminalization, man. We saw your hearings on the tube."

The pungent smell reached Joe.

"Marijuana?" he asked tentatively. Francis shook his head yes.

He started to look at the twins for confirmation but thought better of it. It was best if he did not know for sure. It was best, also, if he left as quickly as possible.

"Look, I have to go," Joe said, starting toward the door. "I just can't say how much I thank you. I just can't thank you enough." He opened the door and peeked out. A man was coming down the hall. Joe closed the door and looked back into the room.

"I mean it, I just can't thank you enough."

He opened the door and looked out again. The coast was clear.

"Don't thank us, man," said Ronald Bimm. "Thank grandpa."

"Grandpa?" Joe asked.

"Yeah, grandpa," said Ronald. "The cat invented toothpicks."

Joe opened the door a bit and slipped out. He walked quickly down the hallway, brushing his shoulders as if the smell of marijuana could cling to him like invisible dandruff. He hit the elevator button and started to chuckle to himself: the toothpick heirs. He laughed some more. Don't thank us, thank grandpa. He laughed some more. He was still chuckling when he got back to his office. He went directly to the phone and called Francis at the hideaway office. Francis's voice sounded thick. Joe smiled.

"Francis, are they still there?" he asked. "Good. Listen, Francis, I have one question for them. Flat or round?"

He sunk into his chair laughing.

Ellie Tynan, at thirty-seven was a wonderful-looking woman, one of those types who gets more attractive with age. She was a natural blonde, and wore her hair a medium length—not too long and not too short. Like Joe, she dressed not to offend voters. She had green eyes and the look of a no-nonsense professional woman who once had been the high school queen but who had worked to outgrow it. When she was in Washington, which was not too often, she was sometimes mistaken for Joan Kennedy, although she was not as tall. But like Joan Kennedy she had learned to live with rumors. In Ellie's case, the rumors were not about Joe, although there were some of them, but about her. It was whispered that she felt herself too good for Washington, that she found politics dull and pedestrian and Washington full of people who cared only for appropriations and expenditures. Finally, it was rumored that she, like some other senators' wives who would not come to town, had a lover—an artist, they said. Some people would even supply the name, a Spanish name, something beginning with de.

"How's your lover, José what's his name?" Joe asked her. The two of them were lying in bed, Ellie in a nightgown, Joe in his shorts, both flat on their backs. Ellie had been reading something in a file folder. She was so engrossed in it that she hardly heard what Joe said.

"What?" she asked.

"Your lover. The bullfighter-artist-guitarist. José de Iturbi.

She put down the folder. "Not again, Joe. Not something in the papers again."

"No, I just wanted to get your attention."

"Joseph Tynan!"

"Did anyone ever tell you you're beautiful when you're angry?"

"Yes."

"Who?"

"José de Iturbi."

"Very funny."

"I just wanted to get your attention."

"Do you realize that I got the public works bill passed? Do you know how many people have tried? And I got it passed."

"I think you must be a genius," Ellie said, giving him the elbow with her voice. "I think that must be it."

"I have got what is known in Latin as clout. C-L-O-U-T. Clout! My little subcommittee, my teenie-weenie subcommittee has POWER!"

Joe looked down and noticed that the covers were

missing. "Hey," he shouted with a laugh, "I don't have any covers."

"No kidding," said Ellie. She had been slipping them off with her feet.

"What are you doing?"

"It's called getting your attention."

Joe reached for her and she rolled into him. He hugged her and then rolled on top of her, clenching his teeth in mock passion. "You can't get enough of me, right?" he said through his teeth. "Power makes women crazy."

"It certainly makes you crazy."

"Yeah?" he said rolling off her and onto his back. He focused on the ceiling. "I got a bill passed today that will put a million people to work. You know how I did it. I said one word."

"Shazam?"

Joe shook his head no. "Subcommittee."

Ellie brought her knees up to her chest, wrapped her arms around them, and rocked from side to side. "Oh my God! Don't say that word. It drives me wild." She reached for Joe's hand and tried to bite his knuckle.

"Stop that," Joe said laughing and pulled away his hand.

"I'll give you five seconds to do something wonderful to my body. After that, I start playing rough. Five . . . four . . ."

Joe rolled on top of her again and buried his face in the crook of her neck. He kissed her there twice. "Better?" he asked in a whisper.

"Yes."

"You know how lucky I am? Do you know that

there are probably dozens of men lying awake right now wishing . . . just wishing . . . they had their name on my public works bill." He quickly rolled off her, breaking up at the shocked expression on her face.

"Okay, that's it!" she shouted. She brought her knees up and started to push Joe out of bed with her feet.

"Hey, wait a second," Joe pleaded, laughing too hard to offer much of a fight. He tried to move his body away, turning over on his side. "Wait a minute," he yelled, still laughing. "No one pushes Joe Tynan out of bed."

With that, Ellie brought back her feet and gave one, mighty shove. She caught Joe in the small of the back, tumbling him out of bed. He broke the fall with his hands and stood up, affecting mock dignity. He got back into bed.

"Very nice," he said, trying to stifle a smile.

"What happened to your power? I thought all you had to do was say one word."

Joe flashed her a smile and then quickly brought his legs up, catching Ellie around her thighs with his feet. He pushed, but she rolled away from him. His feet skidded over her. She laughed, cocked her own legs, let go once again, and caught Joe broadside. This time, he went flying out of the bed, hitting the floor hard. Ellie gasped, bringing her hand to her mouth.

Joe got up and stood by the side of the bed. "How do you do that?" he asked, his hands planted on his hips.

"Jogging. Very strong legs. Want to try again?"

"I've got a better use for those legs."

38

"I think I know what you have in mind." Raising herself on her elbows, she reached for him.

"Subcommittee, huh?"

"Jesus, Ellie, Jesus."

Joe Tynan went up on the balls of his feet and let the punch go from the shoulder. It hit just right, making a nice round sound. The heavy bag seemed to hesitate for a second and then swung out a bit. When it swung back Joe was waiting for it with another punch. This one was a left. He went at the bag for about five minutes, giving it a vicious beating, enjoying the pain throbbing in his knuckles, the sweat rolling down the back of his neck. He gave the bag a final punch and then pushed it away with a mean little shove. He had seen a fighter do this once in the movies and he had been doing it ever since. He took the gloves off and walked over to the rowing machine. He sat down and pulled back on the oars, rowing down an imaginary river in the Senate gym, appreciating how this was a good day for his body, one in which he felt lubricated, well-oiled, smoothly functioning. There were days when there was nothing but pain and everything creaked, but not today.

Tynan had nothing but contempt for physical education nuts. He hated their obsession with the physical, with their bodies, with pain and with fatigue and with, in the end, the pleasure they took from both pain and fatigue. Nevertheless, Joe worked out every day. He did it because he thought he had to do it, because he thought it kept him in good health, and also because he saw himself as something of an actor. He had to watch his body, keep it lean and fit. It was worth votes to him, and although he had never calculated how many, he figured something like five percent. Nothing cynical about it, he would say. The old organizations were dead. They used to provide five percent of the vote, he figured. He was his own organization now. People used to vote the organization ticket for a lot of different reasons—ideology, jobs, maybe even some flowers at a funeral. It was the same with him. He got some votes for his party affiliation and some for his politics and some for his looks. Five per cent for the looks, he figured—two miles a day of running and fifty push-ups and ten minutes on the rowing machine so that public works bills that would provide employment could be passed. He hit the floor for his push-ups.

"You know if you look too good, you lose votes."

Joe spun over on his back and looked up. It was Birney standing behind him, his arms folded over his chest, looking at Joe as if he were watching a man in the process of losing his mind.

"Proxmire does a hundred of these."

"That's how he lost his hair."

Joe gave up on his push-ups. He stood and grabbed for a towel, wiping the back of the neck as he walked over to Birney. The old senator pulled a newspaper clipping out of his pocket as Joe approached. It was from that day's *Washington Post*. The front page announced that the President was going to name Edward Anderson to the Supreme Court.

"You see this?" Birney asked.

Joe nodded. "Edward Anderson, yeah."

"The President has assured me that he's going to nominate him to fill Peterson's seat on the Court. But he wasn't going to announce it for another week. Certain matters had to be taken care of first. I wonder why this was leaked?"

"Well, I don't know."

Birney looked troubled. "Can I see you somewhere? I need to talk to you about this." He stabbed his finger into the newspaper clipping.

"Sure. My Capitol office in fifteen minutes. Give me time for a shower."

"You drink anything other than Gatorade or orange juice?" Birney asked Joe as he looked around his Capitol office for the standard decanter of bourbon.

"I drink ice tea and coffee, Senator, but if you want something a mite stronger, I do have a touch of bourbon in my drawer." Joe walked around to the back of his desk and opened the bottom drawer. He took out a bottle of Wild Turkey forced on him a year or two back by a constituent grateful for the private bill that had made him a citizen. He showed Birney the bottle, holding it up like a hunter holds a dead bird, and then he walked with the bottle to the small bathroom that adjoined the office. He took two glasses, washed them out, and returned. He took one of the wing chairs and swung it around to face the coffee table. Birney did the same to his chair. Joe poured, offered Birney one of the glasses, and lifted his glass in a toast.

"To Edward Anderson, a *landsman* of yours, I presume," Joe said.

"To Edward Anderson," Birney said. "What's a lantz . . . whatever it is you just said?"

"It's a Jewish expression. It means someone from the

41

same country or of the same religion. Anderson's from your state, isn't he? He must be your guy, no?"

Birney took a swallow and nodded yes. He grimaced as the bourbon went down and he reached into his pocket for the newspaper clipping. He tossed it on the table. The senator belched and pounded his chest lightly with his fist. "That really Wild Turkey?" he asked smiling.

"Fellow who gave it to me said it was. Fellow with a strange look in his eye who muttered something about *sic semper tyrannus* when he handed it to me."

Birney laughed, setting off another burp. "Damn!" he said. "If I knew this was going to happen, I would have eaten some beans and saved us all some money." He laughed at his own joke. Joe managed a small laugh.

Birney pointed to the newspaper clipping. "Now what's going on here?" he asked, suddenly very serious. "You've got your ear to the ground. Who's trying to block Anderson?"

"You think someone's trying to block him?"

"Sure," Birney said. "This thing wasn't supposed to be announced for another week. Certain things had to be done. You can understand that, Joe. One of the things, quite frankly, was for you and others on the committee to be informed. You know I just wouldn't have something like this come out in the papers. I wouldn't like it if I read it first in *The Washington Post*."

"It's all right. Forget it."

"No, it's not all right. I've seen this before. I saw it with Haynsworth and again with Carswell. I know when they start to move. Only a couple of places they could have gotten that story. The White House is one. My office is another. You guys on the committee didn't know. The FBI is a possibility and the bar association is a good shot, only I'm not sure they've been informed yet. If I had to bet, I'd say the White House. Someone there wants to see if this thing is going to fly. They want to see what the reaction will be before the President formally nominates and it's too late."

"Is there a problem?"

Birney nodded. "Look, twenty years ago Anderson said a few things during a campaign, I think it was for the state legislature, that wouldn't sound too good today. But, Joe, it was all campaign rhetoric. There was a lot going on at the time. The man's a moderate. You don't have to worry about him."

"Senator," Joe said, perplexed, "I really don't know him." Joe looked at Birney. It seemed as if he had tuned out.

"I don't mind if you vote against the man. In fact, you probably will have to. Just don't make a problem for me."

"Like what, Senator?"

Birney refocused and glared at Joe. "Like leading the opposition, that's what. I shouldn't have any trouble with this unless someone makes a fuss." He pointed at Joe. "Someone like you. Pardew, someone like him, shit, doesn't mean a thing. Everyone expects it. You, it's different. You move to the head of this parade and it'll be trouble. You're everyone's favorite cover boy now. One week I got off the plane at National and saw you looking at me from what looked like a dozen magazines. Could swear your picture was on the cover of *Popular Mechanics*." He laughed.

"It was," Joe deadpanned.

Birney looked at him. "What do you say, Joe?"

"Well, Senator, I'll give Anderson the most careful consideration. You can count on that." It was a response straight from a press conference, the sort of answer you give the press when you don't want to answer the question. Birney didn't even listen to the words. He heard "No comment" in Joe's voice. He sipped some more from the glass, put it down, and leaned forward. He put his hand on Joe's arm.

"You know, Joe, some folks back home are saying that I'm getting too old, that my stroke has left me . . . feeble or something. Me, feeble? Can you imagine that? That's a lot of bull. But they've got somebody very attractive to run against me next time. I don't want to take on this man if I can avoid it. Now let's see if you can guess who he is?"

Joe looked at Birney quizzically. What the hell sort of game was he playing? How was he supposed to know who was threatening to run against Birney in the Democratic primary? Francis would know . . . A bulb went on in his head.

"Edward Anderson," he said in triumph.

Birney nodded. "If he's on the Court, he's out of the running. For life. And he happens to be eminently qualified."

"I understand, Senator."

"Can I count on you?"

"Sure."

Birney stood and looked down on Joe. "Vote against him if you like. Just don't start a crusade, all right?"

"All right."

"You with me?" Birney asked. He started to pace the room.

"I won't oppose you, Senator. I just told you . . ."

"Right," Birney said loudly. "Right. Piss on them. Piss on them and their self-satisfied talk about old age. They think they're not going to get old? They just have to wait a while, that's all. It doesn't take talent to get old. *D'où vient cette idée de jeunesse éternelle?* Huh? Answer me that *mon vieux?*"

"I don't speak French," Joe said, slightly peeved at Birney showing off.

"Look, vote against him," Birney went on, still pacing. "Just don't make a fuss. *Écoutez, mon copain, ce n'est pas la peine. Vous devez lire Monsieur Stendhal au sujet de ces choses. Tout est là. Il a dit tout, lui.*"

Joe smiled, uncertain now of what was happening. Birney passed him on one of his pacing forays, and Joe noticed a vacant look in the old man's eyes.

"I won't oppose you on this," Joe said loudly. Birney stopped pacing and faced him. "Senator?" Joe said just as loudly as before. "Senator, I won't oppose you on Anderson." A weak smile broke out on Birney's face. He started to say something but changed his mind. He left the room without saying good-bye.

"French?" Francis yelped. "He started talking French?"

Joe nodded. He was looking into the mirror of the medicine cabinet in the small bathroom off his personal office. His face was covered with lather and his shirt, jacket, and tie lay on the nearby office couch. He raised the razor and then put it down.

"While he was telling me he wasn't getting senile."

"His mother was French," Francis said. "And of course he's from Louisiana. They all have to know some French down there. Maybe he was quoting something."

"I think his brain pan is leaking."

"And you told him you wouldn't come out against Anderson? You told him *that?*"

Joe shrugged his shoulders. "Maybe he won't remember."

"No way. His guy just had me on the phone nailing the thing down. Said something about this wonderful talk the two of you had. *I* assumed it had been in English."

"Goddamn it," Joe said. He reached for a towel and wiped little islands of lather from his face and walked back into his office. He put on his shirt, tied his tie without consulting a mirror, and walked into the outstretched jacket held for him by Francis.

"I wish you'd made him ask you twice," Francis said from over Joe's shoulder. "At least then he'd owe us something."

"Maybe he did ask twice. Maybe he even offered us something. If he did, he said it all in French and I don't know what we got. Anyway, how bad can this Anderson be? Any calls about him?"

"Arthur Briggs of the NAACP. He called and talked to me. He said Edward Anderson is a racist."

"A racist?"

Francis nodded. "The man has come out in favor of segregated schools."

"Christ," Joe said with a whistle.

Joe's inter-office phone buzzed. He picked it up, listened for a moment, and turned to Francis. "Henry

Goodfellow, the director of the National Civil Rights Coalition, is on three. He says it's urgent." Joe punched the button. His face lit up with his telephone smile.

"Henry? How are you?" Joe sounded as if he were talking to an old friend, instead of someone he assumed he had met but couldn't place. Francis hurried out of the room and returned with an oversized index card. He handed it to Joe.

"Well, Henry, all of this is a bit premature. In the first place, the President has not yet sent up his name. In the second place, I haven't come out in favor of Anderson. I haven't said one word about Anderson." There was a pause. "That's a rumor," Joe said after a while. "It's not true." He looked at the index card. "How's Florence?" he asked reading the name off the card. "Give her my best, will you? And Henry Junior? Must be, what, twelve or thirteen now . . . Thirteen, huh. Wonderful. I hope you didn't get a Bar Mitzvah greeting from us, Henry." A laugh came out of the phone which Joe had pointed toward Francis. Joe held his stomach in mock laughter and then brought the phone back up to his mouth. "See you soon, Henry." He hung up the phone and the smile vanished from his face.

"Jeezus," he said.

"What now?" Francis asked.

"What now? What now?" Joe repeated. "Good question. Wonderful question. Insightful and acute question. What is now happening is that we are getting ourselves caught in what my old high school football coach used to call a shit sandwich. This is all happening very fast. The tom-toms are beating and the wagons are being drawn up and we don't even know what the fight's about. It can't be Anderson. What's an anderson? Who's an anderson? Would you buy a used anderson? Would you buy one from Richard Nixon? How about from George Allen? Fred Allen? Allen Funt?"

Francis went over to the couch and sat down. He had seen this before—his boss free-associating, letting his mind go at its own clip until he came up with either an idea or a phrase for a speech or a solution to a problem.

"Birney said something about the White House," Joe said, suddenly turning toward Francis. "He said something about the White House leaking word of the appointment—sending up a trial balloon, giving our wonderful leader a chance to put his fickle finger to the wind and see which way it's blowing. Francis, get thee to whoever at the White House is your pal and find out what the hell is happening. Gotta move quick, Francis. *Schnell!* Mucho quicko. Let's go." He scooped his hands from Francis toward the door, giving his aide a broad hint. When he had gone, Joe continued to stand just where he had been.

"Jeezus," he said to himself. "A racist. The White House is going to name a racist to the Supreme Court and then torpedo its own nomination, and I'm going to be left holding the bag." He thought of something and ran to the door.

"Francis!" he yelled.

"He's gone, Senator," a young woman whose name he had forgotten told him. "He went to the White House."

"That's impossible. He just left here. He couldn't have arranged things so quickly."

"Oh, he's had the appointment since this morning. He took a call from that nice Arthur Briggs and then he called the White House."

"Thank you," Joe said, walking back into his office. He closed the door and stood before his desk.

"Jeezus, what the hell is Francis up to at the White House?"

CHAPTER 3

The White House is one of the great American misnomers. It is, like Hollywood or Broadway, more of an area, even a state of mind, than it is an actual location. In the case of the White House, for instance, it is more than the white executive mansion with its east and west working wings, living quarters, and the ceremonial room sandwiched in the middle. It is other buildings as well, and the foremost of these is the Old Executive Office Building, a four-story wedding cake of a building created in an era of Victorian excesses. It boasts ceilings where clouds could form and hallways as wide as football fields and magnificent fireplaces in many of the office suites. It once housed the Department of State and War and then, after State moved to Foggy Bottom, just War and then later it was incorporated into the White House compound. The alley separating the building from the White House was closed off and a gate erected, and presidents came to use the building for their staffs. It was Richard Nixon who used the building for himself. He established a hideaway office there on the first floor, and it was to this office, now occupied by someone else, that Francis was heading.

He got out of the cab on Pennsylvania Avenue heading west and jaywalked across the broad street. He pushed open the gate of the Executive Office Building and looked up at the gray monstrosity. Like most Washingtonians, he loved the building. He climbed the steps slowly, purposely, aware that the tourists out on the Avenue were watching him, wondering who he was and wondering also what his business might be. It didn't matter one whit whether any of this was actually happening. It was happening in the mind of thirty-three-year-old Francis O'Connor, who had been smitten with the political bug so long ago that he could not remember when it had first bitten.

From childhood he knew where he was heading—to Washington. He appreciated the power of politics, a lesson he learned early when he applied, at the age of twelve, for the exalted job of picking up litter on the beach. He lived in Queens County, New York City, and the job of picking up beach litter was one of the more valued summer jobs. You got to the beach early and you took your pole with a nail on the end of it and you walked along, sticking the nail into the paper and dumping the paper into a canvas bag. It was easy work with wonderful work rules. One of the rules was that no one worked when it was really hot, and the other rule was that no one worked more than two hours a day. It was a Parks Department job. You applied at Democratic party headquarters.

Headquarters was a storefront under a subway el. There was a large room in the front for meetings and some smaller rooms in the back for the officers of the club and then one large room that was the domain of the local party boss. His name was Manny Gerstein and when he died, the club was named in his honor—the Manny Gerstein Independent Democratic Club.

Francis had gone to see Gerstein by himself. It was his father's idea, the notion being that the boy would do better without a parent along. He was nervous, but he biked down to the headquarters and leaned his bike against the window. An old Italian man wearing two cardigan sweaters and a cap burst from the front of the store.

"Hey, get dat bike outta here," he ordered.

Francis walked the bike over to the curb and leaned it against the parking meter.

"Better feed da meter," the old man said.

Francis looked at him quizzically.

"Put a nickel in da meter, kiddo, or some cop's gonna take your bike." He laughed, showing a gold tooth.

Francis fished in his jeans for a nickel, sensing that he was being teased, but unsure how to handle the situation. He thought the best thing to do was to find a nickel, put it into the meter, and let the old man have his fun. For all he knew, it could be Mr. Gerstein. He took a nickel from a small mound of change and was about to put it into the meter when someone grabbed his hand. He turned and saw a man with an enormous nose, rimless glasses, and dark, dirty hair.

"He's kidding with ya, kid," the man said, releasing his hand. "Gino, you're no good," he said, turning to the old man in the doorway. "You do this one more time and you're out on your ass." The old man slunk back into the store.

"He didn't mean any harm, sonny," the man with the long nose explained. "He's just an old man. Someday you'll be an old man, then you'll understand." Francis leaned his bike against the meter pole. He stepped back and looked at the man with the long nose. He was wearing a heavy tweed suit, the jacket and vest open. His tie had a picture of a rearing horse on it, its border the lasso of the cowboy on the horse. Francis looked at the man and brushed past him into the store.

"Hey, who you looking for, kid?" the man asked.

"Mr. Gerstein," Francis said.

"That's me, sonny. What can I do for you?"

An hour later, Francis staggered out of the store, loaded down with election pamphlets. The next morning, he was up at dawn. He not only delivered all the pamphlets, he actually read them all, too, and he talked to his father about the candidates. He stopped people in the hallways of apartment houses and spoke to them about the candidates—telling them to vote the organization ticket. Word of this got back to Gerstein and Francis not only got his job, he got a virtual uncle as well. The clubhouse became Francis's hangout and from Gerstein he learned the art of politics—old time politics, but politics. He watched jobs dispensed and scholarships awarded and streets paved. Garbage pick-ups were controlled from the storefront, as were liquor licenses and other matters no one wanted to talk about. Sometimes calls were made to the local precinct jail or even to the county courthouse in Forest Hills, after which some people were released from jail, others got light sentences or none at all. This was done, Francis later learned, not only for money but occasionally because Gerstein knew the family.

But there were more than favors involved. Gerstein, Francis learned, was a perpetual student. He was constantly studying his statistics—who was registered and what the turnout had been and how the vote had gone. He spent long hours going over charts and tables of numbers, row upon row of them. He was responsible for the entire Rockaway peninsula of Queens—twenty-eight precincts—and he worked hard at his job. Francis worked alongside him and over the years, in the summer, the city of New York provided his jobs and later a college scholarship came from the state and even later he was awarded a grant to study law, not to mention a job at Borough Hall in Brooklyn, where he was not expected to show up.

"You've worked for it, Francis," Gerstein told him. "Don't let it bother you." But it did.

Gerstein had a plan and as he outlined it one night to Francis in an Italian restaurant, it seemed, as the kids would later put it, neat. Francis, Gerstein said, would soon run for the state assembly. As the organization's candidate, he would naturally win.

"It goes without saying you will win," is the way Gerstein put it. "You will then be the assemblyman from this district and my number one man. You can decide in time whether you want to go to the state senate or not. Maybe a judgeship would suit you better. Up to you. Either way, you take over from me."

The two other men toasted each other in Chianti. Francis cried and Gerstein cried and the two of them shook hands, stumbling out into the street much later, kissing one another, and so it was understandable that the old man's heart broke a year later, 1968, when Francis broke with him and helped organize Queens for Eugene McCarthy. In that primary Francis stole the old man's charts and beat him, and when, two months later, Gerstein died, Francis called him a war victim.

Francis rode the McCarthy campaign like a barnacle. He stayed with it until Chicago, where he saw what happened to the kids in the streets, but instead of the experience making a radical of him, it convinced him that what the Democratic party needed was a dose of the old leadership. By 1972, after a stint hidden as a staff member to a congressional committee, he emerged as Hubert Humphrey's man in Maryland. He just showed up in the state one evening, set up shop in the Lord Baltimore Hotel in Baltimore, and took out what would later be known as the Golden Charts. He had prepared them months before and they showed, of course, for Maryland what Gerstein's charts had shown for the Rockaway peninsula—everything.

Francis did more than merely study the charts. On the day before election day, he organized a giant rally for the Charles Center of Baltimore—a large, open space in the heart of the city's financial and business center. He ordered a huge, wooden platform for speeches, but under the platform he also had constructed a door with a peephole. Inside his workmen—donated, of course, by the local carpenters' union—

built a room. A desk was placed in the middle of the room. On the walls were hung huge pictures of Hubert Horatio Humphrey, and on the day of the rally, after the mayor and the governor had introduced a politician to the crowd, he would descend the steps of the platform, go around to the side, knock twice on the door, and freeze at the peephole for a look-see. Then the politician was allowed to enter.

Francis sat at the desk, the drawers open but hidden to the entering politician. Inside the drawer were large envelopes full of money. The name of the politician and his political club were written on the envelope. It always contained an amount previously negotiated. The largest amount was twenty-five thousand dollars, and it went to a man named Pollack who once controlled the Jewish north side, but now was down to nothing but some alliances with Polish-American clubs in the east end. Still, it was going to be a close election. Pollack delivered. Humphrey took the state and the word spread about Francis.

It was McGovern, though, who was winning the big primaries, and so when the credentials and rules committees met in Washington just before the convention, a coalition formed to try and stop the South Dakota Democrat. The coordinator of that coalition effort was Francis. He challenged McGovern's victory in the California primary, arguing that the Democratic party had adopted rules outlawing winner-take-all primaries like that of California. Some of those delegates, Francis said, would have to be apportioned to the other candidates. The McGovern forces fought back, but they were forced to fight with their contested California troops, trampling over the very rules they had recommended. In the showdown vote, it was Francis who got an anti-McGovern member of Congress to call the mayor of San Juan, Puerto Rico, and tell him to instruct a woman delegate from his city to vote against McGovern or the city would lose a promised public park.

The woman, an extraordinarily graceful and lovely lady, was taken to the phone by Francis himself and given the word from San Juan. She cried. She slumped at the phone and cried, looking up at Francis from where she was sitting, tears running down her cheeks, babbling at him in Spanish.

"Okay," he said. "It's all right. Go back to your seat and forget the call."

She looked at him.

"*Comprende? Comprende?* You understand?"

"Yes," she said. She rose, dabbed her eyes with a handkerchief, and returned to her chair. Joe had seen it all. He had an offer.

"When you need a job, Francis, give me a call."

Two weeks later Francis called from the floor of the convention and Joe hired him on the spot.

Now Francis was standing before a white-shirted member of the Executive Protection Service, the police force that guards the White House and the embassies. The guard was heavyset and mustachioed, with his hair cut close on the sides. Francis showed him his congressional ID. The guard referred to a clipboard.

"Turn left at the corridor directly behind me, sir, then take that corridor all the way to the end. Make a right and watch the numbers. You'll go past the stairway and then it's the first office on the left after that."

The ceilings must have been twenty feet high and the corridors about as wide, and as Francis walked down the hall his heels made a clicking sound that echoed far out in front of him. He seemed almost to be walking ahead of himself. He passed the staircase and turned left at the next office. He walked into a large reception area, a desk directly in front of him. To his right was the main office and to the left a large, but clearly subordinate office. Francis announced himself to the receptionist.

"Francis O'Connor to see Jerry Rappaport."

The woman, a frail thing all in white, started to hit the button of a phone with her finger when the door to the right-hand office suddenly opened.

"Drop dead, O'Connor," Rappaport said.

"Drop dead, Rappaport. How the hell are you?"

The two men laughed at this, a quick variation of an old campaign routine, and shook hands. "C'mon in," Rappaport said. "Let me show you how I've risen in the world." Rappaport, a bear of a man, draped an arm around Francis's shoulder and steered him into the room. The power of the man was astounding. A touch from him was like a strong poke from someone else. He was a large, cigar-smoking man, potbellied and bellicose and very tough. He was once a union man, first an organizer and then a COPE guy in the Midwest and later the number two COPE man in Washington. Labor had lent him to the stop-McGovern coalition in 1972, which is where he and Francis got to know each other. Rappaport was about as thorough a political professional as there was in Washington. He was also deeply committed to the union movement, to "the working stiff," as he put it, and to disguising the fact that he had a doctorate degree in English literature.

The big man strode into the middle of the room. He waved his arms and did an imitation pirouette. "Mon quarters," he said. To one side, facing the window which in turn looked out upon the White House, was a large Federal-style desk. Before the window were two couches, covered in flowery slipcovers. To both sides of the windows were floor to ceiling bookcases, which were virtually empty. He pointed to them.

"Due to my rapid rise in the world of politics, and, in particular, to my rapid rise here at la maison blanche, I have not yet had a chance to have my books brought in and displayed, to the chagrin of all those who think I am nothing but a union gorilla. C'mere, I want to show you something." He pointed to a rip in the carpet under the coffee table. "The famous tapes, buddy boy. The famous tapes."

"You mean this was Nixon's office?"

"I do, indeed."

"Well, drop dead."

"Drop dead, indeed."

"C'mere," Rappaport said, curling his finger at Francis and tiptoeing over to the bathroom. He pointed up to a metal bar set into the door jamb.

"The royal chinning bar," he said.

"Well, drop dead."

"And beyond that, the royal bathroom. Can you see it now? It is 1974, during Watergate. Agnew is in a load of trouble. Ehrlichman is getting the shakes. Haldeman is crying. Pat is walking the halls of the

White House in her sleep crying, 'Abraham, Abraham. I need a drink, Mr. Lincoln.' John Dean, THE John Dean, the one we have all come to know and love, is leaking to half the press and Radio Free Europe, and Richard Nixon calls a meeting. He has the FBI and the CIA and the Army and the Navy. He talks by satellite to other satellites. He lifts the phone and talks to the future. He makes the San Andreas fault move an inch or two. Generals stand and salute. Admirals stand and salute. Spies go out in the cold. Or come in from the cold. I forget . . . And then like you, like me, and like all men everywhere, he comes in here to the royal bathroom and he sits down on the royal throne, looking like a damn fool, feeling like a damn fool, doing what we all do, and he realizes that he is finished. He may be the president, but he is just a man. He sits there with his pants down, he sits right there on that there floor sonny, and it occurs to him that it is all over. Right there. That's where it happened. It had to happen. There should be a plaque put into the floor right there: Here is where Richard Nixon realized his goose was cooked."

"Well, drop dead."

"Drop dead, indeed."

Rappaport walked back to his desk. "I've reserved us a table next door in the Big House," he said. "We can do the serious talking over there. Meanwhile there's something else I want to show you." He walked over to the couch where his jacket had been deposited and slung it over his shoulder. Francis followed him out of his office and then to the corridor, where he turned left. The two of them walked down the hall until Rappaport stopped before a narrow door that looked like it opened on to a broom closet.

"This is it."

"I bet it is," Francis said, not knowing what he was looking at.

"This is the room where the tapes were stored. It is Room 175½ and in it, if you read your court depositions, is where the presidential tapes were stored. It is also where the famous tape recorders were kept and where they did their famous recording. Now I show you this room for a reason. You remember a fellow named Deep Throat?"

"Indeed I do."

"You remember how he knew everything? How he knew what the FBI was up to and what the President was up to and what the prosecutors were up to and what CREEP was up to?"

"Indeed I do."

"Well, everytime I eat over at the Big House, I pass this room. I know this room. I mean, I know what went on in this room. Rooms around here fascinate me. There's one over in the Big House, for instance, that's a little like this one. It's under the stairs and it's where Eisenhower used to sneak away to do his painting. It's also where Warren Harding used secretly to see what's her name. I always wonder if Ike knew that.

"Anyway, one day last week I'm passing this room and I try to imagine what it was once like. It's locked, you see." He tried the door. "I tried the door then, too. I imagine those Sony 800 B tape recorders on some shelves, and I imagine some file cabinets with the used tapes in them, and I imagine a couple of cartons on the floor containing new tape. Pretty simple. Actually, it *was* pretty simple, and there was a lot a system like that could not pick up. It was not a very good system. You with me, sonny?"

"Indeed," Francis said. In fact, he was intrigued.

"Now, I imagine the whole system is operating. Nixon's in there where my office is now and he's talking and the machines are in here and they're recording. They switch over automatically when one runs out of tape, and when they both run out of tape they stop. So I imagine this and then I imagine some guy comes into the room. He's a secret service technician. Some guy you never heard of. He's got short hair and he wears a double-knit suit and he votes, when he votes, for anyone who'll keep the blacks out of his kid's school.

"So he comes in and he sees that both machines are out of tape. He takes out the old tapes and labels them and then he puts in new tapes, and he's about to leave the room, when he wonders whether or not the machine is working. I mean, wouldn't you wonder? It's your job, man. What if those machines are on the fritz? The royal words of the royal president will be lost to posterity, not to mention the royal publishing house. So you take your basic earphones from the shelf and you plung them into the little hole where it says 'monitor' and you give a listen. Your eyes go pop-pop. You can't believe it. You hear about crimes. Crimes! You keep listening. You play tapes. You play the old tapes and the new tapes and pretty soon you know all there is to know about Watergate. You know everything because his holiness, the president knows everything. The FBI is reporting to him and the Justice Department is reporting to him and CREEP and the CIA and John Dean and everybody. You come out of the closet. This room here. You come out after, say, a week of listening and you call an old buddy from the Navy. He's now with *The Washington Post*. You put your money in the slot. You dial the number. It rings once. It rings twice. Someone picks up. You take a deep breath. You say, 'Hello, Woodward, it is I, Deep Throat.' "

"Well, drop dead," Francis said, impressed.

"Drop dead, indeed. Let us now eat."

The two of them crossed West Executive Avenue and entered the White House from a side entrance. They passed under a little canopy and ran smack into a tight group of Army colonels coming out. They walked along a hallway and then down a small flight of stairs until they came to the White House Mess. The Mess, reserved for senior staff and run for the White House by the Navy, is divided into two rooms, nearly identical, seating about thirty persons apiece. Rappaport and Francis were guided to the room on their right and seated at the rear table. They both ordered the tuna fish salad plate and iced tea and they both said nothing, concentrating instead on the people coming in and out and the smattering of conversation they could pick up. They could actually hear very little of what was being said. Usually nothing at all could be heard from one table to the next.

"Have you per chance seen this morning's paper?" Rappaport asked Francis.

"Yeah."

Rappaport smiled. "This Anderson's going to make a wonderful judge, right?"

"I don't know," Francis said.

"Wrong. He will make a terrible judge."

"Excuse me for being wrong," Francis said. "Sometimes I can't help myself."

"It's all right, sonny."

"That story was a deliberate leak by someone here, wasn't it?" said Francis.

Rappaport leaned back in his chair and smiled. "No comment," he said.

"Hey, Jerry, look. What's going on? My guy's getting caught in the middle here and I got to do some downfield blocking. What's up?"

"Don't panic, sonny," Rappaport said, still smiling. He lit a big, wonderful cigar, blowing smoke directly at the ceiling. Then he leaned forward on his elbows, the cigar pointing toward the ceiling, and crooked his finger at Francis.

"C'mere," he said.

Francis mimicked Rappaport's pose, planting his elbows on the table, ready to do some listening.

"There are things I can tell you and things I can't tell you. What I can tell you is this: we are in a terrible situation here with this Anderson thing. Birney wants the guy on the big bench in the worst way. He and the President have had several very long talks about it and they have reached an agreement, I hear. I dunno some of this for sure, but as I get it, Birney threatened to block everything that came to the Hill from the White House unless he can get his man on the bench. We have some big programs coming his way, directly into his committee, and some of them, I don't mind telling you, have to do with labor. Birney could kill them all, kill everything. Sit on them. Refuse to hold hearings. Make us look stupid. Make us look like we can't deliver. Make us look weak. We didn't win very big last time out, you know. No guarantee we got anything nailed this time around either. We could use those bills."

Rappaport rocked back in his chair, took a drag on the cigar, filled his mouth with an enormous volume of smoke, and watched it all float up to the ceiling. Then he pitched his body forward again and resumed his position, his elbows on the table.

"Now on the other hand, this Anderson's no bargain. If I were still just a labor guy, I would be forced to fight him very hard. He's for right to work and all those nice things, and he's about as conservative as you can get without being downright reactionary. I would have to fight someone like that and, I'm afraid, that's just what the unions are going to do. They are not going to like Anderson one bit. If I were the senator from a state like New York, I would have to bear that in mind. I would also have to bear in mind that our brothers of color are not going to like him either. There is some talk that back when he was nothing more than a red-neck lawyer running for office, state legislature or something like that, he demagogued with the best of them—the politics of nigger, nigger, nigger, as the late Lyndon Baines Johnson used to say. God knows what he said and what's on the record. But the thing of it is that the guy is not all bad. He's one of those strange southern birds. You kept running into them during the 1960s. Very funny. They would politic with the best of them, and they would file suit after suit and tie you up in the courts, but when they lost and the court ruled against them, they toed the line. The judges were like that. They didn't like blacks any, but they loved the law. The law! Da law, son is all dere is."

Francis laughed.

"Seriously. That's the way they were. Once it was law, it was law; and Anderson, I'm convinced, is one of those characters. He will not play with the law."

"But you said he'll make a terrible judge," Francis said.

"Right. For us. For labor. He'll be bad for us. We have some right to work and organizing cases moving up the ladder now to the Supremes and we think a guy like Anderson is a real threat. But that's our special interest and that's our informed guess. You never know what happens to a man when he dons them weighty robes of the Supremes. The point is that he's not all that bad. He might even be all right and there's a chance he could be good. It's not a distinguished appointment, but it's not a rip-off either, and what's at stake is more important. If we lose Anderson we lose Birney and a lot of good legislation gets lost. It's not black and white, I'll grant you that. But it's pretty clear to me which way your guy should go."

"Ah, now we get down to business."

"Righto, sonny boy. The reason I called you this A.M. is that story in *The Washington Post*. It blows our strategy and it was probably leaked for that purpose. It went off before we had a chance to get together with fellows like you and for the President to meet with Joe. I mean, it's terrible the story being out like that and members of the committee not knowing a thing about it. Birney went through the roof this morning. Called over here at six. Can you imagine that? Six in the morning!"

"Who'd he talk to?"

"His royal highness himself. Who else would be up at that hour of the morning?"

The two of them laughed.

"This puts us in a box. Before we can get to the right people, they read about it in the newspaper. And then before we can do anything, the honchos from the NAACP and all over are getting on the phone and calling people and getting commitments to kill the appointment. We never even had a chance to get to the civil rights organizations on this one. All we had was this commitment to Birney that if we could see to it, Anderson would be the nominee. We had to trot him out a bit first. That's why not even the bar association had the name. What you think?"

"I'm not sure."

"Francis, my son, thou art not leveling with me. Thou art not telling the square and honest truth with me, lovely wonderful me who goes back a long way with you and is, may I remind you, much bigger than you are."

"Okay," Francis said, turning suddenly grim. "It sucks. Let me tell you why it sucks. In the first place, you've lost control. The story's in the paper and there's no way to get it back. In the second place, this guy Anderson is no winner. You could do better. Blacks don't like him and labor doesn't like him. My guy is the senator from New York State. You think blacks and labor are outnumbered by hunchbacked Lithuanians?"

"The legislation, Francis, the legislation we all need. Our country needs that legislation, Francis, not to mention the reelection of our beloved President. I mean that, Francis. This guy is a good man, a fine President. I want him reelected."

"Sure. So do it. But this Anderson thing is flying blind on faith. Do it for the President. Do it for Birney. Do it for legislation that won't get bottled up. Do it for every reason other than the man's wonderful and a politically sound appointment."

"Your guy can live with him, Francis," Rappaport said. "You can buy him."

"I'm not so sure, Jerry."

"Yeah, well I am. Birney says he's got a commitment from your guy."

"So, drop dead."

"Drop dead yourself."

"Indeed."

The two men smiled. Rappaport grabbed Francis's hand at the wrist and arm wrestled him down to the table with no effort.

"Politics is for the strong, O'Connor."

Before there was a subway in Washington, there was a subway. It ran on a monorail from the Capitol building to the two Senate office buildings and it was, for a time, a wonderful tourist attraction. It was open on top and powered electrically, and it was operated, as was everything else in Congress, by congressional appointees, some of whom, in recent times, were women. One of them operated the subway that pulled out from the Dirksen Building heading toward the Capitol, with the junior senator from the State of New York as a passenger. She gave him the eye. Joe Tynan, however, would not have noticed if the woman had one eye in the middle of her forehead. He was deep in conversation with Francis O'Connor who, having come straight from the White House, felt very much as if his boss were walking into a trap.

Coming over in the other subway, the real Washington subway, which had cost something like $5 or $6 billion to build, Francis had diagramed matters in his head. He had his worst-case scenario and his best-case scenario. His worst case was that Joseph Tynan stays mute, says nothing, and votes in the end against Anderson. To do this, he would have to rebuff the inevitable appeals from the labor-civil rights coalition that he do more than simply vote no—that he take a leadership role in the fight. They would forever see him as a good-looking nice-guy senator without the stomach for a fight, someone who could really not be counted on—a fair-weather politician. The damage would be limited to them. The best case was far different. In that scenario Joe went out in front in opposition to Anderson, earning the gratitude of the civil rights-labor coalition and their allies in the legal and academic communities. He showed the Senate and the rest of Washington that he knew how to wage a fight and win. He would make the Anderson fight his own, and if this meant going up against Birney, so be it. It was time he was weaned. Francis smiled. He could see Joe nodding his head to all of that and then asking, "But what about going up against the President of the United States, Francis?" He would work on his answer to that one.

"I don't understand," Joe said, turning to Francis. "Birney said he's a moderate. What the hell is everybody getting so excited about?"

"Well, it's those statements he made twenty years ago."

Joe shrugged. "My God, I'd hate to get hanged on something I said twenty years ago. Things were different then. When are we going to stop imposing the standards of one era on another? It smacks of McCarthyism, that's what it does." He pointed a finger at Francis. "Where were you twenty years ago?"

Francis looked stunned. "I don't know. I . . . can't remember. High school?"

Joe waved him off the question. "Never mind."

"Never mind, never mind. Senator, if Arthur Briggs of the NAACP wants you to step in there, I think you have to go along."

"Francis, if I fought Birney on this, I'd be going up against the most powerful man in the Senate. Not to mention the President. I'd get my brains knocked out."

They stepped off the subway and walked over to the escalator that would take them to the Capitol building. Joe paused and gave Francis a studied look, considering both what his aide was saying and why he was saying it. Sometimes it was hard for Joe to understand Francis. He knew Francis sometimes worked independently, getting information that Joe did not have access to. Joe liked that. It was even more protection in a town where there was no such thing as too much. No matter. This business with Birney was bigger than tactics or strategy. Birney was different.

"He's also a friend," Joe told Francis. "Birney. He was my mentor when I first came here. He gave me a subcommittee chairmanship long before he had to give me anything. Those were the days, Francis, when a freshman senator wasn't supposed to even speak on the floor, not to mention chair a subcommittee."

Francis looked at Joe. "Well, of course, Senator, that's a decision no one can make for you."

"Yeah, terrific," Joe said. He shot a look at his watch. "See you later," he said, going up the escalator to record his presence on the floor of the Senate. Francis turned and headed back to the subway. He heard his own voice in his head: "Well, of course, Senator, that's a decision no one can make for you." He mocked himself, asking himself if that was the answer he was going to think of. Remarkable what he could do when he had plenty of time.

"Francis," he heard someone yell. He turned around and it was Joe. "Are we still on with Arthur Briggs?"

"Yeah. One today."

"Well, let's just see what Arthur Briggs has to say," Joe said with a good-bye wave. Francis waved and also smiled and walked briskly for the subway. He was feeling better now. He, for one, was not going to wait to see what Arthur Briggs was going to say. He was going to call him and find out ahead of time. Arthur Briggs, he felt pretty sure now, was going to be tough.

"Moderate!" yelled Arthur Briggs. "Moderate! My fat black ass he's a moderate. Anderson may be a moderate to Senator Birney, but he's no moderate to us." Briggs shot Francis a look of satisfaction and then his eyes came to rest on the woman on the couch. Her name was Karen Traynor. She had accompanied Briggs, who had presumed apparently that the mere mention of her name would be enough of an introduction. Joe had said nothing to her, but there wasn't a person in the room, including Karen Traynor, who didn't notice that the Senator spent a lot of time looking at the lady with Arthur Briggs. Briggs himself was getting a kick out of what was happening. At one time he had to stop his presentation to make sure he had the Senator's attention.

Briggs was a performer, but he was also a man of incredible courage, a civil rights leader from the old days, a preacher who had gone to law school at night, who had defended his clients while under indictment himself, who had boned up for his trial appearances in Jim Crow rooming houses where the heat and the flies kept him awake—a man of enormous physical presence, short and strong and bald-headed, and armed with a voice that had been trained to carry to the last church pew on a sultry Sunday. No one ever slept when Arthur Briggs preached, that was for sure, and he was preaching now. He took in the room, his eyes settling on Joe. This was going to be easy, he thought. Joe Tynan was a decent man. He had always liked him. This would take some talking, maybe. But send up the proper flags—human rights, civil rights, the importance of the Supreme Court—and Joseph Tynan would salute and fall into line. He was, after all, a decent man.

"Well, I'm still not convinced that this man is all that bad," Joe said. His voice was weak and lacked conviction. "People do rise to the office." Joe winced when he said it. Even he knew that that one wouldn't work.

"Senator," said the blonde woman on the couch, "I'd like to read you something." She was holding a file folder on her lap from which she had taken an aged piece of legal-size paper. "In my heart I have never accepted integration and I never will." She looked up at Joe. "How would you feel about a man who said that?"

"Not good," Joe said.

The two of them stared at each other. Joe had never seen a woman quite like her—not beautiful in a pretty way, but startlingly attractive. Her features looked as if they had been chiseled, like a face on a cameo. You could see every bone in her face, especially her cheek bones, which were raised and which she highlighted with just the right amount of rouge. Briggs, once again spotting the eyeball contact, moved in to break the clinch.

"Mrs. Traynor is a very fine labor lawyer who is also our counsel in Louisiana," he said. "She *knows* Anderson's background." He turned to Joe. "Now whoever leads the fight against Anderson is going to get a lot of attention. Someone is going to get a lot of ink on this one. Either way, up or down, you cannot lose. You will be fighting a bad man. You can not lose that kind of fight. Anderson can lose. We can lose. The President can lose. Birney can lose, but *you* can not. You or whoever . . . if it is not you." He walked over to the couch where Karen was sitting and abruptly took the folder from her hands. "If you choose not to take him on, then we'll release this statement to the press ourselves."

"At which point," Joe said with a touch of sarcasm in his voice, "as the fiery liberal from New York, I'll have to join the fight against him anyway."

"That, Senator, will be up to you," Briggs answered. He turned and shot Francis a look. They both gazed at Joe, who realized he was caught in a squeeze play—the old rock and a hard place. If possible, he was going to have to figure out a way to turn the squeeze play into a sacrifice. In the meantime, he would be very cautious.

"Very nice, Arthur," Joe said, pointing to the folder. "I would need a lot more of that. I can't quote him out of context, and I'm certainly not going to call a press conference and then read off a piece of yellow paper supplied from who knows where."

"There's a film of him saying this," Karen said.

Joe ignored her remark. He continued to talk to Briggs. "And there has to be a consistent pattern that shows him to be unfit, at the very least hostile to civil rights."

"You'll have it, Senator," Karen said.

"All right," Joe said, slapping his hands together. "All right, you get me that and I'm with you." He looked once more at Karen. He saw something in *her* eyes. She looked away.

Briggs walked over for a handshake, a broad smile on his face. "Thank you, Senator, we'll be in touch." Karen rose from the couch, gathering her material, smoothing down her skirt. She joined the others in the middle of the room. Joe turned to her and extended his hand. "Nice to meet you, Mrs. Traynor," he said. They shook hands and all of them walked to the door. Joe opened it, held it open for them, and then he closed the door behind them.

"Well, it looks like we're in for a fight," Francis said in a chipper fashion.

Joe stared at his assistant. He spoke very deliberately. "This man is no racist."

"He is to *them*."

"You know, if Anderson doesn't get this appointment, he's going to get Birney's seat in the Senate. Birney needs this to get reelected."

"Well, so do you, Senator. So do you."

Joe had no reply. He walked over to the couch and sat down heavily. Francis went to the window and parked himself on the radiator cover, his back to the Capitol. He realized he had spoken out of turn.

"Look," he said in an apologetic tone of voice, "this is also one hell of an opportunity."

Joe gave Francis what Francis later called his Et Tu Brute look. He was impressed and a bit shocked by his aide's cynicism.

"I don't think I ought to turn on a friend for the sake of opportunity, do you?" Joe asked.

"No, of course not. But—"

Joe cut him off. "Let me tell you something about Birney. Better yet, let me ask you something. You know how he voted on all the civil rights bills?"

"Against?"

"Right. No points, though, because you would expect him to vote no. Not that it mattered. We had the votes anyway. But let me ask you this: did you ever wonder how those bills reached the floor? I mean, ask yourself who was chairman of the Judiciary Committee at the time?"

"Birney?"

"Right."

"Then how'd those bills get past him? I don't know. Wait! I *do* know. He got sick. A heart attack. *You* were there, happened at a markup session. I remember it now. What did you do? Slip him something?"

"Almost. What we slipped him was a strategy for letting those bills go without looking like an ass back home. I forget who thought of the heart attack. I think it was Kittner."

"Kittner?"

"Kittner! Then the two of them later filibustered the thing as long as they could. We waited them out and won it, but the real trick was the heart attack. This is a decent man you're asking me to step on. Decent and powerful. You think I could go up against someone like that for the sake of opportunity?"

"No, of course not," Francis said dejectedly. Then his face brightened. "But if you win . . . If you win, you could get a lot of stuff passed around here. You could do a lot of good."

Joe chuckled, Francis was incorrigible—the Sammy Glick of politics.

"Well," said Joe, "let's see what that lady comes up with before we make any decisions. What's her name again?"

"Karen Traynor."

"Oh, yeah, Karen Traynor."

CHAPTER 4

When Joseph Tynan watched Joseph Tynan on television, he was something to behold. There was nothing casual about the way he watched, the way he took mental notes, the way he noticed his own performance, and the way he graded himself. He studied the way he held his body and the cut of his hair—what looked too long and what looked too short. He noticed how television emphasized hair, made it look like there was more than there was, and also how when he had his hair cut short, his ears seemed to stand out. He worked on his smile, trying to keeep it small so it would not look oversized on television, and he practiced hard with his voice, too. When he was tired, he tended to drop his voice at the end of sentences. The consensus of the Capitol press corps was that no one on the Hill was better at using television than Joseph Tynan, but he himself felt there was always room for improvement—always something to learn. Now once again he was learning. The teacher in this case was Merv Griffin.

"Senator, of all the public figures we have, you come off as an exceptionally genuine person. How do you account for that?"

"Well, you get more votes that way."

Griffin threw his head back, laughed, and nodded to the audience as if to say, "Hey, this guy's all right." Joe noticed the little nod, that touching base that enlisted the audience on Merv's side. He liked the way he was looking. He was doing fine, he felt.

"Someone just told me that your son just ran for President," Griffin said.

Joe took his eyes from the television set and rested them on his son Paul, who was sitting cross-legged in the middle of the room. The eleven-year-old boy, still chubby with the fat of boyhood and with his hair long but neatly styled, brought his hands up to his eyes and rocked on his haunches. He was both pleased and horrified that his name had come up on the television show. Once again he would be a real somebody at school the next day. But Paul had been one of his father's props before. Not every time did he find it an enjoyable experience.

On the television screen Joe was nodding. "Of his class, yes. President of his class." He looked straight into the camera. "And suddenly there was this enormous wave of anxiety that went through our house. We all wanted him to win, y'know."

"Sure, sure," said Merv.

In the Tynan television room everyone leaned forward in anticipation. Ellie gave Joe a smiling look, as if to say she trusted him to handle this well. Paul continued to rock on the floor and behind them all Janet, fifteen years old and dressed in a bathrobe and pajamas, stood in the doorway, observing, witholding her presence from the group.

"So we took one of my speeches," Joe told Griffin, "and fixed it a bit, and he was just great at it. *You* couldn't give that speech any better."

"How'd he do?" Merv asked.

Joe deadpanned into the camera. "He lost."

The audience broke up. Merv laughed and gave the audience another one of his isn't-he-terrific looks. The camera zoomed in on Joe. He was smiling. In the television room of the Tynan household, Paul threw his arms over his head. "Oh shit," he said.

Joe turned to his son, a concerned look on his face. "I'm sorry, Paul. Did I embarrass you?"

"That's all right," Paul said, looking away. There was movement in the doorway. Joe looked up in time to see Janet turn and walk off. He exchanged looks with Ellie who signaled him with her head to follow Janet. Joe found her in her room, already in bed, a geometry textbook in her hands, a pouting expression on her face. Like Paul, she was dark-haired, but unlike the boy she had taken the rest of her looks from her mother. She had Ellie's high cheek bones and something of her nose. "Going to have bazzoms like my mother," Joe had once said to Ellie. Most of the time Janet was a kid, dressing in overalls and plaid shirts and wearing her hair parted in the middle, tied back in a ponytail or pigtail. But when she dressed up, put on a skirt or a dress, she suddenly was a young woman. It was those moments when Joe knew the time was coming when the kid phase would disappear all together.

Now he gave her a concerned look and sat down on the edge of the bed.

"What is it?" Janet said, putting the book down on her lap.

"I just want to see how you're doing," he said.

"I'm reading."

"Fine. Go ahead."

"You're just going to sit there?" she said in disbelief.

Joe nodded his head. "I'll watch you read."

Janet looked at her father for a moment, as if waiting for him to show his cards. When he did nothing, she shrugged her shoulders, said "Okay," and reached for her book. She brought it up to her face. As she did so, Joe playfully put his finger close to her eye. It was an old routine of theirs and Janet fought a smile.

"What *are* you doing?" she asked.

"You still reading?"

"Yes."

"Go ahead. I won't bother you."

Janet picked up her book again and again Joe put his finger close to her eye.

"Will you stop it?" she said, giggling.

"If you want to talk, I'm here," Joe said, taking down his hand.

"I notice that," Janet said. "Where will you be if I don't want to talk?"

"Also here."

"In other words, I'm trapped."

"I guess so, yeah."

Janet breathed out in studied exasperation. She eyed the door and then reached for her book, which she brought back up to her face. Suddenly, she bolted for the door. Joe, who had been warned by her eyes, lunged after her. The two of them reached the door at the same time, she standing, Joe on his knees, both of them fighting for the doorknob. Janet collapsed to the floor in spasms of giggles. She sat on the floor with her back against the wall. Joe also sat on the floor, blocking the door. He reached for a straight chair and jammed it under the knob. Then he moved over to her.

"So how's everything going with you?" he said matter-of-factly.

"Lousy." Her expression had suddenly turned stormy.

"Why? What's the matter?"

Janet said nothing. She brought her knees up to her chin, hugged them, and stared directly at the floor.

"You want to know?" she said after a while.

"Yes."

"Really?"

"Janet, what's bothering you?"

"Life sucks."

"I see," Joe said, as if she had just said something sensible. "What do you mean, life sucks?"

"It sucks."

"Yeah, well, in what way exactly does it suck?"

"Every way."

"You know, you're not being very explicit."

"I'm not very happy, okay?"

He put his arm around her. "Why babe?" he asked softly.

She looked up from the floor and at him. "Because," she answered.

"Jesus," Joe said, dropping his arm. "This is like pulling teeth. Is it school? Is it Mom and me? Is it a boy?" She looked away, tucked her knees under her chin again, and once more studied the floor. Joe ducked under her gaze. "Am I getting warm?" he singsonged.

"I don't want to talk about it, Dad," she said, looking away from him.

He straightened up. "Okay, look, whatever you're going through, Mom and I have probably gone through it, too. Use us."

"Maybe I'll talk to Mom," the girl whispered.

"Should I get her?"

"I mean someday," she said, her voice showing exasperation.

"All right, you don't have to tell us anything personal. But when you're ready . . . a little hint, okay?"

"Okay," she said.

Joe got to his feet and extended a hand. She took it and he reared back, hoisting her to her feet. She got into the bed and pulled up the covers. She reached for the geometry book and clutched it to her chest as she used to do with her teddy bear. Joe leaned over. He gave her a kiss on the forehead.

"See you later," he said.

In the world according to Joseph Tynan, there were two entities. There were his kids and there was everything else. Always, the two forces were at war. His job, his speeches, his campaigns, his social life (such as it was), even Ellie conspired to keep him away from his children. They were the expendable ones, the ones who would wait, the ones who would always be there, the ones, in the end, you could push around, who would accept any love they could get. He seized upon the concept of "quality time"—the notion that parents in a rush spend little time with their children, but that the time they do spend with them is not wasted, not empty, not silly, but rich. It is time in which much is invested—emotion and care. He loved the concept and he recited the theory often, carrying on in a very convincing fashion, he thought, on a panel discussion of the father as politician that was held at the American University in Washington. The others on the forum had been Fritz Mondale and Edward Brooke. Afterward Mondale, Brooke, and he had stopped for a minute at their cars in the parking lot and talked over the show. Joe had his key in the car door.

"Quality time," Mondale said. "So that's what you call it."

"Yeah, there's another word for it, though."

"What's that, Joe?"

"Bullshit."

They all laughed. Joe turned the key, got into his car, and drove away.

Something about that night had stuck with him, maybe the realization that he was becoming just what his father had been in his own way. Joe's father, Joseph Tynan, Sr., had been fairly famous around the New York City area. He once had been a vaudevillian, a comedian who had more routines than he could possibly remember, but who later became one of the first hits of daytime television. He did a kid show, *The Officer Tynan Show*, in which he dressed as an old-time cop with a proper helmet and billy club and an Irish accent, and he worked all of his old skits. What had once worked for adults in vaudeville was now working for children on television, a turn of events that confounded everyone.

Joseph Tynan, Sr., was about as Irish as you could get—first generation and somewhat of a professional Irishman. He knew, or he claimed to have known, George S. Cohan, and he hinted that he was the secret composer behind "Mary." He became bitter, his career was going nowhere. He ate and he paid the rent and he had a son and a wife, but most of his days he spent hanging around a candy store in the Bronx, waiting for a call from his agent.

The call came with the advent of television. Joseph Tynan, Sr., took the job, protesting all the time that it was beneath him and that it was only for a short time anyway, and he was as amazed as anyone when he became a hit. All of a sudden Joe Junior's dad was a star and Joe Junior himself was something of a neighborhood celebrity.

With the new money the family moved. Joe Senior had urged a move to Manhattan, but Joe's mother, Rose, wanted to be near her Italian relatives, some of whom lived in Inwood, Long Island. So they moved near there, to Cedarhurst, a South Shore town where the lower class was middle class and the upper class was middle class and even the middle class was middle class. There was no poverty and there was no wealth, and it was the sort of town, at least it was then, where a girl could get a reputation if she wasn't careful and where middle-class values were never questioned.

With the move, though, came the disappearance of Joe Senior. Years later Joe was to learn about other women, but that was never the full story. The full story was money—his career. He was suddenly in demand. It seemed a shopping center could not open without him and a Bar Mitzvah would not mean a thing without him. After a while he all but franchised himself, allowing other actors to stand in for him at some shopping center openings, and the inaugurals of drive-in theaters. And when he accepted an engagement in the mountains for the Christmas-Hanukkah holidays, he told Joe that it was a stand-in who would perform. The family had a little Christmas ritual in which Joe Senior always dressed up as Santa Claus and handed out the presents. Some years they were joined by Pie-Face Pete, an old vaudevillian pal of his father's who did one of the world's great drunk acts. Once a year Ed Sullivan would give him a shot.

"Great man, Shulliben," Pete would say in his drunken slur and everyone would crack up laughing.

That Christmas the family was gathered around the tree in the Cedarhurst home. Joe Senior, who had been away, was set to make his promised entrance as Santa Claus. Joe was told to close his eyes. The boy did so. He was nine years old, in the never-never land of Santa Claus belief—no longer a believer, but not quite an agnostic either. He squeezed his eyes closed with all his might and then, when told to open them, popped them open. There was Santa Claus, the familiar costume, even down to the tear in the shoulder where his father once had actually tried to squeeze up the chimney.

The Santa Claus came into the room, ho-ho-hoing, pounding his chest, and approaching the tree. He tugged at his beard and leaned over to pick up the presents. He took an armful of boxes in his hands, discarding those that were not for Joe. That left three. He went to put the other two under the tree and lost his balance. He teetered for a split second but then seemed to catch himself, only to do a quick step backward, almost into the tree. He straightened up, looked down at himself as if he was concerned, saw the boxes in his hand, and jumped back as if in surprise.

"Shay, shom shonbitch gave me shom presents." With that, he fell down in a sitting position, looked around him, and burped. Rose Tynan cracked up, but Joe just stood and looked at Santa bug-eyed.

"Pie-Face!" he protested. His mother looked at him surprised. "Pie-Face, I thought that was Daddy." He burst into tears and ran from the room, his mother running after him. Pie-Face was left sitting on the floor. He looked around, and according to what Joe later learned from his father, the old vaudevillian said, "From now on, I'm only playing Shulliben."

Later, much later, actually, they would all get a good laugh out of the Pie-Face episode and Joe would never tell his father how much he had hurt him. He figured, though, that the old man knew, because when Joe later ran for office, his father was always there, bringing in the crowds and especially the kids with his routines, sometimes canceling paying dates, explaining only, "I owe ya, Joe." When the old man died, Joe was already in the Senate, already having vowed never to miss a roll-call vote. He missed one for the funeral. He stood by the grave side with his mother and Pie-Face and he tried to look dignified for the photographers, but when the body was lowered into the ground, and they all turned to go, he looked into Pie-Face's eyes.

86

The old man swayed back a little and buckled his knees, and Joe threw his arms around him and hugged him. Pie-Face cried and Joe cried and no one said a word when one week later, Peter Eisenberg reported to work as a case worker in Joe's New York office. Joe knew him as Pie-Face Pete, and when the administrator of the New York office asked why they were hiring a broken-down vaudevillian, Joe straightened up, got red in the face, and said, "Because Shulliben is dead."

While a student at Catholic University, Joe got a job as a Capitol policeman. His father had arranged for the appointment under the patronage of the local Long Island congressman, the about-to-become felon James Tobin. Joe was nothing more than a glorified watchman, but on his rounds he met other young men like himself. Some were elevator operators and others were so-called engineers, but what they all were was young men thirsting to get close to the politics of the nation's capitol. They were all patronage appointees, some of them with no-show jobs, but they were all expected to someday return to their home districts and repay their patrons with a modest amount of volunteer work.

At night the patronage cops and the patronage engineers and elevator operators and janitorial workers would sit in the hallways of the Capitol and sing rock and roll songs. They would bounce the rhythm off the marble hallways, and when they tired of that, they would talk politics. They had all the answers and they vowed that they would come back to this place as congressmen themselves. Some of them did. One of them was Joe.

First he dropped drama as a major and took government. Then he dropped Catholic University all together and switched to New York University. It was there that he met Eleanor Montgomery, a psychology major, a true beauty, and, he said, the first Episcopalian he had ever known. They were married in his senior year, her junior year, in the high-ceilinged and wood-lined office of Surrogate Anthony DeFalco. As the invitation said, a reception followed at the Gramercy Park Hotel. The newlyweds rented a small house in Cedarhurst and both of them commuted to Manhattan on the Long Island Railroad. Already Joe was implementing his plan. He was never going to leave his district. The Tynans lived in that small house during law school and for years afterward. It was there that Paul and Janet were born.

After law school Joe turned down offers from Manhattan law firms. Instead he joined a local firm with a general practice and took everything that came at him. For two years he did what he was told, handled all the cases the firm assigned, and some that he himself brought in. In the meantime he was preparing what later became known as the Four Sisters suits. He filed it one day at the county courthouse in Hempstead, and then he and Ellie, moving very fast, dropped off copies of the suit at all the newspapers and radio stations in the county. They paid particular attention to the weeklies, writing news releases that they thought would hold up even after the dailies had used the story. They made no claims they could not support, and when they were finished, they sat back and waited for the explosion. Nothing happened.

"Why didn't you use it?" Joe asked the court reporter for *Newsday* over the phone the next day.

"I just told you. We never write about suits that are filed. Anyone can file suit. Filing suit means nothing. Getting a hearing is something. Winning is even better."

Joe and Ellie waited. In the law firm word of his suit had gotten around. Joe was treated coolly and then, after a decent interval, asked to leave the firm. He did, agreeing with the senior partners in the firm that he could not stay on now that he had filed the Four Sisters Suit. He practiced law by himself, at least he tried to. He took court-assigned criminal cases and worked with a consumer organization and once a week he took the train to the Brownsville section of Brooklyn and there worked in a storefront office set up by Neighborhood Legal Services. Generally, he handled landlord-tenant cases. Most of his time, though, was taken up with filing briefs and attending pretrial examinations regarding the Four Sisters Suit. Then, four months after the suit had been filed, a story appeared in *The New York Times*. The story ran inside, but it was noticed by all the Long Island papers. In a matter of a week Joseph Tynan was virtually a household name.

The headline read:

LONG ISLAND SUIT
COULD CHANGE
BANKING PRACTICES

There was another smaller headline under that and it said, "Conspiracy Alleged in Political Deal." The story followed. "In a little-noticed suit, a Long Island lawyer has charged that four of Nassau County's largest banks have conspired with the Republican Political Organization of Frank Mattuci to receive county funds without paying any interest. In return, the suit alleges, the banks invested funds and loaned money to Mr. Mattuci and a business he and his family were associated with."

The story was an immediate sensation. It not only charged a deal between the Republican organization and the four banks, something the U.S. Attorney would later prove was true, but it documented for the first time that the county had been depositing its funds in local banks and getting no interest. That charge was proven in a day.

Within days Joe had been interviewed by almost every newspaper and television station in the state. His father was also interviewed when the link became known. For a while Joe was pictured by cartoonists as wearing a policeman's uniform himself. Just when the publicity was dying down, word got out about his firing from the law firm and how he had been supporting himself defending indigents in criminal court. By now Joe was a definite political threat, a potential candidate almost too good to be true. Reporters dug into his past and found nothing. Private investigators hired by some politicians worked the same ground. They, too, found nothing. Dossiers were compiled on him. He was a husband who didn't stray, a father who cared for his children, a lawyer who didn't cut corners, and a man who was incessantly talking issues—the rights of the people. Among the private detectives he was known as the "Boy Scout," and when one of their reports fell into the hands of a friendly newspaper reporter who published it, his father called him collect from a shopping center in Sullivan County: "Don't you even jerk off?" Joe blushed.

In the congressional campaign that followed, Joe was the favorite from the very beginning. Nevertheless, he was up every weekday morning at five thirty and by no later than six thirty he was either standing at a busy intersection, handing campaign literature to commuters, or greeting train-riding counterparts at railroad stations. Often he rode into Manhattan and then rode out again with the late-afternoon commuters, and one day he even worked a train crowded with ladies going to the Broadway matinees. It paid off. An hour after the polls closed, Joe was declared the winner. He got an amazing 69.4 percent—landslide—and went off in January to Washington by himself. Ellie and the children would remain in the neighborhood and he would return most every Thursday night. He stayed, usually, until Monday and then returned to Washington.

At first the arrangement had been something of a precaution—another one of Joe's attempts to put the family first. He had been elected to Congress, a two-year term, and he knew he could be ousted in a very short time. He knew, too, that Congress meant constant campaigning—one campaign ending and the other just beginning—and that it paid to spend as much time as possible in the home district. But more than that Joe and Ellie did not want to uproot the children and plunk them down in a strange neighborhood and school. Even after he had won his Senate seat, it still seemed to make sense for the children and Ellie to remain behind in New York. He toyed for a while with the idea of returning to New York to run for governor, just as when he was in Congress, he flirted with the notion of running for Nassau County Executive. What he was, he thought, was a politician with two goals. The first was to do the most good for the most people. The second he never admitted to anyone, not even to Ellie. It was to become president of the United States. He thought the first goal and the second goal were synonymous.

Joe Tynan, as usual, was running late. He was to have lunch at the Amalfi Café with Oscar Harris, the chief congressional lobbyist for Common Cause, Congresswoman Mary Cenza, and Francis. They were going to discuss Cenza's bill, introduced at the behest of Common Cause, to insure that working women who were married would not be denied life insurance on the ground that their husbands were already covered. He jumped from the cab and looked around the Amalfi, a large outdoor café, the favorite meeting spot for Washington's left-wing liberati. Harris had chosen the place and it was not because he was a left-wing liberatus. It was because of their salads. Harris, as usual, was on a diet.

Joe scanned the tables. He could not find his friends. He asked one of the waiters and the man shook his head no. People by now had noticed Joe and he felt a bit uncomfortable—as if he was being stood up. Then he glanced to the outdoor café next door and his heart sunk. They were over there. Didn't they know it was owned by one of Washington's most celebrated reactionaries, a Greek supporter of the old junta?

Joe approached cautiously, almost on tiptoes. He

walked into the café area, past the boxed hedges, looking around as if he were waiting for someone to say something. Then he decided this was the wrong tack. He barged ahead and took his seat as if he were certain of what he was doing.

"What are you doing *here*?"

Harris gave him a quizzical look, a forkful of salad poised to enter his cavernous mouth. "Eating, Senator."

"No, no," Joe said in an urgent whisper. "What are you doing here? We are supposed to be *there*. This is the bad place. That is the good place."

Harris, his mouth full of salad, tried to say something, but all that came out were weird sounds. Cenza began to laugh.

"Sorry, Mary, but this is not funny."

"Newfellowshers," said Harris, his face reddening. Cenza brought her hand to her mouth and laughed.

"This is terrific," Joe said. "Now everyone is looking at us."

"New arachpccc," said Harris. He started to cough, hitting himself on the back at the same time. Cenza stopped laughing and looked suddenly concerned.

"Oscar, Oscar," Joe yelled.

Oscar was turning blue.

Joe jumped up and ran to the other side of the table. He slapped Oscar hard twice on the back and stepped back in triumph. Nothing had happened. Oscar had himself by the throat now. He stood up, a terrified look on his face. Suddenly he was grabbed from behind by an enormous bearded waiter. The man was a giant. He put his arms around Oscar from the back and locked them in the front just under his chest.

Then he gave a mighty jerk backward. Oscar's eyeballs bulged as he was lifted off his feet. His eyes teared and his nose ran into his mustache. The giant set him down and then whirled him around as if he were a top. He looked at Oscar and then, satisfied that the substance in his windpipe had popped loose, the big man walked away.

"New management," Oscar said to Joe. He reached for a handkerchief and wiped his nose. His eyes were red and teary. "You'll excuse me," he said, walking off to the men's room.

"Lobster salad?" Joe asked.

"Yeah," said Francis.

"Anyway, what are we doing here? We were supposed to meet next door."

"It was packed," Francis explained. "I knew this place had new management and we could see you from here, so I figured what the hell."

Joe was hardly listening. He was looking around, scanning the sidewalk and the tables, searching for someone. Harris returned to the table and noticed what Joe was doing.

"Looking for someone?" he asked Joe.

"Yeah, Oscar. Someone's supposed to meet me here. I mean over there." He pointed to the other café. He turned to Francis. "You think she went next door?" Francis shrugged his shoulders, giving Joe a search-me look. "Francis, you finished with your salad?"

"Yeah."

"Do me a favor? Go next door and look around. Maybe she's over there."

Francis rose, giving Joe a pained look, and went off

in the direction of the other café. Joe turned to Mary Cenza.

Mary was a short, dark-haired woman who wore her hair in a boyish cut. She was flat-chested and possessed of enormous teeth and what some thought was the finest mind in the House of Representatives. There were others, though, who felt that she was a danger to the Republic—a fat-lipped lady who would say anything at any time to gain some attention. There was, in fact, something to that. Mary had often admitted that she had in the past postured for the sake of attention. "No one pays attention to a woman otherwise," she said. Now in her third term, she had settled down into being one of Congress's more effective members, although her reputation as a loudmouth and a disaster for her district still stalked her.

"Mary, how are ya?"

"Fine, Joseph," she said showing him her teeth in a brilliant smile.

"How's the old bill coming?" he asked.

"Not so fine, Joseph."

"You've worked things out with Francis, haven't you? I'm sorry I was so late. Meetings. You know, Mary."

"Indeed, I do, Joseph."

"The first thing is, though, I think we have to see what positions the joint committee is going to take on this."

"Right, Joseph, and then we have to watch and see that we don't get ourselves new assholes carved up in the markup."

"Why, Mary. I am surprised."

"Why, Joseph. You are not."

The two of them and Oscar laughed. He very much enjoyed the company of these two members of Congress. He was an unabashed fan of Cenza's, and he felt somewhat the same about Joe. He feared, though, as Joe grew in popularity and he became mentioned with increased frequency as a presidential candidate, he would drift inexorably to the middle. Oscar kept looking for signs of that in Joe's voting record and was relieved to find none yet.

"Yeah," Harris said. "The markup. That is where we're gonna get hurt if we're gonna get hurt."

Joe stood up and the others at the table noticed Francis leading a striking-looking woman to their table. She was dressed in an expensive, well-tailored dark suit that set off her blonde hair. The two of them approached the table. Joe did the introductions and Karen sat down.

"Now where were we?" Joe asked. "Oh yes." He turned to Francis. "Find out who's against us on this," he ordered in a self-conscious manner. "Let's not get hit from behind. Get a computer run on everyone who's voted on this, and let's see where we stand."

Francis, going along with the act, took out a small notebook and jotted some notes. Oscar looked at Cenza, shrugged his shoulders, and smiled. The two of them stood at almost the same time.

"I have to go, Senator," said Oscar.

"*Moi aussi*, Joseph," Cenza said.

"Okay. Sorry I was late. Mary. Oscar." He shook hands with Harris and planted a kiss on Cenza's cheek.

"Sorry I interrupted," Karen said with a forced smile.

"You're right on time," Joe said, sitting down. "Too cold out here for you?"

"No," she said. "I'm from New Orleans. Cold's a novelty. I like it."

"So how's it going?" Joe asked.

The smile faded from her face. "I'm not crazy about admitting this, but I'm having trouble getting that film about Anderson."

"Well, look, if it isn't there, it isn't there," Joe said, sounding relieved.

"Oh, it's there, all right, but someone's holding it back," Karen said. "A black woman. Can you believe it?"

"Can't you get to her?" Joe asked.

Karen shook her head. "It's Carla Wills," she said, as if the name were supposed to mean something to Joe. She got nothing but a blank look from Joe. "You know her?" she asked.

Francis spoke up. "She's going for a congressional seat in some district north of New Orleans. I don't know which one. Pretty good bet to win."

"Yeah?" Joe said.

"One of her people got hold of a film of Anderson doing his in-my-heart speech and she won't give it up," Karen said. "I think she's cut a deal with Anderson. She gets to go to Congress and he gets to go to the Supreme Court. I think . . ." She looked squarely at Joe and her face lit up. "I think she would love to talk to *you*. How would you feel about calling her?"

"Well, I don't know," he said, a bit startled by the question. If this Anderson thing was forced upon him, well so be it. But that was quite a different matter from going out and looking for trouble.

"Maybe you should," Francis said.

"Senator," Karen said, her voice showing obvious excitement, "I think you're the most exciting political figure in this country today." Francis made a face. She was gushing. "When I think of the splash you'd make if you got hold of this film, I just get weak in the knees." Francis wondered if she was kidding. She caught his look and quickly added, "It's the right thing to do."

Joe hailed the waiter. "A cup of coffee, please," he said.

"Black?"

"Yeah. Give me a minute here, will you? Let me think." The waiter came with the coffee and Joe played with it while he thought. If the film existed, Anderson was as good as doomed. Something like that on network television and the man would be finished as a Supreme Court nominee. No doubt about that. If the film didn't exist, Anderson still had a chance and Joe could postpone his decision awhile longer. Of course, he would still have to vote against him, but he need not bang the drums at the head of the parade. Either way, a flight to Louisiana might clear up the matter. Besides, to be honest, he had to admit that he was looking forward to a little time alone with Mrs. Traynor.

"I'm speaking in Houston on Friday," Joe said, putting down his coffee cup. "I'll meet you in New Orleans Saturday morning. Can we see her then?"

Karen nodded. "This will make a big difference, Senator."

Joe smiled. "Karen, that film, if it exists, is ours."

❂ ❂ ❂

In the spring the garden of the Tynan home in Cedar-hurst became something to behold. Joe loved it and so did Ellie, who had planted most of it with the help of an old Italian man from nearby Inwood. Of the three it was Joe who appreciated it the most. He always commented on how his New York garden was two weeks or so behind the blooming of flowers in Washington, which gave him a chance to see the flowers bloom twice, but also heightened his expectations. Once he joked about following the flowers northward from the South, starting somewhere like Georgia and then going north with the season. He would have months of spring, he said, months of color and flowers.

Now Joe and Ellie and a third person, a woman with sharp features, were standing before a bank of outrageously yellow forsythia on the side of the Tynan home. It was a warm spring day, the casement windows to the house thrown open to the spring air, a gentle breeze coming in from the direction of the Atlantic Ocean. The other woman was Sheila Lerner, a writer for *McCall's* magazine, who had already made a name for herself by injecting herself into her interviews. She was the one, for instance, who got Joan Kennedy to talk about her drinking problems by admitting her own drinking problem. Lerner's celebrity was such that in some newspapers news of her drinking problem shared equal billing with Joan Kennedy's. Now she was standing on the Tynan lawn with her notebook out, smiling sweetly at Ellie and giving Joe the creeps.

"Is there anything about your life you'd change if you could?" Lerner asked Joe.

"Not really," Joe said. The phone inside the house

rang. "We get a lot of satisfaction out of our lives." Ellie looked at Joe with wry amusement. Lerner caught the look and made a note.

"How about your house?" Sheila asked of Ellie. "Is there anything you'd change about that?" The phone continued to ring.

"Yes, I'd pull the phone out by the roots."

"The phone's always ringing here, isn't it?" Sheila asked.

"Only during the day and night," Ellie responded, casting a you'd-better-get-it look at Joe.

"I guess I'd better get that," Joe said. He went off toward the house. When he got to the door, he ran for the phone and lifted it off the hook and swung the window open as far as possible at the same time. He was determined to hear what was going on on the lawn.

"There's a lot of pressure on a political family, isn't there?" Sheila asked.

"Well, Joe's the public figure. I'm trying to do other things."

The two women had their attention attracted by the voice coming from the open window. It seemed to Ellie that Joe was talking awfully loudly, as if he wanted them to hear what he was saying.

"Francis, this isn't working out the way it should," he said. "Look, Francis, I want blacks on that commission. And women. Let's just get them on. Make that part of the deal." There was a pause. "Do it, Francis, just do it." Joe hung up the phone.

Outside the two women had drifted away from the voice on the phone. They were walking back toward the garage.

"You've become a psychologist lately, haven't you?" Sheila asked.

"I've been accepted as a fellow at the Karen Horney Institute. It's very exciting. I have my own case load."

"How did you get interested in that?" Sheila sounded genuinely interested, and while she did not drop her pad, Ellie had already come to the conclusion that the reporter's reputation as a hatchet lady was unfounded. "Were you in therapy?"

"Yes. Yes, I was."

"That's great," Sheila said. "A lot of political people are afraid to talk about their therapy."

"Well, I certainly don't think that treatment of anything is something to be ashamed about. In my case, however, it is a necessary prerequisite for my certificate."

Sheila took it all down in her notebook. She looked up. "What's it been like for you, being a political wife?" she asked. "Has it been difficult?"

Ellie looked down at her shoes and then reached for a flower, taking a dead bug off it. She was impressed even more with Sheila now that the business about the therapy had been handled in such a matter-of-fact fashion. She decided to answer the question frankly.

"Well, it was at the beginning. During Joe's first Senate campaign, they had me out stumping for him. I was flying all over the state, driving at night, eating cardboard sandwiches. I got to know what they mean by rubber chicken. I had to wash my hair once in the ladies room of a gas station and they flew me in a lot of helicopters. God, I hate helicopters. I pleaded with them not to make me fly in them. They scare me to death. God really did not intend them to fly, but they

101

treated me like some silly woman—'Oh, you know, she'll get over it.' Finally, Joe had to put his foot down. 'No more helicopters,' he ordered." She smiled.

"But has politics had an effect on your life? You know, personally?"

"Well, toward the end of that campaign, we were running ourselves ragged and I had a miscarriage. I went into some hospital and Joe couldn't be there to check me in. He had to appear at some state fair somewhere and there was lots of fog and bad flying and he couldn't get to me. Some state fair. I can't even remember where it was. It was that important. Maybe worth two, maybe three votes. He was there and I was in the Catskills region making an appearance with his father. You know his father, don't you? And then we had to go back to the city and we couldn't fly. So we drove. Me and this very nice young man. Some volunteer. Just a kid with brown and white shoes.

"We started off and it was very foggy. I already had some pain but I thought it was back pain. You know, lower back. I had had them on and off in my other two pregnancies, and twice I had gone to the hospital thinking I was in labor when actually it was this lower back thing. I mean, I was way early. So we went off and the pain got worse and worse. I started to shriek in the car and the fog was closing in on us, I mean really terrible, and this poor kid was scared out of his wits. I was screaming and yelling in the car and he was going maybe ten miles an hour. He couldn't see a thing. He got me to a Howard Johnson's and they put me up on a table and there was some guy there and a state trooper and they delivered me there. The kid who drove was pale. White as a sheet. Now I know where the expression comes from. I was so proud of myself. Doing it alone like that. At Howard Johnson's. But no one knew what they were doing. The child had the umbilical cord wrapped around his neck. He strangled. Then they took me to the hospital."

"Is that when you started therapy?" Sheila asked quickly.

"Yes. I felt I needed a few sessions with somebody to get my head straight. Five years later, I was beginning to think my treatment would never end." Ellie smiled at Sheila. "All in all, you might say I'm not too thrilled with politics."

"Then you weren't in therapy just to get your certificate?"

They heard the snap of a twig. It was Joe. He came up behind them and stood behind Ellie, hugging her around the waist.

"Sorry, what did I miss?" he asked.

"You've heard it all before," Ellie told him.

"I guess you can tell for yourself, Sheila, Ellie is a very special woman." Something about the tone of his voice suggested to Ellie that he was covering for her.

"Of course, I was speaking for myself," Ellie said acidly. "As with most politicians' wives, my views don't necessarily reflect those of the management."

Everyone chuckled. Sheila snapped her notebook shut, and Ellie could tell from the way Joe held her that the only thing standing between her and a terrible fight with her husband was a reporter named Sheila Lerner who was, of course, missing nothing.

Later that night Joe and Ellie undressed in their bedroom, watching each other warily. Ever since

Sheila Lerner had left, there had been little skirmishes, usually about nothing. The refrigerator had been slammed when no peanut butter turned up, and there was a ferocious temper tantrum about responsibility when Joe was told that the car was almost out of gas. Ellie knew an explosion was coming and she knew what had provoked it.

Joe took off his pants and picked them up by the cuffs for the hanger. A set of keys fell out of the pocket.

"Shit." He bent down and picked them up and suddenly whipped them across the room. They hit the marble top of an antique dressing table. Even he seemed surprised at what he had done.

"Okay, come on. What is it?" Ellie said.

"It's your life. I'm not going to tell you not to talk about it."

"I think that's a good idea."

"You know what it costs to talk like that to reporters?"

"To say that I've been in therapy? Fifty votes. I didn't say you were in therapy. That would cost a thousand votes. Lithium is twenty thousand votes and electric shock treatment goes for fifty thousand. I know what things cost."

Joe fought to control his anger.

"Look, these people ask everything they can. You don't have to dig into your bowels everytime they come up with some stupid question about the furniture."

"She wasn't talking about the *furniture*," Ellie exploded. "She was talking about *me*. It's taken me seven years, but I think I know how to tell the difference."

"Why did you let her get you to run down politics, Ellie? It's my life. It's what I do for a living. It's not hard to handle them, you know. You don't have to answer the question. You know that. You don't have to answer any questions you don't want to. Just say what you want. I've told you that. You've done it before."

"I didn't want to do this interview. I told *you* that."

"Ellie, Ellie, Ellie. How much do I ask of you? How much do I ask you to do? You have a life entirely apart from politics."

"No, I don't. I can't escape it for a minute. I can't call the plumber without being Mrs. Joe Tynan." She went into a little singsong: " 'Oh yeah, Mrs. Tynan. I worked on the Senator's toilet a couple of years ago and gosh, Mrs. Tynan, it must be exciting as all get out to be down there in Washington.' Jesus, Joe, I'm living in a goddamned fishbowl. Just once I want to go to a party as me. Not as the Missus. Not as Missus You. I want someone to say to me, 'Say, what do you do?' instead of telling me how wonderful it must be to be married to you."

"Don't you think it's a little late to be thinking of that?"

"When was I supposed to think of it?" Ellie yelled. "When you decided to run for another term without asking me? When I heard your decision *on television*?"

"I discussed that with you," he said softly.

"Discussed it, yes. *We* discussed it. But remember *we* had reached no decision. *I* was opposed. *We* were still discussing it. *You* said you were still thinking about it."

"What did you expect me to do? I got the question. It was there, wasn't it?"

Ellie looked at Joe dumbfounded. "It was there? You got the question? What do you mean it was there and you got the question? What do you mean by that?" She was shrieking. "You just put me in my place, that's all. Burned your bridges behind you, right? A fait accompli. No more discussions. No more planning at the breakfast table. You got the question and Ellie was either going to get with the program or get out. And then Joe comes home with this guilty look in his eye and he says he's announced. He didn't mean to, but he got the question and what can they do about it now? So he hugs Ellie and she hugs him back, but she has resented him for that. It was there. You got a question."

"What about today, Ellie? Huh? What about what you did today?"

"I was asked a question about my life and I answered it."

Joe mimicked her. "I was asked a question about my life and I answered it. Try that one on your short friend down at the Institute, Sigmund what's his name? See if he believes that one. See if he says, 'Ellie, dats da vey it was. Noting more. Jew got asked a qvestion and jew answered it, yah?' "

"He doesn't have an accent."

"Maybe not, but if he's got a head on his shoulders, he would know that you were doing something more today than answering a question. He might have something to say about your hostility to my work. My life. Jesus, Ellie, I come home here and I get greeted like I haven't been doing anything worthwhile all week. I feel like I've been doing something vaguely larcenous. Like a pimp or something. I could use some appreciation. I could use some help. Jesus, the next time you get a question like that, handle it. Help a little."

"No, next time, you handle it," Ellie said folding her arms and turning her back on him. She walked over to the clothes hamper and then stopped. She turned around. "And next week when they come to take your picture for the cover you can stand with your arms around your administrative assistant."

"I won't be here next week," Joe shot back. "I'm going to New Orleans." Ellie noticed that suddenly his mood had changed. He was smiling.

CHAPTER 5

She had been very good. Joe was impressed. She had shown up one day, very brazen, walked into the office, asked for Francis, and literally demanded to be hired. She would be needed, she said firmly. She was short, dark-haired and she wore a plain dress, sort of a farm dress. She had worked in both the McGovern and McCarthy campaigns, she said. She had gone the route. There was nothing she could not do. She could schedule and she could canvass and she could set up a telephone bank in no time. She knew about WATTS lines and postage rates and bulk mailings. She could knock out an opponent's phone bank with a fistful of dimes and a half a dozen teen-agers. She had stayed in every hotel in the country and flown every airline and eaten in every restaurant. She was the total political pro, she said, with only two vows in life.

"Oh yeah," said Francis amused, "what's that?"

"Never cry on election night and never go to bed with a Republican."

He hired her.

She was moved into a little cubbyhole and given half a desk (she had to share it with a caseworker) and told that either her duties would expand as Joe did more and more traveling, or she just might have nothing to do and they would have to let her go. Either way, Francis said, they would play it by ear. Her name was Regina but they called her Granny for the glasses she wore. It was she who had scheduled Joe's trip to Houston and New Orleans. He had never traveled as well before.

Instead of the Shamrock Hilton where he usually stayed, he was put in the Warwick, one of the world's great hotels, Joe soon discovered. Granny had gotten Joe's host group to pay for it. She had arranged for a car to meet him at the airport and for the same car to pick him up in the morning and take him out to the airport. There a real surprise awaited him. The car missed the terminal entirely and drove right out to the tarmac. It deposited Joe before the sleek body of a Lear jet, which Granny had finagled for only slightly more than the first-class fare from Houston to New Orleans. Joe's host group had paid for some of it, he was told, but what he was not told was that the charter service was promised more business in the future by Granny—the future, she later explained, being anytime between now and the moment of her death.

Joe climbed into the jet, and before he had a chance to get through the *Houston Post,* he was in New Orleans. Karen was waiting for him. She was dressed in tan slacks and an off-white jacket, with a green silk blouse underneath. Her hair was parted in the middle and tied in the back with a ribbon. Joe thought she looked beautiful. He noticed a white silk scarf hanging from her neck, making her look like one of those old-fashioned pilots from the barnstorming era.

"Hi, Sky King," he said when he got off the plane. "How are things?"

"Terrific," she said. The two of them shook hands and the pilot of the Lear came around the side of the plane and handed Joe his bag. Joe looked around, trying to figure out where to go next.

"This way," Karen said. She walked off in the direction of some hangars.

"You got the plane?" Joe asked.

"Yes."

"Good plane, I hope. These little private jobs make me nervous. Everytime I ride on one of them I have to remind myself I'm not a country-western singer."

Karen gave Joe a puzzled look.

"That's how they all die," he explained. "In private planes. Always in private planes."

"I know what you mean," she said. "But it's always during a storm. They fly during storms because they have to make concert dates. It's not the planes that kill them, or the weather. It's the money."

By this time they had come to the last of the hangars. They walked around to the side where a Beech-craft Commander was parked.

"This it?" Joe asked.

Karen nodded and walked around to the pilot's side of the plane. She took a key out of her pocket and opened the cabin door with it. Joe watched her, not sure of what she might be up to. She noticed the expression on his face.

"Mind if I drive?" she asked.

"No, not at all," said Joe, catching on. "How long have you been flying?"

"Long time. A long time."

She climbed into the plane and then reached over to the passenger door and unlocked it. Joe put his foot on the toe hold and lifted himself into the plane. He watched as Karen prepared the plane for takeoff. She moved it in an arc to the side of the runway and then onto an apron. The plane taxied out to the runway. Joe started to say something, but Karen hushed him. She reached for her mike.

"New Orleans tower, this is Beech four oh nine, ready for takeoff."

"Roger, four oh niner," said an electronically sounding voice. "You gonna see your daddy?"

"That's negative. Gonna go see a lady about a movie."

"You're clear."

Karen gunned the engine and the plane moved off down the runway. In the small plane Joe noticed for the first time how fast they were moving when they took off. Suddenly, the rumble of the wheels ceased and the plane lifted into the air. Karen banked it to the east and then headed toward the northwest. With the sun behind her, she turned to Joe and smiled.

"I think two weeks really is a long time, don't you?"

Joe made a mock expression of alarm, but to himself, the senator from New York was thinking that sometimes two days is a long time.

* * *

From two thousand feet up Mississippi and then Louisiana rolled beneath them, as green and verdant as Ireland. Below them the Mississippi River coursed, wide and fat, rolling down to the Gulf in wide curves, pushing the land out in bulges to suit its whim. The plane flew north, up past the northern suburbs of New Orleans and then into Mississippi and finally, after arching to the west, into Louisiana. It passed over the Delta, large, white clouds rolling by on invisible currents of air. Joe felt transported.

For a time he said nothing. He seemed, to Karen, to be content to sightsee. But he was studying Karen, analyzing, as best he could, what effect she was having on him. He didn't like finding her so attractive and neither, for that matter, did he like the idea that he was in a plane with her, about to go off on a political mission that might be trouble. There were elements about this mission he did not like. He didn't like taking on Birney and he didn't like doing it on behalf of a dubious cause—the alleged racist statements of a man who was probably not a racist. But mostly he didn't like this Karen business.

His family came first and then his job and then there was nothing else. If you had any time, you gave more to the first two. That was one thing. There was something else, though, and he had once stated it to Kittner, who had looked at him as if he was weird when he said it. Women, he said, make you do funny things. All of a sudden, he said, you're introducing bills for them and making speeches to please them. You're not wooing the people you should be wooing—your constituents.

"Your constituents don't love you up, son," Kittner had drawled.

Karen dived the plane. "Hey," Joe yelled. "What's going on?"

"Trying to get your attention," Karen said. "I was right about Carla Wills. She made a deal."

"Why not? Why should she be the only person in this who hasn't? How do you know?"

"I asked the chairman of the Louisiana State Democratic Committee."

"And the son of a bitch told you?"

"The son of a bitch is my father."

"Full of surprises, aren't you? Does your father fly also or is he the one with an ocean liner? No, Mississippi riverboat. How does he know she made a deal? And with whom? And how did a father of yours get to be party chairman? And what am I doing up in the sky with you, anyway?"

"First things first. Yes, my father flies. That's how I learned. Second, no riverboat. Third, he heard that Anderson's organization will support Carla Wills for Congress. It goes without saying that they will not support her if she parts with that film of hers. She's a shoo-in with them, a doubtful if she loses the support of that parish courthouse bunch." She pointed out and down. "See those roads down there? There's not a one of them I don't know. When I was four I'd go campaigning with my daddy on every one of those little brown streaks you see down there."

"And your mammy? How's about your mammy?" Joe asked, mimicking a southern accent.

"She died in childbirth. Cancer. They didn't know she had it. It hit her about the same time as her labor.

Opened her up and closed her up and waited. She was dead that very day."

"I'm sorry."

"It's all right. I was a kid. I hardly knew her. I cried and cried. They took me to an aunt and they told me what had happened and I just couldn't understand. That business about them never coming back. I couldn't understand that. Forever. It seemed so unfair. They put me up in the old attic of this house, an attic that had been converted to a bedroom. I remember it had a big metal bed. Not brass, but metal of some sort. Gray. Gun-metal gray. It was a double bed and it had big bolsters on it and the walls were covered with paper that had pictures of flowerpots on it. I think I just lay in that bed for a day and cried, and then my father came to get me. I heard him coming up the stairs. His eyes were red and he hadn't shaved and he came to the bed and picked me up and held me and told me that we two would never be separated again. He would always be with me.

"My mother was a wonderful woman. People told me she was one of those who acted a bit daffy, so people wouldn't be offended by her ideas. She believed in integration, for instance, and once she went to a colored church. She went with our maid and afterward the sheriff stopped her and arrested her for drunk driving. They put her in jail with the drunks and all and that got the people of the town so mad the sheriff lost the next election. But before that he used to follow her everywhere in his car. She wasn't daffy. She was idealistic." She looked off into the sky and said nothing more.

114

"You were going to tell me about your father," Joe reminded her.

"He's a good man. I think he thought he would pick up where mother left off. He's fought those local parish types for years, and back in the 1960s he helped form the Freedom Party. That was the integrated one. No one would talk to us then. He sent me away to school. To Connecticut. But in 1968 his party got seated at the convention and he became party chairman. He's held it on and off since then, although he's always swearing he's going to kick the political habit and retire to Las Vegas to gamble." She turned to Joe and smiled and noticed that he was studying her. She felt awkward.

"Seat belt fastened?" she asked. And then without waiting for an answer she dived the plane, bottoming out after a thousand feet or so. Joe's stomach seemed to stay at a higher altitude. Karen took the little plane up and down, banked it and rolled it, and then gently arched it on its back.

"Isn't it great?" she yelled over the roar of the gunned engine.

"Yeah," said Joe without enthusiasm. "Just great."

"*This* is flying! Let me tell you, this is flyeeing!"

Joe unbuckled his belt.

"What are you doing?" she asked, alarmed.

"I'm calling a cab."

They laughed and she climbed to her original altitude.

Carla Wills was nothing like Joe had expected. What he had been looking forward to meeting was a

Hollywood version of a black, southern woman—someone stout with a lyrical voice, shouting poetry, raising children, battling menfolk, and wearing, just for good measure, a bandanna. This was an exaggeration, to be sure, but he did expect someone on the order of Barbara Jordan, and he was prepared for some histrionics. He was prepared to deal with that.

But this Carla Wills was nothing like that. She was not heavy, or anything close to it. She was closer to thin than anything else and nothing covered her head. Her hair was worn in a long Afro, and when she came out of the frame house to meet them, she was wearing a light-colored linen suit, nicely tailored, whether in New Orleans or Memphis, a print blouse, and sensible cloth shoes. Her voice was frail and cultured, and when she opened her mouth, she was all teeth. There was no way by looking at her to tell that she had a long list of firsts—the first black woman to become a White House aide, the first black woman to be elected to the state legislature, the first black woman to become a director of a New Orleans bank, the first black woman to be a delegate to the United Nations (on African affairs, naturally), and now, with 55 percent of the district's voters black, she was about to become the first black member of Congress from Louisiana since Reconstruction. She would certainly be the first black woman to serve in Congress from the state since anytime, and without a doubt the first to make no bones about being a lesbian.

She shook hands with Joe and Karen and led them out of the house into the fields. A tractor worked off in the distance. The three of them walked along the furrows, making small talk about farming, which neither Joe nor Karen knew anything about. Finally, they got around to politics.

"Senator," she said to Joe, "let me do the arithmetic for you. This is so simple you don't even need fingers to count. This county is 55 percent black. Registered voters, that is. I am assured of the nomination and after that the election. The reason I am assured is that I have the backing of the organization. They will supply me with what I need to turn out that 55 percent. What I need to get that 55 percent to the polls is money.

"Now in the old days, or even today in the movies, you can get people by having a cause. There are no more real causes, no marching-to-bands causes. So what you need if your cause is black people and women and their rights and so forth is money. Here is what I need." Joe started to say something, but she waved him quiet with her hands.

"I need fifteen dollars for every poll worker. I need that fifteen dollars and I need gas money for every worker who's gonna use his car to take someone to the polls. I need sample ballots, Senator, and I need people to distribute them to the people of this district between Sunday, when they will be given out at church, and Tuesday, which is the election. I need a force that will turn out those two days. I need money to pay them.

"I need even more sample ballots for the people who don't go to church. There are a lot of roads around here, many of them still dirt, and if you go down them, drive say two, three, even four miles, you might find a family or two living at the end. For that drive you distribute two sample ballots. It costs you a lot in gas. It takes you a half hour just to make the drive. If it's just rained, you can't even make that drive.

"I got poll workers that need to be paid and a printer that needs to be paid and drivers that need to be paid and volunteers that need to be paid. Volunteers don't come as cheaply as they used to. All of that, Senator, the organization can supply me. If I want to go out and buy it, it would cost me ten thousand dollars, I guess. That's about what that film you're after is worth." She paused and looked up at Joe, squinting in the sun to see him. "And it's not even in color."

"Yes, but is it a talkie?"

"Most assuredly."

"And does it talk about segregation?"

"It does."

"And about how he is for it."

"It does. It does do exactly what you think it does. But it also buys me a congressional campaign. I can't run a congressional campaign with what I get from soybeans." She reached down and scooped up some dark earth and let it drift through her fingers. "I'm not much of a farmer anyway. This place comes with the name Wills."

Joe loosened his tie. Sweat had popped out on his forehead. He took out a handkerchief, mopped his brow, and took off his suit jacket. He figured he'd wave the flag a bit before he waved the green stuff. Now that he knew the film actually existed the choices had suddenly narrowed. The word would get out sooner or later. Loose lips sink ships and the S.S. *Anderson* was already going down.

"This man is headed for the Supreme Court. He'll

affect matters for the rest of his life, maybe for the rest of our lives. You can stop him."

Carla Wills shot him a look that was a warning against taking her for a fool. "He means nothing to me one way or the other. He won't affect matters much down here. Down here we need federal money—grants programs, aid, anything you can name. A congressperson with some commitment can get that for these people. You ever look at the statistics for this district? We're near the bottom on everything except illiteracy, child mortality, and venereal disease. We have no drug addiction because no one can afford the habit and there's no one to steal from. This is the end of the line, Mister Senator. This is a foreign country you don't have to leave the country for. We got Vietnam veterans—look, there's one right now on that tractor—who say they got sent to Vietnam so they could see how the other half lives. The humor here is as black as the people."

Carla Wills started walking back to the house, Joe and Karen at her side. She walked slower now, stopped and sighed. "And Anderson. I know Anderson." She smiled. "I *know* Anderson. You know your Bible, Senator Tynan?"

"Huh? Yeah."

"Well, I *know* Anderson. Knew him anyway. That was before I wised up. Okay, he's no liberal. But he's not that bad either. They all said something like his in-my-heart speech back in those days. They had to say something like that. The fact that he said it doesn't mean one thing one way or the other. What you have in Edward Anderson is your basic white southern male circa fifty-five or sixty years of age. He could live all right with segregation and he could live all right with integration. What he cared about was his business and his profession. He gave up on resisting integration when it started to hurt business. When the factories from the North stopped coming because the red-necks were hanging people from the trees like Christmas trinkets, it stopped some of that business cold. People like Anderson did not like that. They had money in this county and this state and they did not like losing their money. And lawyers like Anderson don't like people making monkeys of the law. They respect the law. They love the law. The law segregated this whole society for nearly one hundred years and they loved it as justice. When the law desegregated the society, they loved the law just as much, even though they knew by then that there was so such thing as justice. Sometimes I think that would allow any trifling with the constitution because somewhere in there are the guarantees for private property. That, as Lyndon Johnson used to say, is getting close to the nut-cutting. Private property, Mister Senator. That's the nuts of this society. Anyway, Anderson. It's all history. Times have changed. He's not all that bad."

Joe was dumbfounded, speechless. He looked at Carla Wills, his mouth wide open in admiration.

"How bad does he have to be?" asked Karen. "Carla, I was in Catahoula Parish when my daddy came and supported you for the legislature. And I remember what you said that night about people you grew up with and how you would never let them down. You remember that? How bad does Anderson have to be?"

Carla gave Karen a condescending smile. She kicked some dirt and shrugged. "Ask your daddy if I can win this thing if I help destroy Anderson." She turned and walked quickly to the house, Joe and Karen scurrying after her. At the door she stopped and turned to them. She put out her hand. This was going to be good-bye.

"Look, Miss Wills, I don't want to go after Anderson either," Joe said. "I have a lot to lose if I fail at this."

"But you have a lot to win." The message was clear. It was time to talk turkey.

"Miss Wills, just how much money does it take to get out the vote?"

"Bare bones and nothing for no one's pocket?"

Joe nodded his head.

"Five thousand to do the minimum job. Seven hundred or so for ads in the weeklies and some radio spots."

"Miss Wills, have you ever heard of the Bimm Twins?"

She shook her head no.

"They are about to contribute exactly that much money to your campaign. I think you should know. Their grandfather invented the process for making toothpicks."

Carla Wills brightened. "Miss Traynor, Senator, come on in the house."

A half hour later a dusty Buick with a black man at the wheel and two white people in the seat next to him was seen hurtling into town. It entered from the north, near the auto auction lots, and proceeded down Gen. Philip M. Carter Memorial Avenue, popularly known as Memorial Avenue, to the corner of Northwest Fourth. There the car swung right and parked, front end to the curb, before the only modern building in town. It was a one-story brick and glass affair. Mounted on the outside wall, in big chrome letters, were the letters KYVH. The two white people got out. The black man, who had been summoned from his tractor for this task, remained at the wheel.

Through the glass the man and the woman could be seen at the information desk in the lobby. An attractive young black woman at the desk stood as she talked to them. She nodded her head and smiled a great deal and then reached for a white phone with many buttons on it. She punched one of those buttons, looked up and smiled at the couple, and then punched another button. She said something into the phone, asked the couple something, spoke once again into the white phone, and then hung it up. Presently, a short man with a wide smile and a huge belly came out from behind a glass door. He was wearing a short-sleeved white shirt with a clip-on striped tie and double-knit blue pants. He shook hands with the man and then with the woman and the two of them followed him behind the glass door. He was the station manager.

"You-all in luck," the man in the short-sleeved shirt said to Joe and Karen as they walked down a tiled hallway. He talked over his shoulder to them, swinging his arms wide as he walked so there was no getting next to him in the narrow corridor. "We're mostly all tape. Even I had to check to see if we still had one of these movieolas. Especially with sound. Ahm surprised we still got it. In fact," he said, stopping at a door and reaching for a key, "ahm gonna find out why we do. Ah might have to fire someone up for this." He slipped the key into the door, pushed it open with his knee, and laughed. "Well, there 'tis," the station manager said. He waited for someone to do something but neither Joe nor Karen made a move. Slowly, the smile faded from the station manager's face. "Ah suppose you-all want to be alone," he said. "Government business?"

"Check," said Joe.

The station manager turned and left the room, saying he would be glad to assist if they needed help. Karen reached into her purse and took out the can of film. She opened it and the two of them threaded the movieola.

"Lights," Joe said.

Karen walked over to the switch and held her hand up in the air. Joe could see that her fingers were crossed. She threw the switch. On the small screen a man was speaking at an outdoor rally. The black and white film moved jerkily through the movieola. There was no sound!

"Joe? Joe, there's no sound," Karen squealed.

"It's the lead-in. Don't worry."

On the little screen the camera moved in for a close-up. It was Edward Anderson. His hair was shorter and darker but it was definitely Edward Anderson. Karen jumped with glee and threw her arms around Joe. The sound came groaning on. Anderson was covered with sweat. He was wearing a white shirt and a thin, black tie. His shirt was wetted through. He was outdoors at some sort of rally.

"I want the voters of this county to know that regardless of what I've said in the past or what I might say in the future, in my heart I have never accepted integration and I never will."

A great whoop from the audience died like a vacuum cleaner coming unplugged as Joe stopped the machine. Karen jumped again, grabbing Joe around the waist. Then the two of them jumped together, smiling then laughing. Abruptly, they stopped. They held each other in the dark until Joe let his arms drop.

"I'll get the lights," he said awkwardly.

Joe reversed the movieola and wound the film. He put it back into its canister and then into Karen's bag. They turned off the lights and let themselves out of the small room. At the reception area they said good-bye to the woman at the desk and got back into the car with their waiting driver. They drove to a wind-sock airport ten minutes out in the country where Karen had parked her plane and then headed east to Jackson, Mississippi, an alternative airport suggested by the amazing Regina, the staff aide with the brain of a hitchhiker.

Inside his ticket envelope Joe had suggestions on where to eat in Jackson and some people worth talking to if he really got tied up, but he used none of that. He caught the Delta flight to LaGuardia and within hours he was back with his family in the New York suburb of Cedarhurst. He spent the evening with Ellie and Paul and Janet and, occasionally, when his mind drifted, with the woman with the blonde hair and the smile like sun on polished steel. Her scent was still with him.

It started in a corner of the ceiling, up over the lamp, and it continued for a foot or so in a straight line and then it veered hard to the right where it trailed off and disappeared. Joe stared at it. He had been keeping an eye on it for a year now, sometimes asking Ellie if she thought it had grown, asking his children to walk softly over it, wondering if there was a leak of some sort, becoming, after a while, particularly anxious that this crack in the ceiling was the harbinger of terrible things to come—of new pipes needed and new plaster and people coming through the house in overalls, armed with stubby pencils and rulers, thrusting bills at him and talking in the gruff and macho language of construction.

Joe had first noticed the crack about a year ago. He said nothing at the time, almost hoping that by saying nothing it would go away. It did not. It grew suddenly and rapidly and then stopped altogether. Then it started again, shot ahead by an inch, and then stopped again. For a month or more nothing happened. Joe took this as proof that his warnings to his children not to run up and down the stairs had worked. Gentleness, he thought, would pay off here. But then the crack, like the San Andreas fault, went on the move again. For a while it was all Joe could talk about while he was home. The crack became something of a running joke in the family, and while Joe laughed along with everyone, there was something about that crack that was troubling to him.

He looked at that crack and he saw his decision to go into politics. He sometimes wondered about it, not the basic "rightness" of the decision, but what it meant in terms of money. That crack was going to cost him. In the long run that crack was the beginning of the end of the house, a symptom, a sign of a home where the man was never home. This was a house that knew no maintenance—just emergency repairs. And this was a house in which the man of the house, while making what most Americans thought was a good buck, knew he was undervalued by at least $150,000. That, Joe thought, was about what he could make on "the outside."

In the beginning he had not given money any thought. It meant nothing to him. But now Janet was just a couple of years from college and Paul was heading that way and Joe had to think about how he was going to pay for it. The house needed work, he knew that, and the car was old and in need of repair and he spent too much money flying to Washington and back. The government, after all, paid for only twelve trips a year. He had his studio apartment in Southwest Washington, which cost him three hundred dollars a month in rent, and he had the house in Cedarhurst with the mortgage and he had something worse— something far more expensive. He had gotten used to a rich way of life. The men he knew were rich and the places where he went were plush and he realized after a while that other successful men his age were rich. He, too, was a successful man. There were only a hundred others like him in the entire country. In all of New York State there was only one other man like him. He was a senator of the United States, a potential president. It was all very heady, but at the moment he was wondering how he would pay for his ceiling when his two children, who were fighting upstairs, caused the crack to yawn wide, bringing a dusting of plaster down on his head.

A door slammed. He heard the muffled sound of

feet running along the second floor hallway and then a door slammed. There was silence for a moment and then a door opened, two sets of feet ran down the hallway, and another door slammed. Joe eyed the ceiling.

"What the hell is going on?" he asked, rising from the living room sofa and heading to the foot of the stairs. Ellie looked up from the sofa where she had been writing in a notebook. She had been sitting with her legs tucked under her, wearing a green plaid skirt, light green sweater, and an even lighter green cardigan thrown over her shoulders.

"He probably read some of her love letters again," she explained. "They'll work it out."

Joe shrugged his shoulders and returned to his place on the couch. He reached for a copy of *Newsweek* and put his feet up on the coffee table when again there was a loud crash—louder and more thunderous than the mere slamming of a door. Joe checked the ceiling crack.

"Jesus Christ!" he exploded, racing for the stairs.

"Joe, they can work this out without a parent."

Joe cocked his head and listened. He heard footsteps and then the quiet closing of a door and then silence. He nodded his surprise to Ellie, indicating with his raised eye lids that she might have been right, and started to return to the sofa. Ellie patted the cushion next to her and he sat down. She put her left hand on the back of Joe's neck, massaging it in an absentminded fashion, while continuing to write in her notebook with her other hand.

"What are you doing?" Joe asked her.

Ellie continued to write. "I take the same notes after every session. Nothing new. It's almost always the same. It's like following you around in a campaign, listening to the same speech every day." She went back to her writing and then stole a glance at Joe. He was pouting.

"Hey," she said, "didn't I read in *Time* magazine you have a great sense of humor?"

"That's why I'm not laughing."

"Ah, good one." Ellie laughed, dropping her pen and pad, and toppling onto Joe. He put his arms around her, kissed her on the side of her neck, and worked around to her mouth. She moved her head to meet him and they kissed. They parted and kissed again, this time more hungrily. Ellie planted small, light kisses on his lips. She framed his face with her hands and shook her head back and forth slightly.

"I don't like politics, but I love you," she said. She moved in for another kiss, but Joe moved his head to avoid her.

"Ellie, I'm not a politician. I *am* politics."

Oh God, she had done it again, she thought. An innocent remark. Here they were at it again. "You're a good, decent man who's in politics. If you ever *are* politics . . ."

"What?" Joe demanded. "Just what? Would you still love me?"

"I'll have to get back to you on that," Ellie cracked, still trying to keep it light. She pulled him to her and kissed him. He didn't respond. Instead, he waited for his lips to be free for talking. The moment they were he spoke.

"Look, politics is part of my life. A major part of my life, if I may say so."

"Joe, I love you." She pursed her lips. "Go like

this." Joe scowled. "C'mon, go like this." She pursed her lips again. Joe smiled faintly.

"No."

"Like this."

His smile broadened. He reached for her, pulling her into him. They kissed. Ellie locked both hands behind Joe's neck and hugged him tightly.

"If she touches my rabbit one more time, I'm gonna break her camera!" It was Paul. He had come down in his pajamas and he was standing at the foot of the stairs, holding a large Belgian rabbit, either not noticing what was going on with his parents or not caring.

"You got that?" he demanded.

"Right," Ellie said.

Paul turned and shuffled back upstairs. Ellie leaned back on the sofa, covered her eyes with her hand and reached for her notebook with the other.

"God, when will we grow up?" she said. "Any of us?"

In the Capitol building, in Room S-111 on the first floor, the door opened and a red-coated waiter, a black man, as they all are, came out, balancing a tray on his shoulder. He turned to his right and walked across the red-tiled floor to the elevator, where he got into one of the waiting cars. He nodded yes when the elevator operator pointed down with his finger. When he arrived in the basement, the waiter turned right, walked down a short hallway, and then turned left. Here the hallway was long and the rooms along it numbered SB-9 and SB-10 and so on, the SB standing for Senate basement. As the waiter walked, though, the numbers changed and instead of having the prefix SB they had the prefix ST. It stood for Senate terrace.

The waiter walked quickly, crisply, and almost silently in his rubber, treaded heels. He was an older man, gray here and there in his hair, a touch stocky but still muscular. He was a proud member of that diminishing cadre of Washington service workers—the ones who worked with pride at menial tasks for the federal government. They were the drivers for cabinet officers and ushers at the White House and cooks in the private kitchens of the highest officials. They were the ones who made the embassies hum, the ones who lived on top of Big Bertha garages down the driveway from the homes of the very wealthy, and often they could trace their lineage as far back as their employer—even further in some cases. In some cases, undoubtedly, they had a common ancestry—the whites going one way, the blacks another. In the end, skin color determined why one man served, another waited to be served.

The waiter walked toward the west front of the Capitol. On the east side, the side known best to the American public from countless televised presidential inaugurations, the basement was truly a basement. This was the peak of that mound known as Capitol Hill. But on the downtown side of the slope the hill dropped away and what was basement on one side was terrace on the other. Here the rooms looked out on the picture-postcard view of the Washington Mall. Here was one of Washington's premier views. Here, by no accident, were the private offices of the most senior senators.

The waiter glided along the floor. He seemed to

take note of no room numbers, apparently arriving at his destination simply by instinct. He stopped before a door and knocked sharply.

"Come in," yelled Joe Tynan.

The waiter reached down and turned the door handle. He shoved the door open and walked into the room. He noted Senator Tynan and he noted also the blonde woman in the gray suit seated on the couch.

"Senator Tynan," the waiter said by way of greeting.

"Hi. Gee it's good to see you. We're famished. Put it there." He pointed to the coffee table.

The waiter handed Joe a dining room bill for his signature.

"Anything else?" the waiter asked. Joe shook his head and looked down again at the papers that were spread out on his desk.

"Senator Tynan, ma'am." The waiter left.

Joe stood up and waved his hand across the top of the desk. "This is sensational stuff. How did you get this sort of stuff?"

"A lot of digging."

"Well, it's terrific." He moved around to the coffee table and sat down on the couch next to Karen. "Let's eat," he said, lifting the white napkin from the top of the tray. Underneath were two tuna salads, no mayonnaise, and two ice teas. Joe set himself the task of serving everything. "Take lemon?" Joe asked. Karen, some tuna fish in her mouth, shook her head no. "Good. They only sent one." He squeezed it into his tea.

"You're working very hard on this," Joe said. "I'm very impressed. Getting hold of this stuff must have taken some time. Are you getting something out of it for yourself?"

"Just don't forget me when you get to the White House," Karen said.

"The White House?" He waited for her laugh. It didn't come. She was serious.

"You're going to be very hot after this. For you not to make it, they would have to find you in bed with an elk."

"I hear they give good antler."

She managed a weak smile. "I'm *serious*. You could be serious, too, for a minute. It doesn't mean you have to run and open up a campaign headquarters. It just means that if this thing works you're in that inner circle, the starting gate. Call it what you want. It will be you and some others, but *you* have what it takes to go all the way. You're the right age and in the right party and have the right record and come from the right state. You're good-looking and there are no elks around here." She gave him a so-there look, and Joe could not help but contrast her enthusiasm with his wife's.

"I'll tell you what I want," she went on. "I'd love to work with you when you make your move. We'd knock them on their fannies."

"You like to win, don't you?" Joe said.

"When I want something, I go get it." She leveled him with her eyes. "Just like you, Joe."

For a moment they said nothing and instead wondered how the conversation had gotten off politics onto something else. Joe felt as he had in that small room at the television studio. He wondered what to do next. It had been years since he had made a pass.

Karen sensed something coming. She suddenly stood up.

"I have other notes in my briefcase," she said awkwardly. She walked over to the desk and rummaged through the briefcase, taking longer to do it than she needed to. She pretended to be looking for something, taking out one document and then another, looking at them and then slipping them back.

"Oh, here it is," she said finally. She started back toward the couch but pivoted for the wing chair at the last minute. She sat there. Joe smiled at her ploy. She was no good at this either.

"I have a 1970 decision that makes him look pretty bad," she said, holding the paper in her hand. "*What* are you smiling at?"

"I'm not sure," said Joe, holding the smile.

"What do you *think* you're smiling at?"

"Well, I think something's happened we didn't expect. What do you think?"

"I was hoping we were going to have the brains not to mention it."

Joe looked startled. "We don't have to do anything about it. But I don't think it hurts to be honest. I mean, do you have any idea how many times I've thought about you since New Orleans?"

"Yes."

"Really?" He was dumbfounded.

"You *know* I have a husband."

"Look, I'm not suggesting anything." He smiled. "But I do notice that I want this Anderson thing to go on forever. I think I'm infatuated with you."

"Why?"

"You remind me of John F. Kennedy."

"John F. Kennedy!" Karen broke up. "Well, I never heard that one before."

Joe was surprised by her reaction. He had not meant to be funny. "You do," he insisted. "If you looked just behind his eyes, you could actually see his intelligence and wit and compassion. Just like you."

"Did you make a pass at Kennedy?"

"Is this a pass?" He seemed annoyed. "He had something else behind his eyes, too. A little spark of anger, of flint."

"Oh?"

"Cynical lady. I wonder if anyone can really get to you?"

"You're making this a challenge. I have trouble resisting a challenge."

"Yeah, me, too," he said, rising to the invitation. He walked over to her chair, leaned over, and kissed her softly on the lips. "I think this *is* a pass." He kissed her again, only this time harder and longer. He slipped down on the arm of the chair and leaned across her. They hugged very tightly. The phone rang. They ignored it, but on the third ring Joe reached across her to the top of his desk and groped for it.

"Yes," he whispered into the phone. "Mary Anne, I thought I told you . . . Well, tell him I'll call him back a little later. Oh? Okay, put him through." He pushed away from Karen, got to his feet, and covered the receiver with his hand. "It's my son," he explained. "He says it's an emergency." He turned his back to her and faced the window. "Paulie? Hi. What rabbit? Oh yeah? What's wrong?"

Joe faced Karen. He leaned against the desk, the telephone propped on his shoulder. Karen reached for his hand and began kissing his fingers, lingering over each one. She looked up. Joe's eyes were closed in concentration.

"Why won't she let you keep it in your room?" he asked his son. "Uh huh . . . well, Paulie, it *will* smell up the house. I can't talk to her right now. No, Paulie, not now. Okay, put her on. Hi, El. Yeah, maybe we can keep it in the basement. Maybe you won't smell it there." He paused. Suddenly his face crinkled and he laughed. "Well, maybe it's not the rabbit," he said. "Maybe it's him." He laughed some more, his eyes still pressed closed, and then, suddenly once again aware of Karen, he looked down. She dropped his hand. "Listen," he said, his voice businesslike once again, "I'll be home for the weekend. I have to get off now. Me, too. No. Now now. Can't. Yeah, yeah. Me, too." He hung up the phone and walked completely around the desk, not turning to look at Karen. He was hoping to give himself time to plan his next move. Karen stood and brushed down the front of her skirt.

"I think I'd better go," she said.

"Wait a minute, please."

She shook her head no. "You weren't faking with her," she said.

"So?"

"So I don't think I want you faking with me."

She gathered her papers, stuffed them into her briefcase, and walked up to the door.

"Good-bye, Joe," she said at the door.

"Yeah, see you soon."

She went out the door and down the hallway with the click-clack of high heels on stone floors. Walking toward her was the waiter who had brought in the tray.

"Quick lunch, ma'am?" he said, as they passed. Karen, deep in her own thoughts, stopped. "Pardon me?" she asked.

"Quick lunch, ma'am. Something wrong with the tuna fish?"

"Oh. Oh, no. Nothing like that, thank you. The tuna was fine. The rabbit was lousy."

The waiter was still trying to make sense out of that one when he ducked into a phone booth tucked under the stairway at the end of the hall.

"It's me, Reynolds," he said into the phone. "She's a very pretty lady. Very pretty. And a lady. You can be sure of that. A real lady. Brought them the lunch and she was gone in fifteen minutes." He waited while the voice on the other end said something. "Don't worry about that. Reynolds starts each day with a fresh memory. Minute his head hits the pillow at night, he forgets everything he seen and heard and done that day. The only way to get a good night's sleep around here, if you knows what I mean. Good-bye. Yes, sir, you, too. Good-bye, Senator."

CHAPTER 6

In the French Quarter of New Orleans, on a narrow
street where the houses were colored a decaying pastel
and the fine gardens were hidden by walls from the
nosy eyes of the tourists, there was one house colored
an overripe pink. It sat back from the street, guarded
by a peeling cement wall with a wrought-iron gate entrance. The gate opened onto a drive paved in old
brick that widened, like a keyhole, in a courtyard. To
one side stood a brick wall, mossy and covered with
vines, and to the rear an old brick house, mossy also,
once a cottage, now the garage. Behind it and to the
right was the swimming pool, but before it, in a blaze
of incredible yellow, stood a beautiful old house. It
was banked by lovely flowers, some standing nearly as
high as the two-story house itself. Down at the base of
the house, just to the right of the door, a plaque had
been affixed that said that the house had been built
by Philip DeLacaeux Carter, the scion of one of New

Orleans's foremost French families and one of up-state's foremost Anglican families, who had used his family fortune to become one of the city's cotton brokers and squandered a good piece of what he earned supporting a fine newspaper, the legendary *Vieux Carre Courrier*. The plaque was neatly polished and shined every day at the orders of the owner of the house. His name was Barry Traynor and he was in the export-import business.

At forty-two years of age Barry Traynor had led the sort of life that made other men sick with envy. He had, for one thing, lots of money and he had, for another thing, no compunction about spending it. He felt this was his due, his obligation, since it was he who had made it.

"All by myself," he used to say, stabbing a finger into his own chest. "Me, myself, and I. It's a family company."

He had started years earlier as a travel agent. He realized then that with more and more people traveling abroad, there would be a demand for someone who knew how to buy things overseas. He became a purchasing agent of sorts, a fellow who developed the idea of having the tourist pick out the item and let someone else do the buying. He did the shipping and he paid the customs and he handled the paperwork and he worried about breakage. He did it all and what he became, in most European countries and twelve Latin American ones, was a middleman. He started his business on very little money, most of it borrowed, and within three years he was a millionaire. If that was not enough, it was also the same year he married Karen Harmen, daughter of one of the state's most influential political figures, a labor lawyer, and, everyone agreed, a beautiful woman. Barry Traynor was doing all right.

The living room of the Traynor house was especially created just for parties. It once was actually two rooms. A wall had been taken down to make it one of the largest private-party rooms in all of New Orleans. It ran the length of the house, with the exception of the kitchen in the back, and it was a spectacular place to entertain. It had two fireplaces and it was cross-hatched with huge ceiling beams. The furnishings were Spanish style, and the room itself became something of a showcase for the antiques Barry brought home from his travels.

One of these pieces was a long oak table and on it now was placed a suitcase, an attaché case, and a canvas overnight bag of the sort that you can sling over a shoulder. Barry Traynor walked over to the table and mentally inventoried his luggage. He was handsome, sharply featured with dark, curly hair. He was dressed in a summer-weight brown suit, cream-colored shirt that was worn open at the neck, and dark brown slip-on shoes. The tie was in the attaché case. He opened it just to be sure and checked. The phone rang.

"Taking attendance, darling?" Karen asked him.

"Uh huh."

"You have your raincoat?"

"Raincoat? Raincoat? In the bag. Isn't that your line?"

Karen nodded. "It's probably the office. Maybe a break in the strike. Let it ring. I'll get it later. Shall I drive you to the airport?"

He checked his watch and shook his head no. "I should have a driver outside."

"Tell me again where you're going?" Karen said, glancing over her shoulder at the still-ringing phone.

"New York then Rome then Warsaw then Tunis," he said, thumbing through the ticket book. "No. Tunis then Warsaw. No, that's not right either. Something's wrong. Oh, yeah. It is Tunis and then Warsaw." He looked at Karen and smiled. "Didn't my girl send your girl my itinerary?"

"She probably couldn't believe it was our only way of communicating." She walked over to him and smoothed down his collar. "You look sharp as usual, darling."

"You look pretty terrific yourself."

She spun around in the living room, billowing the bathrobe and nightgown she was wearing. "It will be here when you return, sir, from your trip to Cathay."

"Cathay? They sell stuff in Cathay?"

He walked over to the table, the canvas bag over his shoulder, grabbed the other two bags, and leaned over for his good-bye kiss. "Plant it, baby," he joked.

Karen walked over and kissed him. "Good-bye baby. When you get to Italy, call me. I'll just be getting up."

"Good. And listen, Karen."

"Yes?"

"If you get lonely . . ."

"Yes?"

"Have your secretary call my secretary."

They both laughed, kissed, and he was out the door. Karen realized that the phone was still ringing. She walked lazily over and picked it up.

"Have you noticed a strange ringing in your apartment for the last several minutes or is that the sound of the New Orleans cricket?"

"Who is this?"

"Karen, it's Joe."

"Oh, hi," she said, brightening.

"You *are* kind of hard to reach. The phone's been ringing and ringing."

She made no response.

"What?" he yelled. "Listen, you'll have to talk up. I'm in a booth at National Airport and it's kind of noisy. Listen, can you hear me?"

"Yes."

"Okay, good. Listen, on this Anderson thing . . ."

"Yes?"

"I need to work with you a little on that. Could you come up to Washington?"

"I can't, Joe," she said.

"No? Wait a minute. The hearing's coming up soon, I need you to help me work out a line of questioning."

"No one else can do that?"

She sounded cynical and distant. He wondered if the call had been a mistake. He had batted the thing back and forth on the way down from New York and had finally decided to do it. Now that he had done it, he had real doubts about his decision.

"You've done the research. No one could do it as well as you could."

"I don't see how I can. When would you want me to be there?"

"How about tomorrow?" Joe suggested.

"I have a problem. I'm involved in settling a strike down here. I thought that's what this call was about."

"Okay, Wednesday. I really need you. I need your expertise."

Karen hesitated. "Well . . ." she paused.

Joe pressed her. "Are you going to drop it when we're so close to winning?"

"It's not that," she said. "It's . . . Okay, Wednesday. But listen . . ."

"Yeah?"

"This is just work, right?"

"Karen," he said sternly. "The hearings are coming up soon. I need help."

"Yes, well, if you sit on the couch and I sit on the desk, that's not going to make you smile, right?"

"What?" Joe protested. "Why would that make me smile?"

"I'll see you Wednesday," she said. "Good-bye, Joe."

Joe hung up the phone and checked the coin return for any change. He swung open the door of the booth. He was smiling.

Francis paced, a worried look on his face, up and back on the rug before Joe's desk. Joe was confused by the young man's concern, his failure, actually, to get the point.

"I'm just not sure that she's worth the expense, Senator," Francis said, shaking his head back and forth. Francis thought what Joe was about to do was more than just silly, it was downright dangerous.

"She'll be very useful, Francis," Joe said.

"Look, don't get me wrong. I think Karen Traynor's terrific. I just don't know if we can get that much mileage out of her. Besides, where can we put her?" He took a computer printout from the coffee

142

table and once again looked at it. "The best Lou can come up with is that we put her on the subcommittee staff as a per diem consultant. But that's it for the fiscal year. No more per diems unless we go back for more money. And I wouldn't advise that. You're already using Birney's own committee to torpedo his own nominee. It's a bit unorthodox. It is also living very dangerously."

"I'd like to keep her working with us on this," Joe said. He was beginning to sound irritated. "Francis, I've already asked her."

Francis got the picture. "Oh, well, fine, I think she's very knowledgeable."

"I think she can make a difference," Joe said.

"Yes, make a difference," Francis muttered.

"She'll need a place to stay."

"I'll get her a room at the Embassy Row Hotel. You can work with her there."

"Fine."

"I'll take care of that personally."

"Fine."

The Embassy Row Hotel is on Massachusetts Avenue, just down the street from most of the major embassies. It presents a contemporary glass front to the regal avenue, something new in an area dominated by homes built once for the very rich and used now by foreign countries as embassies. The location is perfect—neither downtown nor uptown, neither city nor suburban. For this reason it is a hotel that is not frequented by Washingtonians, particularly not by reporters. They go elsewhere for lunch, and the hotel has built up an underground reputation as a fine place for assignations, for lunch when you do not want to be seen—for anything when you are afraid of whom you might meet in the lobby.

It was to this hotel that Karen Traynor headed, her cab pulling into the semicircular driveway not more than thirty-five minutes after leaving Dulles Airport in the farm country of Virginia. Karen got out, paid the driver, and was already registered and on the way up in the elevator when Joe's cab pulled into the same driveway. He walked briskly into the hotel, checked in the lobby for Karen's room number, and went directly to the elevator. The knock came so soon after Karen had walked into the room that she assumed it was the bellhop returning for some reason. She opened the door. It was Joe.

"You?" she said softly.

He stepped into the room and she closed the door. They looked at each other, Joe noticing something in the look of the eye. She saw the way his chest heaved. They moved toward each other. They kissed, at first softly and tentatively and then hungrily, enjoying the taste of each other, the feel of holding one another close. Karen fought for a respite.

"Listen," she said breathlessly, "I spent a lot of time working on notes for this meeting."

"Good, we'll go over it together," Joe said.

"Yes. Good. Because . . ." They kissed again. They stood in the little entrance alcove. Joe moved Karen against the wall and held her tightly. She pushed gently against him, running her hands up and down his back, dipping a hand underneath his suit jacket and then up the back of his shirt. Joe glanced around.

"Does this place have a bedroom?"

144

"I don't know, I just got here."

They moved into the living room, Karen backing up, Joe advancing on her. She stopped in the middle of the room and threw her arms around him. They kissed. She began pushing his jacket off. He fumbled for the buttons on the back of her blouse. It had been a long time since he had undressed a woman. He worked two of the buttons free but his arms got tangled in his jacket. The two of them moved over to the cream-colored couch, aiming for that. They missed and sank slowly to the floor, a tangle of clothes and arms trying to get free.

"My God, you taste good," Joe said.

"I can't get my . . . let me get my arm out of this." Karen sat up and slipped her arm out of her blouse. She looked into his eyes, imploring him, asking him something, telling him something. He didn't know what.

"Listen," he said, "I'm going to sound like an idiot talking about this now, but I want to be honest with you."

"I know, you're married."

He shook his head no. "You can't count on me. I'll never be able to get involved beyond a certain level."

"Okay, so you're married. So am I."

They kissed again. He eased himself up to look down at her, shaking his head back and forth as if he couldn't believe what he was seeing. Her hand trailed his chest, opening the buttons on his shirt.

"You know, you're very demonstrative," she said.

"You never made love to a Democrat?"

* * *

Later, they went into the bedroom and made love once again. He devoured her. He studied her. He looked at the way she was built, noticing secretly the difference between her and Ellie. He had to give some thought to his lovemaking. Nothing could be taken for granted. There was no just knowing when to do what, no ground rules about what was off-base and what was considered fair.

She, too, groped for the rules. She learned things the first time and then the second, but she made no comparisons as she went along. Joe was different, that was all. Just different.

In the early evening, with the light fading and the room growing dark, they took turns going to the bathroom. Joe turned on the television set to watch the news. Karen got into bed and watched him watching the news, kissing him frequently, running her hands over his body. A half-smiling, half-painful expression on her face. Behind her on the television screen, the weatherman was pointing to a map. He was wearing a hat made of a watermelon rind and when it slipped off and fell to the floor, breaking, Joe laughed.

Later he had her call down to room service. He hid in the closet when the waiter arrived, trying to suppress his laughter as the waiter counted out the order—"two beers and a cheese order for two and shrimp cocktail for *two*." Karen said nothing. She found the waiter obnoxious, but she tipped him well anyway, somehow thinking that *that* would teach him a lesson. When the door clicked shut, Joe emerged nude from the closet, a look of helplessness written all over his face. He took two large bounds across the

146

room and vaulted back into the bed, pulling the covers over him. Karen slipped off her white terry-cloth robe and followed him under the covers. They put the tray down between them and ate.

"This affair is going to put twenty pounds on me," Karen said, bringing a beer to her lips. "How come you just don't smoke afterward like normal people?"

"I'm very oral," he said.

"I noticed," she said.

"What's his name?" Joe asked her.

"My husband?"

Joe brought the bottle to his lips and nodded.

"Barry."

"Barry," Joe said, as if he was tasting the word. "Sounds very upper."

"He worked his way up. You'd probably like him."

"What's he doing while you're here?"

"He's in Tunis. He travels a lot."

"*That* I like." Karen let that one go by. She reached for a cracker, placed a slice of yellow cheese on it, and plunked it all into her mouth. The crumbs fell on the bed.

"Is your wife as smart as they say she is in the magazines?" she asked, staring straight ahead and brushing the crumbs down toward her toes.

Joe turned toward her. "I'm sorry," he said gravely. "I wish I could tell you that she has the brains of a chorus girl. Unfortunately, just the body of one."

Karen forced a chuckle. She reached for her bottle of beer, took a modest swig, uttered another forced chuckle, and quickly poured the beer on Joe. He arched his back and threw his arms up into the air.

"I love a girl with a sense of humor," he said dryly.

"Okay," Karen said, trying to stop her laughter. "Okay, let's be serious. I didn't mean to scare you."

"Jesus, you southerners are all nuts."

Karen smiled and placed her head on his chest and snuggled in, making cooing sounds as she did so.

"Talk to your father lately?" Joe asked.

"I did talk to my father. I have some terrific stuff you can use against Anderson."

"What kind of stuff?" He asked.

"Campaign . . ." She stopped and looked up at him. "Campaign contributions. Two corporations made secret contributions."

"That's great," Joe said. "The contributions. I won't even have to . . . I won't have to use it. I'll just let them know I have it. Jesus."

He reached down for her and she came up to meet him. They kissed.

"Good. Good," she said. "Fantastic. You're going to be fantastic in those hearings."

Joe leaned on his elbows, looking down at her. "I want to write you secret notes from the floor. I want to fly two thousand miles just to spend an hour with you. And right now, I want to make love to you again and again and again."

"God," she said, "what took you so long?"

Senator Hugh Kittner was bombed. He had started the evening with bourbon, that was certain, but later moved on to his drink—anything. Whenever the waiter passed him, tray of drinks held shoulder-high, Kittner reached and took anything he could get. His arm was like one of those devices for snatching mail bags from moving trains, but the fact of the matter was that all his drinking made him no drunker than ordinary drunk. He had reached that level early in the party and stayed that way, as if he had peaked. It was as if he needed more drinks just to maintain his state of drunkenness, if he stopped drinking for, say, five minutes he would instantly sober up and have to come to terms with what he had been doing all night. This he was definitely not going to do.

He had, for one thing, not talked to his wife all night. He had, for another, made a pass at nearly every woman at the party. He had spilled drinks on the rug and then on the patio beyond the French doors, on the street side of the house. Because he had been so loud, the French doors had been closed and the party contained inside of the house.

It was one of those Georgetown parties that would make the papers. The house itself was one of the area's newer ones, built in a French provincial style at the end of a block of Federal-style brick homes. Its facade was mostly stone and cement, and inside the rooms were large and bordered always in pale-colored, creamy wood. The place boasted a good deal of terrazzo marble on the floors and around the fireplaces and it had the usual pool out in the back. It was worth somewhere between $300,000 and $400,000 and it was owned ostensibly by a lawyer named Duncan whose main job was to represent the government of Kuwait in Washington. A corporation he had formed owned the house outright. The major stockholder in the corporation was the government of Kuwait. It had supplied the house for Duncan so he could do his entertaining.

To most of Washington Duncan was known as Duncan Duncan. His real name was Warren Robert Duncan, but years before the name Duncan Duncan had been pinned on him when in answer to the question "Is Duncan your first name or your last name?" he had said, "Suit yourself." With that the woman who had asked him announced that henceforth his name would be Duncan Duncan and henceforth it was. The name stuck. He even had a listing under that name in the phone book. He explained to the phone company that it was the way most people tried to look him up.

Duncan Duncan was a short man, totally bald at the front of his head, but holding his own from the middle back. He had a slight paunch, a bright, intelligent, warm face, and an infectious laugh. He had never married and although he was occasionally linked to women around town, the rumor persisted that he was a homosexual. One of the town's foremost party givers, he was a wonderful host, determined to have the government of Kuwait finance his good time, in exchange for which he would give them the sort of information they could get by carefully reading the morning paper.

This night he had invited seventy-five persons, but it was obvious that more than that number had shown up. Some had asked if they could bring guests and he had said yes, and others had just assumed that they could bring guests and they had assumed right, and some assumed that their lack of an invitation was merely an oversight on Duncan's part. They might have been right there. Everyone knew that Duncan cared little about who came and who did not. His expense account paid for the party and his caterers did the cooking and the cleaning up, and all he had to do was retire to his study sometime after the party was over and write down in his book the names of everyone who had been in the house that night. He kept these records for two reasons. The first was for the Internal Revenue Service and the second was for his employers. In the morning he would cable the names to Kuwait. The Kuwait government, he long ago discovered, loved names.

Tonight, though, Duncan was having trouble with names. For instance, the buxom young woman who kept going upstairs with various men, sometimes singly, sometimes in pairs—he did not know her name. Two men over at the piano were perfect strangers and several more people he knew only by sight. When Duncan tallied things up, he realized that he did not know fully half the people at his own party. They, of course, could reciprocate. They did not know him either.

Duncan panned the room. He saw Richard Cardoza, a former member of the Kennedy administration and now the preeminent oil lobbyist in town. Duncan worked with Cardoza but did not like the man at all. Unlike Duncan, Cardoza was anti-Israel; unlike Duncan, he also was Jewish. Duncan spotted Evan Meyer, a reporter for *The Washington Post* whom he recognized from Sunday afternoon talk shows. He had not invited him. He spotted Kittner and made a face. The old fool was drunk again, Duncan observed. Kittner must have cost the government of Kuwait the equivalent of a battleship just in booze alone. Duncan noticed that Kittner had cornered Joe Tynan and was chewing his ear off. Duncan recalled the story about Kittner, probably apocryphal, that there had been a clumsy attempt to blackmail him by distributing compromising pictures of him in bed with some woman. Kittner refused to pay a cent for the pictures on the ground that, as blackmail, they were useless since they told people what they already knew and as pictures they were a poor likeness. Duncan's eyes rested on Paul Mortangale, a notorious gate crasher. Mortangale flashed an insolent smile at Duncan, knowing that his host would never create a scene. Duncan walked over.

"And the horse you came in on," he said as he passed, smiling. He wound up bumping into Jerry Rappaport.

"It's R-A-P-P-A-P-O-R-T," said Rappaport. "Two *p*'s."

Duncan looked puzzled.

"You know, for your cable."

"Oh," he said smiling. "Don't worry. I got your name, my boy. Trouble is some of the others here. Do you know them?"

"Search me."

"By the way, Jerry, did I invite you?"

"Well, I am mortified. I am abashed. I am cha-grined."

"I do apologize."

"No. You did not. And for that I humbly apologize. I will make it up to you. I will have the French cable their embassy saying that they should have you as a guest. We'll make sure Kuwait intercepts. Or should we have the Israelis intercept and have them give it to Kuwait. The Israelis have credibility."

Duncan smiled. "How are you, Jerry?"

"Fine. I'm enjoying myself. I love your little parties. Invaluable for me. If there wasn't someone like you, we would have to invent one." He slapped his gut. "I am, however, putting on a little weight at these things. The food's too good." He looked around as if he was casing the room. "The truth is you did invite me. I would have come anyway because I'm your friend and you need my name in your cables."

Duncan smiled and shook Jerry's hand. "See you later," he said, moving off.

He walked around the room, introducing himself. "Hello," he would say, "I'm Duncan." Usually he got a nod, sometimes a name in return, but a few times he was simply ignored, treated like some gate crasher. One of them, a young man with a short haircut, asked him if he knew the "asshole lobbyist who owned the place."

"Not well," Duncan said.

Over by the piano Kittner was still going at it with Joe. Duncan picked up a bit of conversation but what he heard was not the sort of thing he was likely to put in a cable to Kuwait.

"I'm not kidding you, Joe," Kittner was saying. "I said, 'Listen young lady, I'm a United States Senator. What if somebody comes in here and finds us together?'" He gave Joe a comrades-in-arms wink. "And then, by Christ, she threw a fit. It was wonderful. I mean, she acted so needy. I couldn't resist." Kittner slapped his knee, letting out a belly laugh.

"Hugh, you're the genuine article," Joe said, forcing a smile to his face.

"Joe, it was a religious experience," Kittner said, in a confidential tone. "I felt close to God." He dropped his voice. "Listen, I got a visit today from a couple of guys from the labor unions. They tell me they have you on this Anderson thing."

153

It took Joe a moment to realize that Kittner had changed the subject. It took another second to realize that the old bird was far from drunk and still another moment to compose an answer. In the meantime Joe's face registered nothing but shock, an expression that pleased Kittner no end.

"They *have* me?" Joe said.

"I said, 'Listen, it's time the South was represented on the Supreme Court. It means a lot to Senator Birney and it means a lot to me. And I'm sure that Senator Tynan would talk this over with us before he came out against us.'" Kittner eyeballed Joe, pushing right up against him. The smell was overpowering. "Wouldn't he?" he said into his face.

Joe backed up. "Hugh, I'm sure Senator Birney will get what he wants. He usually does." Kittner studied Joe hard for a moment. Then his face relaxed and broke out into a wide grin.

"Listen. What do you say we go partners on those two over there?" he asked Joe, pointing to two women across the room.

"Jesus, Hugh, are you crazy? That's somebody's wife."

"Go on, she ain't nobody's wife," Kittner said, dismissing the thought with a wave of his hand.

"That's Hutchison's wife. The freshman from Minnesota."

"Jesus Christ," he said, shaking his head in disbelief, "those goddamn hippies. They don't even marry women who look like wives."

"Hugh, you're the genuine article," Joe repeated, trying to draw away from Kittner.

Kittner noticed. "G'won, son, beat it. I see you got

some politicking to do." The old man turned and walked away. Joe started across the room when a hand reached up from a couch and tugged at his sleeve. He looked down. It was Aldena Kittner, the still-attractive wife of the Senate's most notorious womanizer. "Come on, sit down here," she said.

Aldena Kittner was one of those women the press calls sharp-tongued. It meant that she was usually bitter, occasionally obscene, and frequently drunk. She was most of those things tonight, but sober or drunk there were certain rules that applied to conversation with her. For one thing her husband's playing around was never mentioned, although she sometimes mentioned it herself, and for another no one ever intimated that her husband was considered an old fool. She was holding a glass of bourbon and wearing a black taffeta dress that showed an ample amount of what was once a formidable bosom. She tugged at Joe's sleeve. He collapsed into the couch.

"You shouldn't be seen talking to that horse's ass," she said.

"Which one?"

"My husband. Look at him talking to that fool Cardoza. He has the same taste in lobbyists as he does in women."

"How're the kids, Aldena?"

She smiled, took Joe's hand in hers, and patted it. "Away in college. And last month the dog died. How would you like to come over and have an affair with me sometime?"

"When was the last time you and Hugh took a vacation together?" Joe asked, wincing at the stupidity of the question.

She laughed. "Lots of good that would do. I not only don't sleep with him anymore, I won't drink out of the same cup as him." She downed what was left of her drink and peered into the bottom of the glass as if she couldn't figure out where it all had gone. "You want to get me another bourbon, honey?" she asked, offering Joe her glass.

"You sure?" he asked.

Her face went ugly. She reached for the arm of a passing waiter. "Hey," she yelled. "Gimme a bourbon."

"Yes, ma'am," the waiter said, taking her glass.

Joe rose. Aldena took his hand and placed it to her lips. Now, once again, she had turned nice and solicitous.

"Is Ellie okay?" she asked softly.

"She's fine," Joe said, patting Aldena's cheek.

Aldena straightened up on the sofa. "Don't you ever lose her if you know what's good for you," she said. Joe was about to say something when he saw Karen come in the door. She was with Congressman Wayne Tiller, a good-looking bouncy guy with an addiction to double-knit suits, white shoes, and a matching white belt. Joe thought Tiller was an asshole, an assessment generally accepted on the Hill. Despite that Tiller was one of the great ladies' men in Congress. He was not only better looking than most of his colleagues, but he had an unfair advantage: he was a bachelor.

"How are the kids?" Aldena asked, noticing Jack's distraction.

"They're great, Al," Joe said, keeping his eye on Karen. She and Tiller were coming his way. Joe wanted very much to be somewhere else.

156

"Can I get you anything, Aldena?" he asked.

"No," Aldena said, catching on. "Go mingle."

He patted her hand and walked off, trying to escape from Karen and Tiller, who were approaching to say hello. Karen stopped just where Aldena Kittner sat. A woman had taken Joe's seat. "My God," Aldena said to the woman. "Would you look at that over there?" She pointed to a woman in a low-cut dress who was dancing suggestively over by the piano. The woman was a free-lance writer who had once made a reputation for herself when she managed to get the diary of a former first lady. Since then she had become better known for her incredible body and what she did with it.

"Who the hell brought her?" Aldena asked the woman next to her.

"I don't think anyone brought her," the woman answered.

"You mean she's free-lancing?" Aldena said. "That girl's gonna make herself fifty dollars easy . . . if she can make it up the stairs ten or twelve times." The other woman laughed and they both looked back at the dancing woman. Someone was playing "The Stripper" on the piano, and the woman, a tall blonde, was gyrating back and forth. All in all, she couldn't dance worth a lick, but she sure was a sight. Joe, who had given the dancing woman a look, had worked his way over to the other side of the room where he was talking with Betsy James, a reporter for *The Washington Post*. Wayne Tiller came over.

"Senator, you know Congressman Tiller," James said. Joe assumed Betsy was another of the congressman's conquests. Joe turned. Tiller extended his hand.

"Hello, Wayne, how are you?" Joe said. Karen emerged from behind Tiller.

"Senator Joe Tynan," Tiller said, waving his hand toward Karen, "Karen Traynor."

"Yes, we've met," Joe said curtly. "How are you?" The smile was as phony as could be.

"Fine," she said. "How've you been, Senator?"

"Fine."

Nothing more was said. Joe's face was cold and tense while Karen's seemed to be pleading for an explanation—"what did I do wrong?" No answer came from Joe, just silence and that stare.

"I'm starving," Tiller said, clapping his hands and forcing up a hearty smile. "Do they have any food here?"

"In the dining room there's a big chicken salad the shape of Louisiana," Joe said.

"You wanna stay?" Tiller asked Karen, putting his hand on her shoulder. "There's a good restaurant at your hotel."

"That sounds convenient," Joe said.

Karen shot Joe a look of reproach. "Let's see what they have inside," she said, taking Tiller by the hand. They walked off in the direction of the dining room. Joe stood for a moment, thinking about what had just taken place, wanting to kick himself for being so obvious, when suddenly he was slammed in the back. It was Kittner. He brushed Joe out of the way while rolling a baby grand piano by him. Four other men helped.

"Watch out, give her room," Kittner yelled, swinging his arm in the direction of the dancing woman. "Help us get this thing out of her way." Joe made no move to help. He feasted his eyes, instead, on the woman who now seemed to be in some sort of alcohol or drug trance. The music had stopped, not that it mattered to the dancing woman. She moved into the space vacated by the piano and did her routine— hands above the head, a clap, hands down the length of the body, hands cupping the breasts, and then all over again. Duncan watched also, his arm resting on the marble mantelpiece of the fireplace, a glass of warm Scotch in his hand. By the time he saw what was happening, he was too drunk and too far away to do anything. Duncan would later confess that he no longer had the moves.

"Give us a hand here," Kittner bellowed, pointing a finger at several men who, like Joe, were simply watching. "You just wait, honey," he said, turning to the unhearing woman. "We're making room for ya."

Four more men took their places at the piano. One of them went around to the keyboard and started to play a bump-and-grind rhythm. The dancing woman took it up, thrusting her pelvis to the beat. With each hump of her body, the men at the piano pushed into it, mimicking her, chanting "ah oomph" with each thrust. It was as dirty a show as Washington had seen since they closed down burlesque.

The man playing the piano accelerated his rhythm and so did the dancing woman and so did the men humping the piano. With each thrust they moved the thing a bit, and when the music had built up and the "ah oomphs" were reaching a peak, something told the piano player to step away. The men behind the piano gave it a final, climactic hump and the piano took off. As it moved, the men on the side gave it a shove. It really took off. It went right for the French doors, hitting them at the point where the doors met. The doors sprang open and the piano rolled out, clumping down the small steps easily, hitting the driveway, picking up speed, and then hurtling down the asphalt drive. People ran to the window. The piano zoomed down the driveway, hurtling to the street where it stopped and was hit by a moving car. It crumpled like a sick camel. The front leg buckled, then the hind two. It just sat on the road.

The car was a white MG sports car with Virginia license plates. The door opened and a middle-aged man in a business suit climbed out slowly. He was wary, dazed, looking around at the growing crowd. Up and down the block porch lights flicked on and people came out of their homes to see the car that hit the piano. The driver walked around to the front of his car and saw the piano. He slapped his forehead. Blood trickled from his nose, where he had hit the steering wheel. He stared down at the piano and then very purposefully walked back to the car, trying very hard to show all the world that he was as sober as could be. He tottered as he walked.

Back in the house Aldena Kittner was still glued to her couch, holding on to it like a sailor holding a rail during a storm. She turned to the woman next to her. "Tell me, did my husband just push a piano out the window?"

"Well, not all by himself," the woman answered.

"What an asshole," Aldena Kittner said.

Outside the street was bathed in the flashing red lights of police cars. There were three of them, two at either end of the street, detouring traffic, the third

160

one in the middle. The driver of the MG leaned against his car, trying to sort things out, while in front of him Kittner was explaining matters to the police.

"Listen, son," he said, jabbing the cop in the chest. "I voted you D.C. cops every raise you ever had."

"Senator," the cop said, ignoring the remark, "I'd just like to know how the piano got into the street." He stood before Kittner, holding a pad of traffic summonses, trying for the life of him to decide if he could ticket a moving piano. Around him the people from the party watched, some of them with drinks in hand. Every house on the block had its lights on, and in some of them people were already calling the newspapers. Back on the lawn of the house, Duncan sat on an aluminum beach chair he had fetched from the garage. He held his Scotch and smiled. In his head he was playing newspaper headlines—the ones that would be written about his party. In each headline the word lobbyist appeared and then next to it, a picture of Duncan, the one always used—the one taken before he got his hairpiece. Duncan reckoned he might be through in Washington. He downed his drink and sank into the webbing of the aluminum chair. Senator Joseph Tynan, who had lots of things to think about, drifted unnoticed down the street and into the Georgetown darkness.

At the accident scene, Kittner held forth. First he recited his voting record in favor of pay raises for the Washington police force, then he reminded the policeman who he was, and then he claimed diplomatic immunity, and finally worked himself into a fine fettle of moral indignation. He coiled himself up like a snake, released his body like a whip, and pointed a finger at the still-stunned driver of the MG. "I want you to give this man a breath test," he demanded.

With the lights behind him Joe kept walking. He made his way to the end of the street, turned right, walked to Q Street, N.W., and followed that for a while. The houses on both sides of the street were among the nicest in Washington—old Federal-style houses, many of them actually dating to the Revolutionary War period. It had become fashionable to knock Georgetown, but it was Washington's premier neighborhood, a truly lovely area, made all the lovelier in the darkness by the occasional gaslight sputtering upward from some large gate.

Joe walked some time. He took Q Street to Scott Circle, and then to Massachusetts. He walked for a while, finding himself in front of the Embassy Row Hotel—"finding himself before the Embassy Row Hotel," he said to himself. He was sort of writing the thing out in his head, realizing that he had not "found himself" there at all, but instead that he was heading that way all the time. The thought depressed him. He realized how much he wanted to be with Karen. He looked up at what he figured would be her room, counting the floors with his fingers. The lights were out. Good, he thought. He checked himself. Maybe it was bad.

He recognized all the symptoms. He was taking it seriously. But he had always taken it seriously. Sometimes he thought he was one of the few left who took it seriously. Sex—raw language. He had no vocabulary like that, no gratuitous feelings. He took it all very seriously. And he resented the way Francis had looked at him when he said Karen would be joining the staff. Francis assumed so much, Joe thought. He assumed it was just sex. He stopped and recalled the other night. God, he wanted to be with her.

"You don't understand," he imagined himself saying to Francis. "I'm taking this seriously."

"Do you love her?" Francis would ask.

"I don't know," Joe would answer. "I'm studying it. I'm considering all the options, but I'll tell you this, right now all I want is to be the best senator the State of New York ever had." He chuckled to himself. "All I want to do is continue to serve the people of the State of New York because, as we all know, they are assholes."

Joe valued Francis. He considered his young aide to be almost amoral, a necessary complement to his own softness. He needed to have a Francis around as a sounding board to say, "Now here, Francis, is the right thing to do. And here, Francis, is the wrong thing to do and now from you, Francis, I want five-hundred words, skipping every other line, on what the political things to do would be. I want all the options, all of them set out, and then all of the options that flow from that. And while you're at it, Francis, I want to know something else."

Francis would stop at the door and hesitate. "Come back in here and sit down," Joe would say in a fatherly way. "Francis, if I told you that under no circumstances would I ever run for president, would you quit me and go work for someone else?"

Francis hung his head.

"Francis?" Joe implored.

"Yes," Francis finally said. "You bet your sweet ass."

"Why, Francis?"

"'Cause I want to work in the White House," he said. "I want to be your top aide, your Sorensen, your Haldeman, your Hamilton Jordan, your Colonel House or Harry Hopkins or Sherman Adams. I want to be one of them."

"Why, Francis?" Joe asked.

"Because I can't be president," he answered. "Because I'm short and I grate on people and I went to a second-rate college and law school that taught you how to chase ambulances and make wills and pass the bar exam. Because my name is Francis O'Connor and I'm half-Irish and half-Italian and even the Italian is half-Jewish. I couldn't get two votes anywhere in this country and so the only way I can get to the White House is with someone like you. I'll work twenty-five hours a day and I'll do anything I have to do, but I'll do it and I'll make you do it, too."

"Why, Francis?" Joe asked.

"Why?" Francis repeated. "Whadya mean, why?"

"Why do you want to work in the White House?" Joe asked.

"Why do I want to work in the White House?" Francis said, stalling for time. "I don't know," he said after a while. "I never asked myself that." Then he brightened. "You've been there," he said to Joe. "There's something special about the place. Even the bookcases seem so nice. I love those offices. Everything painted white, the bookcases with the Sony colored television sets, the mess in the basement with the two dining rooms, the cars and the Secret Service and the airplanes. I love that. I don't think that's wrong. I love that sort of thing. You have to live your life somehow, and I love power or being around power or exercising power or whatever. I don't see anything wrong with that. There's nothing wrong with that, is there?"

Joe said nothing.

"Something else," Francis added. "You don't die if you get to the White House. People know you and they remember you and when they write history books they write about you and your influence on the president and on events. That sort of thing. Your name is in books and people can point to it and say that this man lived at this time and he did this and that and it made a difference. He told the president to start a war or lift an embargo or send food to some starving kids somewhere. You don't die if you make it to the White House."

Joe had reached Dupont Circle. He crossed into the little park with the fountain dedicated to the memory of Admiral Russell L. Dupont and watched the water doing high-kicks among the floodlights. Joe paused for a moment, turned his back on the fountain, and resumed his walk and his imaginary conversation with Francis.

"How about me, Francis?" Joe asked. "Why should I run for president?"

"'Cause it's there," Francis said. "It's the top of the line. The last stop. The spot you shoot for. You don't go into anything to be second-best, second-rate or whatever. You don't join a corporation to be a vice-president or something. You join to be president. You join to go to the top. You've done that all your life,

Senator. Always moving up. Always one rung and then the other and now you're a United States Senator. Very exclusive club."

Joe shot him a look.

"No, really," Francis explained. "I mean, there are only one hundred of you—two hundred and fifty million of us, one hundred of you. Think about that. How exclusive can you get."

Joe nodded his head in understanding.

"You've got to move up," Francis continued. "First, by making yourself into a candidate, you automatically become a better senator. You get power you never had before. You have the power to define issues. You take this Anderson thing. Your going out in front on this one is going to be big news. You're not just another senator. You're a potential president. A potential president does not make nonchalant moves. You're going to carve up this guy Anderson." Joe winced at the imagery.

"But I don't have any program," Joe complained. "I have no broad vision. I even agree with the guy who's in there now and I'll probably agree more or less with whoever runs next time out. What will I say? 'Ladies and Gentlemen, I more or less agree with everyone.' I have no broad program. I have no new vision. What I would like to do is tinker with the programs of others. I think we should call my program the New Tinker. We can fine-tune everything. Francis," Joe said excitedly, "we can resurrect zero-base budgeting and reform the civil service. Those are big tinkers worthy, don't you think, of the New Tinker."

"Terrific," Francis said, laughing.

"My wife hates politics, Francis," Joe continued. "What do I do about her? She's walking dynamite, Francis. She gave an interview the other day in which she admitted that she's been in analysis. Good-bye Idaho or something, right, Francis?"

The aide nodded in agreement. "Idaho?" he said. "At the very least, Idaho."

Joe envisioned a map of the United States made out of puzzle pieces, all the states west of the Mississippi separating from each other, spilling off the edge of a table.

"But she hates it," Joe went on. "She genuinely hates politics. I can't blame her. I mean if you look at it from her point of view, Francis, you can't blame her. She's some sort of objet d'art during the campaign, sitting on all those damned platforms, one leg tucked under the other ankle, like Queen Elizabeth reviewing the royal horse dragoons or something. She hates it. She hates that and the silly airport statements—'Do you think your husband will win, Mrs. Tynan?' 'Actually, no. He and I stayed up all night talking about his pending defeat. We talked about how it would probably leave him very depressed. I am a psychologist, you know. Well, almost a psychologist anyway. I know about these things. It will be rough on us, but we will manage. Sometimes these things are followed by divorce. Quite common, actually.'" He envisioned the reporter recoiling in shock from what Ellie was saying.

"What'ja expect me to answer when you ask me if I think my husband will win?" Ellie snapped. "You expect me to say no? God, I can't stand any more of these dumb questions." Joe was full of admiration for Ellie. She was tough. A mind of her own, old Ellie. Looking good, standing there, giving that reporter the old what for. God she was terrific, he thought. God, he loved her.

"You love her so much, what are you doing at Karen's hotel?" Francis asked.

"She doesn't admire me the way Karen does," Joe explained. "She doesn't like what I do. She finds it shallow. It's simple, Francis. There are things we have to do, right, Francis? You have to campaign to get elected. You have to compromise and do the show-business routines and shake hands and snooker up to power and kowtow to money. But you get something done. You help some people. Take that public works bill of mine. I helped people with that. People are going to be working because of me. That's good tinkering. The New Tinkering works, Francis. I wish Ellie could see that."

"If you quit politics, it'll be the end," Francis observed. "It will be the end of you and the end of Ellie and the end of your marriage. You'll do it for her. I've seen this before. You'll do this for her and you'll feel so good about it, a real angel, a wonderful martyr, but the thing will sink in your stomach like a lead baby—heavy. All the old juices will be flowing, the energy will be there and the adrenalin will pump up, but there'll be nowhere to go. Boy, I've seen that. It happens when they lose. I worked for a guy who lost. He went to Florida at first, then to California, then he became a lobbyist here, and then he went to Europe for a year. He came back here to sell his house and while he was here, maybe a day or two, he blew his brains out."

"Francis," Joe said in exasperation, "that was Milliken and he was dying of cancer."

"Yeah," Francis admitted. "But he also lost."

"Boy, I wish I was as sure of everything as you are, Francis," Joe said. "I've got a seat in the Senate and a wonderful wife and two great kids and a woman in a hotel room back there, and I don't have any idea of what I'm doing. Here I am forty-two years old and I've become a cliché. I'm a senator with a mistress in a Washington hotel, Francis. I will not be a cliché, Francis."

A horn blew, chasing Joe onto the curb. He had walked down Connecticut Avenue to the Mayflower Hotel. He bought the morning *Washington Post*, hailed a cab, and went home, determined not to become a cliché.

Joe was pacing once again. He worked a path in the carpet of Karen's hotel room, trampling it flat where it had been lifted by the vacuum cleaner. Karen, sitting in an armchair, watched.

"How could you do it?" Joe asked. "How could you go there with him?"

"I thought you weren't going to get involved," Karen said coolly.

"How could you go anywhere with him?" he persisted. "The man is a renowned jerk. They had a survey to name the biggest jerk in Congress and he won second place."

"Well, he was perfectly adequate for what I needed him for, which was to pass the evening," she said.

"How do you know him?" Joe asked.

"He's my congressman," she replied.

"You're in bigger trouble than I thought," Joe said.

"So are you," Karen said, smiling.

CHAPTER 7

Francis O'Connor was fast becoming an accomplished liar. He knew that and he liked that. He considered it a sign of his personal progress since arriving in Washington. For years he had been no good at lying, a weakness he attributed to a Catholic upbringing reinforced by a Catholic education. He saw it as a handicap in the world of politics, in the world of anything, actually, and he considered his inability to lie, well, a bit childish, some sort of hang-up that had to be expunged. Francis had noticed how common lying was and how it could be used as yet another political way to get ahead. Francis thought that Spiro Agnew was the best liar he had ever seen.

Francis reserved a special admiration for Agnew. He marveled at the way the man had called press conference after press conference to deny his guilt and assail the Justice Department when he was as guilty as a street-corner pimp. He had to applaud Agnew's performance when he said he would never resign and then went ahead and did just that. In Agnew's hands lying had become another political tool, another weapon in the arsenal, as good as, or maybe better than, a terrific staff or debating skills or a large plurality. It was something that could be used, and while Francis never wanted to lie like that—in the long run credibility was important—he did want to be able to refrain from telling the truth, the whole truth, the complete truth. He wanted to be able to play some games with the truth, withhold some of it or maybe bend it a little. This was different from Agnew's lying style, and this was what Francis thought he was doing with John Cairn, Senator Kittner's administrative assistant.

Cairn was a short, intense fellow, addicted to bow ties and hair blow-dried into a bush at the front of his head. He gave the appearance of a man constantly perplexed, which is what he was most of the time. He was thirty-eight years old, going on sixty-four, which was the standard joke about him—a man with more than the usual number of worries. On the Hill he was both envied and pitied. Some envied him because he was virtually a senator himself. It was he who decided most matters for his womanizing, frequently drunk boss, and so Cairn wielded vast, if unheralded power. For the same reason, he was pitied. He had to work harder than his colleagues and he was also, unlike most of them, something of a baby-sitter and wet nurse combined. He really had to watch over his boss, make sure the man stayed out of trouble or, at the very least, limited his trouble. Now, however, Cairn thought his boss was heading toward serious trouble.

That thought had been growing for the last several days, but it became clear that morning with the arrival of *The Washington Post*. There, on page one, was yet another story about Anderson, the Supreme Court nominee, this one saying that he belonged to a segregated and exclusive club that never in 145 years had admitted a black. The story went on to say that Anderson was on the membership committee when a black federal judge was rejected for membership, although Anderson's role in that and his position on the matter was not clear. The story reported speculation that Anderson had voted in favor of the black judge, but the proceedings of the admissions committee were secret and no one could find out what had happened. No matter. Anderson did not look good. Someone was sure to suggest that the only thing for him to have done was resign from the club. Cairn was tempted to agree with that himself.

Cairn had read the story while standing on the stoop in his pajamas. He had a feeling about the story, about all the Anderson stories that had been appearing in both the *Post* and *The New York Times*. He had seen this sort of thing before with the Supreme Court nominations of Clement Haynsworth and G. Harold Carswell, and he suspected that something similar was happening now. He dressed and went to the office, where he started right off by making phone calls. He made dozens of them, all over the country, waking people in Chicago and getting them out of bed in Los Angeles. He even placed a call to a certain law professor taking a sabbatical in Hawaii and found him about to go to bed. By midmorning the outlines of what was happening were apparent, and by noon

173

Cairn was uninformed no more. Edward Anderson was on his way to fast becoming a dead duck.

As best Cairn could figure it out, the initial opposition to Anderson had come from civil rights groups. The president had goofed there, Cairn thought. He should have checked with the civil rights groups first. The civil rights groups, in turn, had turned to their allies, the progressive unions and they, in turn, had put the elbow on a couple of senators, Pardew being one of them. Some law firms, some of the city's biggest, had also been enlisted in the fight. They had researched Anderson's record as a judge, his reversal rate. Only the biggest law firms had the manpower to do that sort of research. If a client had asked for it, it would have cost a million dollars. Now they were doing it for free, or as a favor to someone.

Still, Cairn thought, the damage was containable—limited. It could all be stopped here. No one claimed Anderson was a liberal. No one argued that he was a progressive. He was just not a racist, not a muldoon. He was not a great legal mind, but no dummy either. The nation could live with his appointment. There had been worse. In fact, there were worse on the court right now. The important thing, Cairn thought, was to see who was going to line up against Anderson. Pardew and his ilk were one thing. No one expected them to go for anything other than a blazing liberal. But Tynan was something else again. He was a moderate liberal. He was a big gun. If he came out against Anderson, it was all over. Tynan had what it took either to say Anderson was no racist, in which case the appointment was almost guaranteed or, on the other hand, to lead the opposition. If he did that, he would define the issue, draw the line, and Anderson would be dead. Cairn had received assurances from Francis O'Connor that this was not going to be the case. The phone calls, however, said otherwise. They said the man behind the newspaper stories, the enlistment of the law firms was none other than Joseph Tynan. He would lead the opposition. He had uncovered something really big. Cairn headed to see Francis O'Connor.

"Look, somebody's leaking this stuff about Anderson," he said to Francis. They were talking in the hallway, Cairn pointing to a newspaper in his hand. "Was it your guy?" he asked Francis.

"John, I really don't know anything about it," Francis said.

"Who else could it be?" Cairn asked.

"I don't know, John," Francis said. "Really." He was sorry about that "really"—too sincere, he told himself. Have to be more careful.

"Senator Tynan's not going to go out in front against Anderson, is he?" Cairn asked in a plaintive manner.

"No, he's just voting against him, John," Francis said. "I'm sure that's as far as it will go."

"Francis, please, you gotta level with me," Cairn pleaded. "I don't want Kittner to lose another big one. He's losing his credibility. I've gotta watch out for him."

"Senator Kittner always lands on his feet," Francis said.

"God, I don't know sometimes," Cairn said.

"He's a hard guy to work for, isn't he?" Francis said.

"He's driving me nuts," Cairn admitted. "He's a

wild man. We go to lunch and instead of talking about legislation, he talks about sex. I'm trying to go over the defense authorization bill with him and he wants to bet me fifteen dollars on what underwear the waitress is or isn't wearing. Then he comes late to a staff meeting with a grin on his face. He tells me I owe him fifteen dollars."

Francis nodded sympathetically. "His last two AA's had the same problem," Francis said. "He'll muddle through. He flies by the seat of his pants."

"He doesn't keep them on long enough," Cairn cracked. Both of them laughed. "Francis, tell me," Cairn said, suddenly serious again, "how big a problem do I have? Is your guy going to make a big thing out of this?" Francis hesitated for a moment. He felt sorry for Cairn. "Nothing your guy can't handle, I'm sure, John," he said.

"Oh, Christ," said Cairn.

John Cairn walked back to his office with his mind in a fog. He recognized no one in the hallways. He was thinking of what he was going to tell Kittner—how he was going to get him to salvage whatever he could from the situation. Cairn paused at the door that led directly from the hallway to Kittner's personal office. It was a door used only by the senator himself, and then only to avoid someone in the reception area. Staff were forbidden to use it. Cairn, without thinking, went right in.

"Senator, we've got a problem," he announced.

Kittner was seated behind his desk. He grabbed for a yellow legal pad and studiously read from it. A pained expression settled on his face. Cairn didn't give it much thought.

"We've lost Senator Tynan on this Anderson thing," Cairn said.

Kittner answered with a silly smile. "Uh, John, I'm kind of busy right now." He looked at the pad. "I'm reading here."

"I don't mean we've just lost his vote," Cairn went on. "I mean he's going to lead the opposition. You know what I mean?"

Cairn noticed a purse lying on Kittner's desk. He looked around, panicked. No one else was in the office. He felt relieved. God knows who might have been there. He moved closer to the desk.

"Yes, well, John, I'm reading here from my pad," Kittner said loudly.

"Senator," Cairn said, approaching the desk, "we may have a . . ." A woman's head! He saw the top of a woman's head under the desk. He saw it for just a second and then he jumped back. The head did not move. Cairn kept backing up.

"Uh, maybe we can discuss this later," Cairn said.

"Yes," Kittner said with a big smile, "I'm reading right now, at the moment."

"Right," John said. "I'll just . . . Right." He backed up some more. By now he was at the door.

"Ask Tynan to come down for some gumbo in my private office," Kittner said to Cairn.

"What?" Cairn said, dumbfounded.

"My office in the basement," Kittner repeated, annoyed. "Right," John said. "I'll get right on it."

* * *

When Hugh Kittner thought about it, which was often, he had to wonder how in his advancing age God had not only increased his sex drive, but also provided him with the wherewithal to do something about it. He had, for instance, no less than three offices in the city of Washington alone, not to mention four others back in his home state. All of these he used for liaisons. In addition he had his seniority, his committee and subcommittee chairmanships, increasing numbers of staff people, some of whom were women, some of whom, Kittner used to say with a laugh, could even type. But that, he was quick to add, was hardly a requirement. The more he thought about his present situation, the more he had to wonder at his luck. He was an ugly man and he had been an ugly boy, only now he had power. "If I felt this way as a boy, I would not have known what to do," he once said. "Now I go out and hire myself a typist."

There was a tendency, especially among the younger senators, to dismiss Kittner as a buffoon. He played his role to the hilt. He loved the part and what was more the people back home loved it, too. He was considered the personification of basic virtues, the average guy, someone who did not have to give matters much thought, whose wisdom was instinctive. All that to some extent was true. But he was also a very savvy politician, a man blessed with a marvelous sense of timing. He knew when to make his move.

He had begun his career some thirty years earlier in the state legislature. He was one of those few men still left in the Senate who had been nothing more in his life than a politician. It was what he did for a living, a life he loved, and he was good at it. Early in his career he recognized the importance of timing, how to hold back and not commit himself. In the state legislature, for instance, he was known for his ability to make his one vote count, to wait until things were deadlocked, at which point others had to do business with him. As a result, it was his county that got the state hospital and later a new fairgrounds. Both installations were worth a lot of jobs, more money. It was this sort of thing that propelled Kittner first into the House of Representatives and later into the Senate.

Along the way, though, Kittner had also picked up a reputation for buffoonery and for theatrics. Once he held up passage of a bill by faking a heart attack, which nearly turned out to be real when he was given mouth-to-mouth resuscitation by a black physician who happened to be visiting the legislature. On another occasion, he returned unexpectedly to his hotel room and found two members of the hotel staff making love in his bed. He not only insisted on having the sheets changed but also had the bed changed. He said he would never give up the room.

Now his sense of timing was telling him that something had to be done on the Anderson matter. He was going to bring Joe and Birney together, bring them together in such a way that somehow the Anderson thing would be settled. A meeting would be no good and a conference would be no good, and so he simply invited everyone to his private office for some gumbo and beer—plenty of beer. Kittner had cooked the gumbo himself, even shopped personally for the ingredients, and had it all brought over to his private office in the Capitol so everyone could be close to the floor in case of a roll-call vote of some importance. He knew about Joe and his obsession with not missing a roll-call vote. He considered it silly, but then he never could understand any of the new guys with their attention to voting, their methodical approach to committee meetings, their constant search for expertise in their staffing, their reluctance, really, to have any fun.

"Lookie here," he said with a wave of his arm over a huge pot of gumbo. "Look at all this. Ain't it beautiful?" He took a large wooden spoon and stirred the stuff, withdrawing the spoon and looking at it in mock wonder. "Wonder why it didn't catch on fire," he said. "This stuff is hot." He looked around the room to gauge his audience. With him were Joe Tynan and Senators McMillan, Worthy, and Spencer and off in a corner, sitting by himself and pouting, Senator Birney. It was time to tell some stories.

"There was this guy once," Joe was saying, "who was a professional thrower-upper. The Republicans used to use him in New York." He looked around the room. "This was before my time," he explained. "I heard about it from some of the old-timers, but what the guy used to do is hit all the functions in midtown Manhattan. The Democratic party would have fund raisers going at maybe three midtown hotels like the Roosevelt and the Biltmore and maybe the Commodore and they would promise that the candidate would make all three. The poor guy would have to stand in a receiving line and shake hands and then make a short speech and then go on to the next hotel.

"Well, the professional thrower-upper would go to the first hotel and he would go through the receiving line and when his turn came to shake hands with the candidate, he would throw up all over him." Everyone laughed. Joe took a swig of beer from a can and went on.

"Well, there would be panic and the professional thrower-upper would mumble how sorry he was. And they would have to take the candidate up to some hotel room and wait there until they could bring him a fresh suit and then he would be late for his appearance at the next hotel.

"When he got there, the professional thrower-upper hit him again. No one would remember what the guy looked like. Well, the candidate would just get sick. He would have to be taken to yet another hotel room and change into another fresh suit and not only would he be way behind schedule by now, but he would be a nervous wreck. Some of them wouldn't go on and the people at the last fund raiser would be pissed. I'm told one candidate went in and just quit politics." Everyone laughed some more.

While Joe talked Kittner poked at his gumbo with the wooden spoon, moving the stuff around like it was hot lava. He took a stack of paper plates and began dishing it out. They all dug in, offering the appropriate oohs and aahs.

"Hugh, that is the best gumbo I have ever been attacked by," Joe said approvingly.

"I got a real pepper in there that grows only on the shores of hell," Kittner said. "Fred, some more?" he asked Senator Worthy.

"Not for me," Worthy replied, shaking his head. "I might need my stomach later."

"How about some more, Joe?" Kittner asked Tynan. "You only live once."

"Or some portion thereof," Worthy added.

"Come on," Kittner challenged.

"Hugh, I just can't," Joe apologized. "I just swallowed the roof of my mouth."

"Jesus, in Baton Rouge this is baby food," Kittner said, warming to a routine. "If we don't give our kids something stronger than this by the time they're six months old, they don't grown any teeth. If . . ."

"Hugh," Joe interrupted, "you are so outrageous I can't believe it." He flashed Kittner a smile. "You haven't had one spoon of that stuff. You just want to see everybody else sweat. You're a sadistic son of a bitch, you know that?"

Kittner laid down the spoon. "I'll match you bite for bite, son," he challenged.

"Yeah? Divide that in half," Joe said, pointing to the pan of gumbo.

Kittner looked startled. "In half?" he said. "There's four pounds of this stuff."

"Put your stomach where your mouth is," Joe shot back.

"That's where it's going to wind up," cracked Worthy.

Joe drew a line through the gumbo with the wooden spoon. He picked up the pan, scooping half of the gumbo onto one plate, the other half onto another plate, setting one before Kittner. He pointed at it with the spoon. "I know that's just an appetizer for a country boy like you," he said.

"You're never gonna see the bottom of that plate, kid," said Kittner. "The blood's gonna rush up your body like a giant thermometer and shoot right through your scalp."

Senator Worthy took off his watch and laid it in the

palm of his right hand. "I'll give the winner a buck for every second under two minutes." He looked down at the watch, waiting for the second hand to sweep to twelve. "Ten. Nine. Eight. Seven. Six," Worthy called out. He looked up. Joe and Kittner were poised over their plates, spoons at the ready. "Three. Two. One. Go!" Worthy shouted.

The two of them plunged in. Kittner held the plate to his chin and shoveled the gumbo. Joe, falling behind, broke into a sweat. The back of his shirt was wet and his eyes teared. The stuff *really* was hot. Kittner looked over at Joe and smiled. He reached for a beer. Then he put the plate back up to his chin and resumed the shoveling. Suddenly Kittner's expression changed. He looked like he had taken a shot to the stomach. He touched his fingers to his stomach.

"I think I'm going to be sick," he blurted.

Joe ignored him and kept on eating. Kittner walked off toward the bathroom, moving slowly and then quickening his pace as he neared the door. He lunged for the knob and threw the door open, closing it quickly behind him. Joe finished to cheers and much pounding on the back. He threw his arms over his head in a victory sign. Then there was silence, everyone listening, looking in the direction of the bathroom. They heard the sound of heaves. Joe applauded and the others joined him.

"This is a goddamn Shriner's convention," growled Birney from his chair in the corner. He stood up and headed for the door.

"You want something, Sam?" inquired Senator McMillan.

"Yeah," Birney snapped. "How about a noisemaker and a funny hat."

The bathroom door opened and Kittner stepped out, looking pale and blowing his nose. "That's never happened to me before," he said to no one in particular. He saw Birney standing at the door looking stern and unamused. Kittner walked over. "Is everything all right?" he asked.

"It is not my opinion that this man will change his mind just because you two have thrown up together," Birney said, waving his left hand at Joe. He turned and faced him. "Are you going to fight us on Edward Anderson or not?" he demanded.

A trap, Joe thought, a goddamned trap. Southern-style trap. "Senator, you know I've always respected your—"

"Yes or no," Birney demanded, cutting him off.

"I'll answer." He tried to stall. "I'll answer you that," he started to say. "But I first—" Birney interrupted again.

"Écoutez, mon ami," he said. *"Je pose une question toute simple."*

Joe looked into Birney's eyes. They focused on the middle distance. He decided to be direct. "Senator," he said sternly, "now hold it."

"Oui ou non?" Birney asked. *"Dépêchez-vous, monsieur. J'en ai assez de ces jeux. C'est pas un . . ."*

"Hey?" Joe said sharply.

Birney focused on Joe. "Cut it out," Joe said. "You understand what I'm saying?"

Birney nodded. "Yes, I do," he said softly.

"Well, I sure as hell don't," Kittner bellowed, still working his nose with the handkerchief.

"He doesn't like to be pressured," Birney said, nodding in Joe's direction.

"Who does?" said Kittner, still puzzled. He poured Joe a beer. "The thing is I think we can find a way to see each other's point of view." He turned to Joe. "Don't you?"

"Sure," Joe said. "Why not?"

Joe slid a glass of beer across the table to Birney. "How about a beer, Senator?" he asked him. Birney picked up the glass and took a sip, leaving a mustache of foam on his lips. "No thanks," he said smiling. "I don't drink." He downed the beer looking all the time at Joe, saying thank you with his eyes.

He had planned very carefully. He could not use his own car, the one with the senatorial license plates, NY5, and he could not rent a car with a credit card because that would not only leave a record, but the receipt would be sent to his office and be seen by his office manager. He thought of renting the car with cash, but then he wondered what the rental agent would think of that—why a U.S. Senator didn't have a credit card and had to pay a fifty- or a hundred-dollar deposit. In that case he would either look like a man trying to hide something or a man who had lost his credit rating. Either way, it was the sort of thing that would find its way into columns.

This business about getting away for an idyllic country weekend was getting complicated. Joe wondered how other people did it. In the movies it was so simple, but when you thought about it, it got involved—a succession of steps that could lead you straight into trouble. The whole car thing, for starters, was a major headache, and then what would happen if there were an accident? My God, Joe remembered that Henry Ford had been in an accident and not only was he with a woman not his wife, but in a Chevrolet as well. And then there was the case of the guy who took his girl friend to the Superbowl and his wife spotted him on television.

He thought of having Francis rent the car for him, but the more he thought of that, the more he didn't like it. He wanted no more knowing looks from Francis, no winks either real or implied. The obvious solution, of course, was to have Karen rent the car, but there was something about that he didn't like either. It meant he could not, that he was hiding something, sneaking around—cheating on his wife. He was doing just that, of course, but somehow he did not think of himself in just those terms. This was different. Karen was different. And it had nothing to do with Ellie. Ellie was in New York and what was happening in Washington was happening in Washington. It had nothing to do with her. It had to do with what was happening in Washington and with himself, but not with Ellie. He was not cheating on Ellie. He was merely having an affair with Karen. In the end he did what he had to do. He had Karen rent the car.

It was some sort of Pontiac, steel gray in color, slung low and flared in the back with a picture of a mild and menacing-looking bird painted on the hood. Karen said it was the only car available, so she had taken it, and now it was parked in the parking lot of a grocery store in Arlington, Virginia. Karen was inside, shopping for their planned picnic lunch. Joe sat at the wheel of the car, being stared at by an eleven- or twelve-year-old kid who kept pointing to the car and yelling, "Firebird!" He said it with admiration in his voice. "Firebird, Firebird!" the kid kept yelling. He pointed to the car and then at Joe who was dressed as usual in a dark three-piece suit.

Karen emerged from the grocery store, a bag in her arms, a French bread poking out of the top of the bag like a periscope. She was dressed in a checked blouse, blue blazer, and tan slacks. Joe thought she looked terrific.

"Firebird!" the kid yelled.

Karen looked startled and then burst out laughing. She walked around to the passenger side of the car, placed the groceries on the back seat, and got in. "Floor it, Joe," she said, laughing. Joe shot her a look and turned the ignition key. The motor turned over, sounding like a Saturn rocket in launch. He backed the thing out to the highway, put it into gear, and floored the car. Their necks snapped back and the car zoomed off down the road, hitting sixty miles per hour before it even kicked into cruising gear. It made an awful noise.

They headed south and then west toward the mountains. They drove for an hour or so, watching the suburbs fade into farms and the farms become fewer and fewer, dairy giving way to apple orchards. Off in the haze they could see the mountains.

"They're really purple," Joe said.

"Huh?"

"Purple. Purple as in purpled mountains majesty above the fruited plain. This is the spot. The mountains are purple and the orchards make this a fruited plain. This must be the spot where the song was written. Look for one of those roadside markers. If there isn't one, I'll introduce a bill first thing in the morning." He laughed, threw back his head, and sang an off-key version of "America the Beautiful." Karen sang along with him, the two of them mangling verses largely forgotten since grade school—"God shed thy salt on thee," was one version they came up with.

Soon, they began to see signs for the Hotel Mountview. The sign showed a green alpine peak and a white-columned big house beneath it—a picture representing what would happen if the old South moved to Switzerland. They cruised through apple country and Joe told Karen stories of the Byrds of Virginia.

"Wonderful apple growers," he yelled to Karen over the noise of the rushing wind. "Rotten politicians." She laughed. Joe braked the car hard. He had passed a sign showing Mountview off to the right. He backed up, turned, and headed off to what turned out to be first the town of Mountview and then the hotel itself.

It was nothing like what was pictured on the sign. The main building was not an antebellum southern mansion, but an old, northern-style wooden hotel, the sort you can still find at some ocean resorts. It had only three stories but it went on forever—wings upon wings upon wings. It had an ugliness all its own, and a charm that came with it. It left no doubt that no cutesy architect had been at work here. Here was a hotel built by someone who had come out from time to time to look at the work in progress and said, "Add another wing, boys," and then had gone back to town or somewhere.

Actually, that is precisely how it happened. The hotel had started as a cabin, and the middle section of the place was still called The Cabin, and it had been turned into a hotel after the Civil War. The place proved popular and wings upon wings had been built. Now there were 312 rooms, six public rooms, tennis courts, horseback riding, a golf course, several ponds, a swimming pool, and, of course, the famous Mountview springs, noted for their curative powers.

"What curative powers?" Karen asked.

"Impotence," Joe said.

She smiled. The car door was opened for her by a pimple-faced kid dressed as an old-time jockey.

"Welcome to Mountview, ma'am," he said.

"Well, thank you very kindly," Karen drawled. Joe stared at her. "You forget where I'm from," she said. She turned the drawl on again. "This here is my kind of place, Yankee."

"Jesus Christ," Joe said smiling, "I got myself a Scarlett O'Hara." He took her by the arm and the two of them entered the hotel. They stepped into a spacious lobby. The registration desk was to their left. Above them a fan rotated very slowly. The dining room was straight ahead, past the lobby.

A woman wearing Bermuda shorts and a sleeveless turtleneck rushed at them. "You're my favorite senator," she gushed, taking Joe by surprise. "You're just wonderful. Would you give me your autograph for my daughter? She just thinks you're wonderful." Joe reached for his pen, feeling Karen's grip tighten on his arm. "Keep up the good work, Senator. You're one of the few good ones." She turned to Karen. "And you're wonderful, too. I read you're a psychologist. My son's interested in that." She took the piece of paper from

Joe's hand and walked off. He smiled weakly at Karen.

"Yes, Senator, can I help you?" the registration clerk asked. He had been watching the scene with the woman.

"Yes, uh . . . I have a reservation," Joe said. "Uh . . ." He looked into the dining room and saw Senator Aikers of Minnesota eating with a woman who most definitely was not his wife. She was, in fact, his legislative assistant. Joe knew her because the two of them had worked closely on a bill the year before. Aikers waved and then, noticing Karen, gave Joe a long nod of appreciation. Joe nodded back, uncomfortably, not understanding what the rules now were, not understanding if he had caught Aikers or Aikers had caught him, or whether he had been caught at all. After all Karen might just be a woman standing next to him.

Joe turned quickly back to the clerk. "Can you tell me where the pro shop is?" he asked.

"Yes, right over there, Senator," the clerk said, leaning over the counter a bit and then pointing around the corner.

"Right," Joe said, starting off immediately for the pro shop, leaving Karen to follow. She did.

"Just out of curiosity," she said in a low, conspiratorial voice, "why are we going to the pro shop?"

Joe answered out of the side of his mouth. "The guy who just said hello to me over there is Senator Aikers from Minnesota."

"Ah so," Karen said Charlie Chan fashion. "So now we have to play golf?"

"Not me," Joe said. "I don't know how to hold a club."

They walked along the long porch, heading for the pro shop. They had to pass before the dining room window. Aikers, a stupid smile pasted on his face, waved to them, and so did the young lady with him. Joe stared straight ahead, feeling very foolish, not knowing whether he should nod to Aikers or to the young lady or what. He wanted to disappear in a puff of smoke. They arrived at the pro shop, a converted old barn. A young man dressed in white shorts and white Ban-Lon shirt stood at a counter fashioned from the bottom part of a barn door. "Hi, Senator," he said cheerfully. Karen groaned. God, she thought, he's known everywhere.

"Yes, we'd like to rent some clubs, and a golf cart," Joe said authoritatively. "And balls and things."

A moment later the two of them were seated in a golf cart, Joe still in his three-piece suit. He pushed his foot down hard on the accelerator, forcing the car to lurch forward and then stop suddenly. He tried to get the hang of the thing but couldn't, and his driving kept Karen laughing. Joe headed down a fairway and then veered off into what looked to him like weeds. He had a determined look on his face.

"Where are we going?" Karen asked.

"I'm looking for some privacy," he answered.

"Here?" she asked startled. That set her off again. Soon she had laughed herself into a jag.

"Will you shut up," Joe said, a smile creeping onto his face. "Try to look like a golfer. People don't laugh like that on the golf course." He headed for some bushes and pulled behind them.

"How's this?" he said, turning to her in triumph. Karen looked around and burst into laughter again.

Joe threw the cart into reverse, hit the bushes, shifted into forward, and stepped too hard on the accelerator again. The cart shot forward, brushed past some weeds, and nosed into a pond. The front of the cart filled quickly with water. Karen, convulsed with laughter, hugged the bag of groceries. Joe turned to her, the water now up almost to the seat.

"Oh my God, will you stop laughing," he said, starting to laugh himself. "Let's eat," he shouted, reaching for the groceries. "What do we have to eat?"

"Fruit compote," Ellie said.

The Tynan family was gathered around the dinner table—Joe, Ellie, Paul, and Janet, the last two wearing the long-suffering looks of children who would rather be someplace else.

"Terrific," Joe said to Ellie. "I haven't had that in a long time."

"Don't give me any," Paul said. "It's got prunes in it." He said "prunes" as if he had said "worms." Joe looked over at him.

"When was the last time you tried it?" he asked.

"When I was too little to fight back," Paul said.

"Come on, try it," Ellie beseeched. "It's something new."

"Where's your curiosity?" Joe put in.

"Come on, it's an adventure," Ellie said, realizing too late that she had gone too far.

"Eating prunes is an adventure?" Janet asked.

"Not really," Ellie said. "We lie."

Janet shrugged and pushed her chair away from the table. She rose to leave the room. "Where're you going?" Joe asked. "We're still eating."

"I don't want dessert," she told him. "It has sugar in it."

"I haven't really been home in three weeks," Joe said, exaggerating a bit. "Let's have a little conversation."

Janet sat down with an air of resignation. She had seen this bit before—her father's come-let-us-talk-together routine. It usually followed periods of extended absence and always followed a campaign. The kids always knew when it was coming.

"What do you want to talk about?" Janet asked Joe, in a put up or shut up tone of voice.

"Whatever comes up," Joe said. "Sit."

Nothing came up. Around the table were four glum faces, two of them waiting for the topic of conversation to be chosen, the other two wondering what it would be. After a while Joe turned to Janet.

"How'd that paper you were doing on Roosevelt turn out?" he asked.

"I told you, I got an A on it."

"Right, I'm sorry," Joe said. "I'd like to read it."

"They're keeping it for the student fair," Janet said. "Are you coming for that?"

"When is it?" Joe asked.

"I told you," Janet said. "May eleventh."

Joe's face dropped. "I can't Babe," he said with a touch of hurt in his voice. "I'll be in Washington. I wish I could."

"That's okay," Janet said, expecting that to be the answer anyway.

"I think you made a great choice in Roosevelt," Joe said to Janet. "He's fascinating. There was a man who amassed great power and yet used it for tremendous good. Usually you have guys who try for either one or the other, but you can't do much good without power."

"Can I go?" Paul asked. He had put his head down on the table. "You always talk about things that don't interest me."

"So we'll include you," said Joe. "How's your bike? You get the chain fixed?" An image popped into Joe's head. He saw himself being handed an index card by Francis with topics of conversation for his children. It said "Bike, FDR Paper, Rabbit," and so on. Joe shook his head and came out of it.

"In that case, can I go?" Janet asked. "I'm sick of his bike."

"I have a good idea," Paul said to her. "Why don't you shove it?"

"Hey, Paul," Joe admonished.

Janet was on her feet and nearly out of the room by then.

"Bye," she said.

Paul turned to his father. "Dad, the game's almost on."

"All right," Joe said. "I'll talk to you later."

Paul got up and left the room.

"I really love a close-knit family like this," Joe said to Ellie.

"I think you were pushing them a little," Ellie said. "You have to let them talk about what interests *them*."

"I *was* trying to talk about what interests them."

"But you were doing all the talking."

Joe Tynan looked as he did when he lost a close vote in the Senate—foolish.

* * *

The senator from New York sat in an old chair. A kitchen towel hung around his neck. His legs were crossed. He had a stoical look on his face. Behind him his wife, Ellie, moved back and forth looking at the back of his head, sometimes patting it, sometimes taking it in her hands moving it this way or that. At his feet and behind him, locks of his hair rested on the grass. He was having his hair cut on the lawn.

"I'm sorry about last night," he said after a while.

"Well, that's the advantage of being married," she said. "There's always the next time."

"I was in the mood," he continued, "and then for some reason . . . I don't know." He shrugged his shoulders and moved his head. She held him harder.

"Maybe you're working too hard," she said.

"What would you think about working in Washington?" he asked, trying to sound blasé.

"You mean *move* there?"

"I think I need you down there."

Ellie said nothing. She chopped away at the hair on the back of his head and then patted it down. She looked at what she had done, peering at it like a sculptor examining his work. She put the scissors into the hand that was holding the comb.

"You know, I wanted to move to Washington when you first got elected," she said. "You said to stay here. So we could have weekends to ourselves."

"I don't have weekends anymore," he said. "I have to speak."

"You *have* to speak?"

"You think we can live on what I make as a senator?" he asked. "You think a round-trip shuttle flight almost every weekend doesn't cost plenty?"

"Well, now the children have roots here," Ellie said. "Their school, their friends. What about my work?"

"Isn't there a psychoanalytic institute in Washington?" Joe asked.

"I suppose there is, but the one that's accepted me is in New York," Ellie said. "And the man I work with, the man who brought me along to the point where I am now, is also in New York. I don't just work in a building, Joe. There are people there who mean something to me."

"Well, it seems so, doesn't it?" Joe said, a touch of sarcasm in his voice.

"What do you mean by that?" Ellie demanded.

"That there are people who mean something to you in New York," Joe said flatly. "That's why you can't come to Washington with me."

"You must be kidding," Ellie said. "You're not implying that I have some kind of attachment to Asher, are you?"

"Well, what is it?" he asked, the businesslike tone gone from his voice. "What's keeping you from bringing up your family in one place?"

Ellie looked shocked. "The same thing that's keeping *you* from doing it," she retorted. "My work! God, are you actually accusing me of having an affair with Asher? He's sixteen and a half years older than me with a potbelly."

"Sixteen and a half?" Joe said like a detective who had just found a clue.

"Yes," she said firmly. "The reason I'm so aware of

it is that we were talking about that in another context."

"You were comparing ages on a strictly intellectual basis?" Joe said.

Ellie laughed. "Joe, please. *Asher?*"

"Think about Washington," he said. "Okay? Will you do that?"

Snap. A hunk of hair hit the grass.

CHAPTER 8

Joe Tynan burst from the Capitol elevator with about a dozen other men, two of them also senators. He had a look of mild panic on his face. Five lights had lit on the clock in his office and five times the buzzer had sounded, meaning that there was only seven and a half minutes remaining on a roll-call vote. Joe had to be there. From all over the Capitol area, senators were moving on the Senate chamber, summoned by the bells. It was like a call to the volunteer fire department. One by one they put down what they were doing and left their office or committee room or dining room or wherever and made it, if they could, to the floor of the Senate. At the moment Joe was one of them.

He looked around for someone from his staff. Angie spotted him and hurried to his side.

"It's the Pardew amendment on the coal mining bill," she told him. "Safety measure and health standards. He's given up some ground, but what's left is plenty good. It's all stuff you've come out in favor of."

Joe nodded. "How are you?" he said to a passing lobbyist whose name he had forgotten. He strode directly into the Senate chamber just as his name was being called.

"Mister Tynan," the clerk said.

"Aye," Joe called out in a loud voice. He walked down the aisle to where Pardew was sitting.

"How's it going Ed?" he asked Pardew.

Pardew shook his head. "They're killing it. My God, Joe, if we give them this mining stuff, we're putting millions in their pockets. The least they can do is let us enforce a couple of health standards."

"It's an excellent amendment," Joe said, hoping to shut off the flow of words from his colleague. It was just like Pardew to argue the merits of his cause even after he had your vote. The man, Joe thought, was all indignation—cause and principle and everything fine. Trouble was, everyone knew, he couldn't get a damn thing passed. He never traded, never swapped, never did any of that. He always stood on principle and he nearly always stood alone. One time someone had written a piece of graffiti about Ed Pardew and pasted it up in the Democratic cloakroom where it hung for a day. It said, "Pardew doesn't care." It was, of course, the cruelest thing anyone could say about the man. It was Joe who took it down.

"Well, it will save a few lives," Pardew went on. He lowered his voice in a conspiratorial fashion. "I mean, they're getting their money, what's wrong with giving us a few lives?" A couple more nays sounded in the chamber.

"You're taking this personally, Ed," Joe said, sliding into the seat next to Pardew. "You shouldn't do that."

"I've been here twenty-four years," Pardew said.

Joe ignored him. "Look, if you don't pass it this time, you will the next session."

"I won't be here next session," Pardew said. "I've had enough."

"Ed," Joe said, taking Pardew's arm in surprise, "you're the most respected man here."

"Yeah, I'm respected, but I don't get any bills passed," Pardew said. "Listen, Joe, you and I know what you have to do to get bills passed around here."

Joe nodded and started to say something but changed his mind. He knew this particular amendment was going to lose. He considered it a good amendment, but like many of those introduced by Pardew it had no give in it. It was good—too good, and what it managed to do was scare both the mine operators and the unions. It would have forced the closing of several old and marginally profitable mines, throwing men out of work. The mine operators didn't want to lose their mines and the union didn't want to lose the jobs. They thought that the several deaths caused by faulty machinery were worth the price of keeping the mines open. With a little compromising Pardew could have split the unions off from the operators. He refused to do that and his amendment was losing. The nays kept coming in.

"I've been thinking of what you said a few weeks ago here on the floor," Pardew said. "Remember? 'What are we here for gentlemen?' After a while you start to forget. And then getting clout and keeping it is all there is. You start lying to your constituents and your staff and your family and everybody. You forget what you thought you cared about.

"I know about this amendment. I know what you're thinking and what the others are saying. I know all that. But let me tell you, I've given it a lot of thought. This was a good amendment. There was no need to compromise. Everyone knows that. Lives are at stake. You compromise and you compromise and you compromise and pretty soon you've given away more than you ever got. All the time you're making arrangements and cutting corners and compromising and telling yourself that you're doing it for the bigger ones. To win the bigger battles. To make your vote count even more. I don't know. I don't know if it works that way. It seems to me all you do is move up some ladder where you get to make bigger compromises and tell bigger lies. I'll tell you, if I'd known as a young man what I know now, I would have thrown myself under a truck."

Joe gripped Pardew's arm even tighter. "Ed, how can you do it?" he asked insistently. "How can you just leave?"

"It's not that hard," he said. "You think about what you want out of life and you ask yourself if you're getting it here. You get an answer pretty quickly." He looked away. The votes kept coming in, the nays piling up, the outcome in no doubt whatsoever. The clerk continued to call out the names.

"Mister Verentoulis."

"Nay."

"Mister Warren."

"Nay."

Joe got up to leave. He looked down at Pardew.

There was a thin smile on the old man's lips. He was saying something. Joe leaned down to hear.

"Vote yes," Pardew was saying. "Vote yes you sons of bitches. Yes!"

There was a tear in the old man's eye.

The waiter pushed the room-service truck right into the middle of the room. He put his foot under it, found a lever with the tip of his shoe, and set the truck down onto legs. He hurried to the sides of the table, opened up the leaves, and flapped the white tablecloth to fit. He turned to Karen.

"Shall I open the wine, ma'am?"

Karen nodded yes. She eyed the closet doors.

The waiter put a corkscrew into the cork. He worked it free with a flourish, smelled the end, and placed it on the table for examination. He gave the table one last look and presented Karen with the check. She signed it. "Thank you," the waiter said and left the room. The closet door opened and a man stepped out.

"What are we having?" Joe asked.

Karen consulted the table as she spoke. "Broiled trout, baked potatoes, white wine, smuffd—" Joe muffled the word with a kiss, moving her toward the bedroom. She stopped him for a moment.

"I just have to call my office," she said. She picked up the phone and gave the hotel operator the number. Joe kissed her once more. "I'll hang on," she said to the operator. Joe walked around her and kissed the back of her neck. "I'm trying to avoid a transit strike over a lousy twelve cents—" Joe cut her off with a kiss.

"—an hour," she said. "I love this room," she said, looking around. "Green walls."

"I thought about your hair all day yesterday," Joe said.

"Yeah?" Karen said, interested.

"I could smell it," he said. "It's all I could think of through three committee hearings."

"Very nice," she said. "I fly two thousand miles so you can have an affair with my shampoo." Suddenly the phone in her hand came to life. "Tom?" she said, as Joe dived his nose into her hair. "How're we doing?" She listened. "Look," she said, "call Billy in the mayor's office and tell him to have these guys knock it off." Joe moved away from her and started to pace the room.

"Call me back here in an hour and a half, okay?" Karen said into the phone. She hung up and gave Joe a very serious look. "I'll race you to the bedroom," she said. For a moment neither one of them moved—then they broke for the bedroom at the same time, colliding at the doorway, pushing at each other, laughing. They collapsed on the bed, laughing, a jumble of feet and arms, intertwined.

"I thought about *you* all day yesterday," Karen said. "And it wasn't about your hair."

"My eyes? My teeth?"

"I never noticed your teeth," Karen said. "Let me see." He made a grimace, exposing his teeth.

"No, that's not it," she said.

"My nose?" he went on. "It's been getting longer lately. I've been telling a lot of lies."

He kissed her quickly before she could react. She began taking off his tie when the phone rang. Karen reached for it. "Hello? Yes, one second, please." She gave the phone to Joe.

"Yes?" he asked. It was his office. "Okay," he shrugged. "Right." He handed the phone back to Karen. She looked at him for an explanation.

"I have to get back to the Senate for a vote," he said. "I've got about eight minutes."

"You must be kidding," she said, dismayed.

"I'll vote and come right back," he said, working his tie back into a knot.

"What are you voting on?" she asked.

"I haven't any idea," he said walking into the living room. "I never miss a roll call. It's a campaign promise. My opponent missed a lot of them and I made an issue out of that. I said I would never miss any, barring sickness and that sort of thing. It's silly, I know."

Karen trailed behind him as he left the room. "I don't know whether you noticed, but this has been a very short visit," she said as he opened the door to the hallway. Joe ignored her sarcasm.

"I'll be back in a half hour," he said. "We'll have the whole night."

She shook her head. "I have to get the ten o'clock plane back to New Orleans," she said.

"You have to?" Joe asked.

"I have to be in court in the morning," she explained. "Why don't you come with me? Spend the night at my place."

Joe's face dropped. "I have a fund raiser in New York tomorrow," he said.

"Vote fast, okay?" she said.

They walked the length of the hotel corridor, kissing all the way.

* * *

Ellie sat absentmindedly in her car as the gas station attendant filled the tank. For a time she studied herself in the rearview mirror, patting down her hair, and then something drew her attention to the traffic out on the road. She watched the cars, noticing that one of them had stopped. A young girl got out, leaned over, and said something to the driver through the window. The girl smiled and the car pulled away. The girl climbed the curb and stuck out her thumb, walking backward as she hitched. After a step or two, she descended into the street.

The girl was too young to be hitching, Ellie thought—about Janet's age. Ellie gasped. Janet! It was Janet!

Ellie bolted from the car and ran to the edge of the service station. She screamed Janet's name across four lanes of dense traffic, but it was no use. The girl kept moving backward, away from the gas station, her thumb still out.

"Janet, Janet!" Ellie yelled.

She ran back to her car and looked desperately for the attendant. The nozzle was still sticking out of the gas tank. She yanked the thing out herself and then stood there, the nozzle dripping gas, wondering what to do with it. Finally, the attendant arrived and Ellie thrust the gas hose into his hands. She threw some money at him and looked across the street. She saw Janet climb onto the back of a motorcycle.

"Oh my God," Ellie gasped.

She jumped into her car and pulled out after the cycle. She sped up the avenue, switching from lane to lane, trying to spot the cycle. Finally, she saw it—way ahead. She followed, unable to gain on it because of the traffic. After a while the cars thinned out and she was able to stay comfortably behind. At an intersection the cycle stopped and Janet climbed off. She waved good-bye to the cyclist and put up her thumb once again. Ellie cruised up.

"Hi, you need a lift?" she asked. She tried to sound nonchalant, but her heavy breathing gave her away.

"Oh, hi," Janet said, achieving a nonchalance that Ellie envied. The girl got into the car and Ellie drove off in the direction they had all been going. Up ahead the motorcycle turned off to the right.

"Where are you going?" Ellie asked Janet.

"I'm seeing some friends," Janet said cryptically.

"Uh huh," Ellie said. "Janet, I don't want you to get your defenses up, but what the hell are you doing hitchhiking?" She had blurted it out.

"Don't worry," Janet said. "I'm careful."

"You're careful?" Ellie repeated. "What do you mean you're *careful*? You could be murdered."

"I knew you would say that," Janet said in a bored fashion.

"You're not allowed to hitchhike."

"Why not?" Janet asked. "That's dumb. I'm not gonna get murdered."

Ellie pulled the car over. She was angry and made no attempt to hide it.

"Listen, pal, you're not going to go around doing any damn thing you please," she said sharply. "You're getting your wings clipped."

"What does that mean?" Janet asked, fearing the worst.

"We're going to start living a normal life, that's what it means," Ellie answered.

"How? What are you talking about?"

"I'm talking about the whole family living in the same house," Ellie said.

"Where?" Janet asked.

"I'm thinking of moving to Washington," Ellie said.

"Oh, no," Janet said, shaking her head and getting teary-eyed. "I'm not going."

"Look, it won't be easy on any of us," Ellie said, trying to soothe her.

"Mom, no!" Ellie exploded. "I don't want to go. I *can't*. You can't make me leave my friends. Please." The tears rolled down Janet's face. Ellie looked at her daughter, sympathy quickly replacing rage. Her anger over the hitchhiking was gone.

"All right, look, we'll all talk about it," Ellie said. "I didn't mean to hit you with it all at once."

"Please!" Janet wailed, still crying. "No."

"Janet, it's not good for us like this," Ellie said. "Dad misses us a lot."

"Then let him be the one to move," she said.

"He can't," Ellie said. "His work is there."

"Well, I'm not going," Janet insisted. "I'm not going." She reached for the door handle.

"Come on home with me, okay?" Ellie asked. "We'll have a cup of tea and we'll talk."

"What about?" Janet asked, a tinge of insolence creeping back in her voice.

"About nothing. Let's just calm down together."

The girl released her grip on the door handle. Ellie pulled away from the curb and headed toward home.

* * *

"Ow!" Karen screeched, stepping back from the shower stream.

"Too hot for you?" Joe asked, adjusting the water. "You know what Harry Truman said. If you can't stand the heat, get out of the shower."

Karen craned her neck to give him a look. He continued to massage her back, working a soapy washcloth into it. Karen looked around the stall and sighed.

"Why is it I'm in a different hotel room every time I come here?" she asked.

"So I won't be recognized coming through the same lobby."

"Well, at least I won't have to look at *this* place again," she said, unimpressed with her surroundings. "What happens when we run out of hotels?"

"I guess we'll start at the beginning again," Joe said.

"Well, that's certainly efficient," she snapped.

"What's the matter?" Joe asked.

"I haven't seen you outside of a hotel room yet, except for that lyrical afternoon on the golf course," she said.

"I'd like to avoid meeting strangers who think you're my wife, and friends who know you are not," he said, an uncomfortable smile spreading across his face.

"So far you haven't written me any secret notes," she said. "We haven't walked in the snow and talked about life. And you haven't flown two thousand miles just to spend an hour with me. But you have shown me nine of the most depressing hotel rooms in Washington. I think our romance needs a little fresh air."

"Let's go out on the balcony," Joe said.

She ignored him and stepped out of the shower, reaching for a towel. She wrapped the towel around herself, cuddling into it at the same time.

"Look, Joe, it won't do anymore to say you don't want to be hooked," she said. "You are hooked and a hooked person gives a little more."

Joe started to say something but the phone rang. Karen glared at him, turned, and headed into the living room. She grabbed a pillow from the sofa and without breaking her stride threw it at the telephone. She knocked the receiver off the cradle. She could hear Francis: "Hello? Hello?"

Joe rushed from the bathroom in a terry-cloth robe. The phone was ringing. It was a different hotel. Karen reached for the telephone.

"Jesus, I hate that sound," she said. "Hello. Yes, Francis, he's right here."

Joe took the phone. "Yeah," he said. "Okay, thanks, Francis." He hung up. "I have to go," he told Karen. "They're voting." He paused and gulped hard. "This is a bill I *have* to vote on. I've been pushing it hard."

"Go," Karen said loudly. "For Christ sake, go."

Joe got suddenly angry. "Look, what did you think this would be like?" he demanded. "You of all people should have known. Your father's been in politics all his life."

"I thought you were different," she said. "I thought you were a person."

"I *am* a person," he said. "And I can't be in two places at once."

She sat on the couch, her head buried in her hands.

Joe looked at her. "Karen, I have to go," he said. "I'm sorry."

She looked up. "Your wife's a psychologist," she said, her eyes red. "Ask her something for me. What does it mean when you ache all through your childhood because your father's never there, and then you grow up and have a *husband* who's never there, and then you take one lover after another who's also never there. Is there a name for that? Besides stupid."

"Look, I'll stay," Joe said. He reached for her.

"Go," she said softly, but with determination. "Go. Your damn country is calling you."

At the Executive Office Building, Jerry Rappaport was also hearing the call of his country. He was working late, making lots of phone calls, saving this part of the day for the West Coast. By now, he was working California and Hawaii, checking things for himself, carrying on long, chatty conversations. Rappaport belonged to the give-'em-time school of politics, the one that held that it is important to listen and to listen and then to listen some more. He had spent the day listening to the country. He called Democratic party officials and union leaders and civic association types and heavy hitters in the financial community. Always he had asked about the nomination of Edward Anderson to the Supreme Court and always he had listened patiently to what they had said and always he took notes. He also kept a score of sorts, rating his respondents from one to four—one being strongly for Anderson, four being strongly against. It was an old campaign survey technique, and what Jerry Rappaport had found out was that if Edward Anderson was a candidate, his campaign would be in trouble. It was time to report to the President.

Rappaport stood and checked his watch. He collected his suit jacket from the back of his chair, grabbed his notes, and left his office, going through the reception area without turning off the lights. He walked down the hallway and through the passageway to the White House and then up to the visitor's area, where he was met by a young marine, his hair closely cut and nearly white. He followed the marine up the grand staircase, past a large reception room to his left, and then down the hallway to the Lincoln sitting room, recently painted a canary yellow on the orders of the First Lady.

The President was sitting on a couch as Jerry walked in. He motioned for Jerry to sit across from him on a facing couch. For fifteen minutes the two of them talked alone, setting the strategy for the handling of the Anderson nomination. Jerry recited in an abbreviated form what he had found out on the phone, showing the President his tabulation on his one-to-four scale. The President made a face at that. Soon after that Rappaport left the Lincoln sitting room.

Later when news of the meeting was reported, some said that the President instructed Rappaport to fight as hard as he could for the nomination, and others said that the President said to give it nothing but a try, while others said that the President told Rappaport to do what he saw fit. Rappaport insisted he fought for the nomination of Anderson as hard as he could and the President, when asked about it, said that that was mostly right. But the fact of the matter was that Jerry Rappaport then did some things that were pretty strange for someone who wanted "more than anything in the world"—his words—to see Edward Anderson wearing "the robes of one of the Supremes"—again his words.

Rappaport found the marine waiting for him at the door when it opened. The young man escorted him down the stairs and then out to the doorway facing south. Rappaport walked out of the White House grounds and then circled the mansion until he came to Pennsylvania Avenue. There he hailed a cab. His work was not yet over. He settled into the back of the cab, working strategy in his head. He was tired and he wanted to go home. Instead he had to go to a party. Some days were nothing but work.

The cab moved toward Georgetown, taking Pennsylvania Avenue until it merged with M Street and then M Street to Thirty-first. It turned right there, climbing the hill away from the river, and stopped, after a left turn, at an old Federal-style house, lit with gaslights at the fence and ringed with waiting limousines. It was the home of Senator Richard Halloran, the Pennsylvania Democrat, the heir to the famous Libby mustard fortune—Beatrice Libby Halloran being his mother.

The house was a grand affair. It contained an immense entrance room, painted a sort of peach, and decorated in early American with furniture that was probably authentically early American. Rappaport thought he would give Halloran the benefit of the doubt on that score. Some of the furniture seemed to have been moved away for the party. Toward the left as Rappaport walked in was a coatrack, manned by a black man who politely took coats in exchange for white metal tabs that matched the numbers on the hangers. A bar had been set up at the extreme right-hand part of the room. The bar seemed to be blocking another room. The door was closed.

To the left was yet another huge room. It was decorated in green with yellow trim, giving it a garden look. Beyond that to the right was a dining room and then past that a living room, and off the dining room straight ahead was the kitchen. In these rooms, with the exception of the kitchen, had gathered around a hundred people, most of them having paid one hundred dollars apiece as a donation to the National Women's Equality Fund, some of them, like Rappaport, having paid nothing.

Rappaport got himself a club soda at the bar—nothing more, when he worked—and ambled off through the house searching for his patsy. He scanned the room, looking for a journalist. He needed a certain kind of journalist for what he had in mind. He saw Al Hunt of *The Wall Street Journal*, one of the best political journalists, but no good for what he had in mind. He saw Jim Dickenson of the *Washington Star* and put him onto his possible list. The *Star* was an afternoon newspaper and that was what he needed—he needed speed. He thought a television reporter would be best. He smiled. There talking to William Cohen of Maine was just the person he wanted—Leslie Stahl of CBS.

Rappaport waited for Stahl to finish her conversation. She would have to turn his way to leave the room and when she did she would notice him. They were old pals—old in the Washington sense. In 1976 Rappaport had taken a leave from his union job and gone to work for the presidential campaign of Henry Jackson. He did that with the full support of his union and with the understanding that he was a union man. Even now in the White House, he was first and foremost a union man, and while he might never again work for the union—go back on their payroll, that is—he would always be their guy—a mole, a union mole, ready to surface. It was in the Jackson campaign that Rappaport met Stahl. She had covered it for CBS and the two of them struck up a quick campaign friendship, a relationship born out of hours spent on planes and days riding the same buses and nights in the same motels. You got to know someone really quick that way. Rappaport had gotten to know Stahl really quick and he liked what he knew. She was smart, tough, honest, and a damn fine journalist.

"Jerry!" Stahl shrieked, breaking into a smile when she noticed him. She walked quickly toward him, forgetting for a moment that she was holding a drink in her hand. Some of it splashed on her dress. She stopped, concerned, looked down, and then looked up at Jerry. She laughed and started toward him again.

"How are you?" she asked, with a hug.

"Terrific," he said. "Look," and he danced around on his toes like a bear. She giggled and patted his stomach.

"Yeah, terrific," she said, nodding her head for emphasis.

He backed over to the wall again. "The baby? How's the baby?"

"She's fine," Stahl answered. "Are you here representing the White House?"

214

"I don't know. Is there anyone else here? I just got an invitation and decided to come. Is it any good?"

Stahl shook her head. "Not much. There's one of your speech writers here, I think, and some guy from the Domestic Council whose name I can't remember." She broke into a smile. "Hey, what's it like on the inside? You finally made it to the White House, but not with the candidate you thought. Huh. That's funny." She laughed.

"I like it some days and I hate it other days. This happens to be one of the days I hate it."

"Poor baby," Stahl said, exaggerating her concern. "Tell Leslie all about it."

"I think we're gonna lose the Anderson nomination."

"No," said Stahl, genuinely surprised.

"Yes," Rappaport said, shaking his head up and down. "Yes."

"But why?"

"A combination of things. How we talking, by the way?"

"Background?"

"Okay, just protect me. No source close to the President or anything like that. I don't mind if you pin it on the White House, but keep to the White House. Nothing more specific than that. Deal?"

"Deal," Stahl said, extending her hand. They shook.

"Number one, some of my union friends don't like him. They think he's too conservative and probably anti-union, although there's not much evidence of that. Some of them don't like him because he's also your basic southern moderate on civil rights. With unions like the UAW it's worse for him that he's bad on civil rights than not too hot on labor issues. Their Washington reps have been feeding them some bad stuff and they're stiffening.

"Number two, the civil rights organizations don't like him one bit. Arthur Briggs of the NAACP is hopping mad about this appointment. We shouldn't be in a jam with Briggs. We should have cleared it with him, but the damned thing leaked before we had a chance to line everything up. That leak could cost us the whole ball game before we're through.

"Number three, the Washington law firms are up to their usual games. They don't like Anderson and they've been researching him to a fare-thee-well. I think they have every legal opinion he's ever written, or maybe even read. And not to put too fine a point on it, Leslie my dear, they are less than awed by his legal acumen. Nothing horrible, mind you, just all right. Nothing more.

"Last but not least, they all have got themselves a champion—the honorable Joseph Tynan, senator from New York."

"Tynan?"

"Yes, Tynan. He's gonna take us on on Anderson. We were hoping they would get somebody like Pardew to lead the opposition. Then no one would follow. But Tynan is a different story. He'll not only attract a lot of attention, but he won't polarize the Senate on this—make this a liberal, conservative issue. The thing about Tynan is that he's no knee-jerk liberal. Picks his shots carefully, he does, and he's picked this one, we hear.

"I tell you, Leslie. I'm worried. We want this appointment. The President wants this appointment and

I'm supposed to get it for him. I just left him and all he could talk about was how much he wants it. Anderson is all right. In some ways he's very good. I'd hate like hell to see someone good like that get sold out in some political battle."

"What are you saying?"

"Call Tynan's guy, what's his name—O'Connor. Francis O'Connor. Call him and ask him if what I just told you is right. And then ask him if they have anything on Anderson. Ask him what there is about Anderson that so upsets the senator from New York. I bet you five bucks and a box seat at the first Washington baseball game that he can't name you a thing. Call me tomorrow and let me know what he's said."

"Call him yourself and do your own reporting," Stahl said.

Rappaport smiled and chucked her under the chin. "I get too cute sometimes. Huh?"

She nodded.

"Okay, I need information. I need information if I'm going to fight. This is getting tricky. Call me tomorrow if you can. Even if you can't, I'll be watching the Walter show anyway. See you later."

Rappaport deposited his drink on the mantelpiece and walked swiftly from the large room. He retrieved his coat and left. He walked until he hit Wisconsin Avenue. He looked for a cab. He walked down Wisconsin, looking over his shoulder for a cab, and finally found one near the intersection of M Street. He jumped in, gave the driver the address of his home, and leaned back. In a moment he was asleep.

* * *

Very early the next morning the phone rang in the Southwest Washington apartment of Francis O'Connor. It was 6:30 A.M. and O'Connor was asleep. He groped for the phone, thinking that he must have overslept. He tried to remember if he'd been dreaming, but could recall nothing.

"Hello?"

"Is this Francis O'Connor?" a woman's voice asked.

"Yes."

"The Francis O'Connor who works for Joe Tynan?"

"Yes. Who is this?"

"It's Leslie Stahl. CBS News."

"Oh, hi. What's up?"

"You're the second Francis O'Connor I've called. The first one was really furious."

"Yeah," Francis said, noticing the time now himself. "It is early, isn't it?"

"Yes. I'm sorry, but I thought maybe we could get something on the morning news. I understand that Senator Tynan is going to come out against Anderson. The Anderson nomination?"

"Probably so." Francis was puzzled. It was generally assumed that liberal senators like Tynan would vote against Anderson.

"No, not just come out against him, but lead the fight to beat the nomination."

"Oh. Where did you get that?"

"C'mon, you got to be kidding."

Francis checked himself. No use asking about sources. He was fighting now to clear his head, understanding instinctively that he now had the chance to paint his boss into a corner from which he would have no choice but to do exactly what Leslie Stahl said he was going to do.

"How are we talking?"

Stahl stated, "On the record."

"Good-bye then. Six Jehovah Witnesses just came to the door asking for money. I have to go."

"Background?"

"There are four Jehovah Witnesses . . ."

"Deep background."

"They just went away. No attribution. You fly on your own with this one. No sources close to the senator, nothing like that. I've never dealt with you before, Leslie, but don't burn me. No fingerprints. Nothing. Yeah. You're right."

"You have the votes?"

That stopped Francis. He had no idea how many votes the anti-Anderson forces had. He had done no work on that at all. "Do we have the votes?" he repeated, stalling for time. "Yeah. Yeah, we have the votes. I think before it's over we'll have more than enough. It won't even be close."

"Why?"

"Why what?"

"Why are you going to fight Anderson?"

"Oh, why that? He's anti-union, anti-black, anti-everything and pro-nothing. You know what you should do. You should call Arthur Briggs of the NAACP. He's staying at the Capitol Hilton. Call around to the law firms, too. Check with Joe Ranch, for instance, and then maybe run a couple of calls up to the UAW. Ask for Howard Paster. Tell him I told you to call."

"Do you have anything special? Something I don't know about?"

"We might. I would not miss the first day of the confirmation hearings, I'll tell you that. In fact, the first day just might be the last day."

"Will Tynan make his position clear to Anderson today? Isn't the courtesy call on today?"

"Christ, is that today?"

"Yes."

"Sure. No. I don't know. I really don't know. Maybe not. I mean, you're supposed to wait for the hearings, aren't you? Isn't that the idea of having the hearings? I don't know what he's going to do, Leslie. Check with me later, okay?"

"Okay. Thank you. Good-bye."

"Good night," Francis said. His head hit the pillow and in very short order he was once again asleep. He was smiling.

Eric Barnston was on his hands and knees, crawling around on the carpet in Joe's office. Finally he spotted an outlet, rose, went over to Joe's desk, took the television set he had set there, and put it on the coffee table. Then he took the cord, got back on his hands and knees, and crawled the plug over to the outlet behind the couch. He had to stick his arm under the couch and then throw the plug a little way. Finally, he had everything set up.

One by one members of the staff trooped in. They had been tipped by a producer at CBS that Anderson's courtesy call on Joe would lead the show. That meant CBS considered it the most important news of the day. Most of the staff had reacted with glee to this piece of news, none of them, apparently, questioning why a simple courtesy call on their senator would be so important. By and large they thought everything their senator did was important. There were maybe two or three who doubted the veracity of the tip, and then there were others, Francis among them, who did not doubt that they would lead the show but worried about what the story might be. After all a simple courtesy call is not earthshaking news.

It had, in fact, been far from simple. Anderson had come down the hallways of the Senate Office Building like a moving sun. He was engulfed in a blaze of light from television crews, a moving white heat, smiling, nodding, answering simple questions with simple statements. He had been courtly and polite and everything he said had been nice and to the point. He had paused before Joe's office and smiled for the camera and then Joe had come out and invited him in. It was all staged and very polite. Joe had said that he had not yet decided how he would vote. He would have to see what developed during the hearings, but he was inclined to vote no. He was sure Mr. Anderson understood that, he told CBS, and NBC, and later ABC which somehow missed the moment of Anderson's arrival. The two of them then walked into Joe's office suite and then into his private office. Both networks showed pictures of the door closing, and then showed it opening again. It was apparent something had happened. Anderson looked grim and Joe looked upset, and while Anderson was willing to go through his routine again, answer the same silly questions and make the same silly jokes, Joe was not. In fact, Senator Joseph Tynan told the press that he had some very important matters to attend to and he would like to be excused. He closed the door.

Later that very day Joe rushed into his office. He nodded to everyone and plopped down on the couch in the space reserved for him. Just as he did so, the *CBS Evening News* came on. Joe did the theme from the old *Movietone News*, cranking his fist on the side of his head and generally playing the moment for laughs. As promised, the Anderson story led the show.

Anderson was shown walking down the hallway toward Joe's office. Some of the banter between him and the reporters could be heard, and then the camera focused on Leslie Stahl. The camera closed in on her and then switched to Anderson.

"Edward Anderson started his day in Washington by paying courtesy calls on the men who will be the first to pass judgment on his qualifications to serve on the United States Supreme Court—the members of the Judiciary Committee. Anderson made his first call on the chairman of the committee, Senator Edward Birney, and then moved on to Senator Joseph Tynan. Unlike Birney, the New York Democrat probably gave Anderson a very cool reception."

"What?" yelled Joe, coming out of his seat. "What the hell is she talking about?"

Francis looked straight ahead.

"CBS News has learned that Senator Joseph Tynan will lead the opposition to the Anderson nomination. Senator Tynan believes that Anderson is anti-union, too conservative on civil rights, and too conservative generally. The opposition of Tynan and his willingness to lead the fight both in committee and on the floor of the Senate has plainly worried the White

House. CBS News has learned that the White House now believes that it might lose the Anderson nomination, yet another rebuff for the President after a string of them. Senator Tynan could not be reached for comment."

"What?" Joe yelled again. "What the hell does that mean? I was here all day."

"I didn't tell you she called," Francis said.

Joe glared at him. "What do you mean you didn't tell me she called. What . . ."

"I thought I was doing you a favor. I knew what she was going to ask you. If you talked to her, you would either have to confirm it or lie or say no comment. No comment is a confirmation. There was no way out. This way you get some more time to think and come up with something."

"Like what?" Joe said, cooled off by Francis's explanation.

"I don't know."

Barnston spoke up, "It doesn't matter now anyway. It's out of the bag. I'll get up a statement for you."

Joe nodded. "Francis, give him a hand, will you?"

"I wonder if Birney's heard this yet?" Francis asked.

"He can't expect you to lose votes at home," Angela said. "The man's a realist, isn't he?" Everyone looked at her in dismay. Angela was where American began. She *believed*. She looked around the room and could tell by the expressions on various faces that she had said something wrong. She did not know what.

Mary Anne, Joe's private secretary, poked her head into the doorway. "Senator Birney's office just called. He would like to see you. Right away if possible."

Joe looked at Francis. "That answers your question," he said. "That only leaves the question of what I say."

"You're supposed to see a group of Boy Scouts," said Mary Anne.

"Say the truth," Francis said. "Just tell him what the score is. We'll get out the press release and get the whole thing over with. No more games." He clapped his hands together.

"No," Joe said. "No. Don't do a thing. Let me talk to him first. See what he has to say. No press release until I come back, of course. But no comments, either, to anyone who calls. Remember. Just say . . . Just say . . ."

"Barnston will take the calls," Francis said. "He'll say you didn't see the Cronkite show and you have no comment at the moment."

"Fine," Joe said, agreeing and heading out of the room. "I'll be back in a half hour." He stopped and turned to the group still in his office and smiled. "Geronimo!" he yelled, pulling an imaginary rip cord and walking into the hallway.

"The senator is expecting you, Senator," said the fat lady at the desk before Birney's office. She smiled pleasantly.

"Fine," Joe said absentmindedly. "How are you, Joyce?" he asked.

"Why just fine," the fat lady said. "Just fine. And you? And Ellie? It's been a dog's age since I've seen that pretty wife of yours." The voice was southern and the tone was caring. Joyce had been with Birney for more than thirty years, everyone knew, but no one knew just how long. If you asked Joyce, she would just smile and shake her head and say, "All you need to know is that I was with him when he was a county judge." That was thirty years ago.

Joe walked into Birney's office. A decanter of bourbon sat on the desk, the late afternoon light coming through the cut glass. Birney stood with his back to Joe.

"Afternoon, Senator," Joe said.

"Looks like we're in for some warm weather," Birney said without turning around to face Joe.

"Yes, I believe we are," Joe said, feeling the heat coming up. He suddenly realized this was going to be painful.

"I never see spring come but I think back to when I was twelve years old," Birney said, still looking out the window. "The smell of spring that year was black mulch and I was just becoming a man. And how proud that made us then. We wore our vulnerability on the outside of our bodies, where it was dangerous. And by God how we swaggered. Of course, we'd get these gently condescending looks from those girls who had already arrived, who for a year or so had held the power of life in their bodies. And we vied with each other. We fought and cursed and beat each other silly for the right to have one of those girls hold us to her breast."

He turned suddenly around. "We're grown men, Joe. What do you say we put away our rulers and stop measuring each other?" He glared at Joe, waiting for an answer.

"Senator, I'm not looking to dethrone you," Joe said after a pause. "I've always thought we were friends."

"So have I."

Joe looked away. "What do you do if the Senate starts lining up against you on this?"

"I was counting on you to stop them," Birney replied in measured tones.

"Isn't that asking a lot?" Joe asked.

"Of a friend?"

Joe looked away again. He was losing this one, strike two already. Birney was hitting him easy.

"Joe, they're after me," Birney said, coming around the desk to him. "I stand convicted of being an old man. I'm telling you straight out, I need your help. And I'll owe you."

"Why does it have to be over *Anderson*?" Joe asked him. "Anderson can destroy me."

"I didn't draw the lines for this battle," Birney said.

"Neither did I," Joe said. "I hope you'll remember that."

Birney looked down, shook his head slowly from side to side, and then looked back at Joe. "You know I can't let you do this to me," he said. "Not with the whole Senate watching."

"Senator, I'd get very badly hurt at home," Joe said.

"That's not what it is," Birney said, waving his hand. "You can live with this. I know you can because I've lived with worse. You just want to get some mileage out of this. Save the country from a so-called disastrous appointment and look like a hero."

"No, I don't, Senator."

"The hell you don't," he yelled. "Well, I wouldn't have the presidential seal embroidered on my shorts just yet if I were you. You do this and no bill of yours will ever get out of my committee. I'll cut off your funding for your subcommittee. I'll strip you of half your staff. You're gonna look about as glamorous as a toad with a tire track down its back. How does that sound?"

Joe stared at the decanter of bourbon. Birney had forgotten his manners, he thought. He pointed to the decanter.

"Thanks for the bourbon, Senator," he said, turning and heading toward the door.

"How's the blonde?"

Joe stopped in his tracks and turned around. "You wouldn't dare."

"You're right," Birney said. "None of my business. Do what you want. You're the moral one. You're the one who's right and sees things the right way and all. None of my business what you do with your personal life. Take anyone and anything you want. But not my money. Not my committee's funds. Not the taxpayer's dollars."

"What the hell are you talking about?"

Birney reached into his desk drawer. "I am talking about a Karen Harman Traynor, Social Security number 076-032-1577, who's been paid on a per diem basis by my committee. She has been paid for twelve days' work and she has not once been seen in the committee's offices. She has, however, been seen having lunch with you in your office. Tuna fish, I think."

"You old . . ."

"Shut up!" Birney yelled. "There's more. Shut up and listen." He referred back to the file. "Mrs. Karen Harman Traynor has stayed at eight different hotels. We have paid the bill for eight different hotels. Here are the receipts." He reached into the file and fanned hotel bills at Joe. "Eight of them. What's the matter?

There some kind of bedbug problem in Washington? Something else that's funny. She always orders food for two. Here's a lady, in town to work for the people of the United States, a little thing, as I've been told, and she eats for two people. She's never seen where she's supposed to work and she changes hotels every time you turn around. And just about every time she checks into a hotel, you show up right after. One thing I'll say for you, lover boy, you didn't have the government pay for that place in Virginia. Nice spot. I used to go there with Mrs. Birney."

Birney looked at Joe. The old man's face had softened, the redness of anger still lingered, though. He motioned to a chair before the desk. "Sit down, Joe. Let's talk about this."

Joe walked over to the chair and sat. He crossed his legs and waited. His heart pounded. He was scared, a jumble of thoughts, some about Ellie and some about the kids and some about his father and some about his political career. He was fast becoming sick, getting an awful pain in his stomach.

"Joe, you don't look well," Birney said. "You're in a tough spot and you're hurting. You're no killer, boy. You wouldn't last two days at 1600 Pennsylvania Avenue. They kill people every day over there. Got to have some stomach for that. Got to think clearly. You're scared. That's no good. You have a right to be scared. But it's no good when you act scared. I been in worse spots than you are now. Much worse. But you're in a pretty bad spot. You put some lady on the Senate payroll so you could have a party. I can prove it. I can prove everything up to and maybe including that you were bedding down with this lady. I got the receipts and the witnesses and the names of reporters who can get even more information. You, my boy, are in a shit sandwich of mammoth proportions."

Joe sat stunned. "Is this the way you play?" he whispered.

"Not if I can avoid it," Birney said. "I hate this sort of thing, especially with you. You're not the type. You've been a good senator and a good family man. You've worked hard here. That business of your not missing a roll-call vote. I know what you say about it being a silly campaign promise, but you mean it. You're a senator. Born for the Senate, Joe, and it's a good place for you to stay. But you won't. You want to be president and that's all right, too. You won't make it. I'll tell you that. You won't make it because you're no killer. You're probably in love with this Traynor lady, and you're so naive you go ahead and charge everything to the committee. You think if *you* do it, it can't be wrong. If some old guy like me does it, then it's wrong." Birney chuckled to himself.

"Only I never do it. I never spend the public's money this way. I . . . never mind about me. The question here is you. You have a decision to make. I want my man Anderson on the Supreme Court. I have given my word to many people on this matter. I have also given my word to Anderson. There is something going on here, Joe, something you don't know about. I don't know all of it either. I'm not sure Anderson wants to be on the court or that the President wants him there or that the two of them or maybe one of them is not the source for these stories. There's games within games going on here, Joe, and you are going to get into the middle of something that you will not be able to control." He brought his fist down on the desk and yelled. "You are over your head, boy."

Joe said nothing.

"There are people in the White House playing games. There are people in the law firms in this town playing games. There are people on your own staff playing games. The President may be playing a game and maybe Anderson is playing a game. I've been through this sort of stuff before. I can handle it. You cannot.

"Joe, I want you to go back to your office and issue a statement saying that CBS is wrong. You have not made up your mind about Anderson. You may vote for him or you may vote against him. You will wait until after the hearings and you may not even decide until the day of the vote. Vote as you wish then, but until then, be noncommittal and keep your mouth shut. Otherwise I will have Mrs. Traynor's name in every newspaper in this town. And I will have an ethics committee investigation. I promise you that, Joe. And I never break a promise."

"What will it get you?" Joe asked. "You'll hurt me a bit, but I'll get over it. You'll destroy my wife and maybe she won't get over it. The lady you referred to will be ruined, I suppose, and my children will suffer, and all this will happen even though what you're saying is not true. You should bear that in mind, Senator—it's not true."

"What's not true?" Birney yelled. He opened the drawer and took out the file. "Is this not true? The Embassy Row Hotel bill. Is this not true? The Capitol Hilton? How about the Sheraton Park and the Shoreham and the Madison. My God, look at this bill. You have expensive tastes, my boy. You like to live well. Is all this not true?"

Joe was worried. He had to be careful about what he said. Birney might have the room bugged. He might have a tape recorder in his drawer or he might have an open line to his faithful receptionist who could be taking everything down in shorthand.

"Maybe she likes to change hotels a lot?" Joe said.

"Bullshit," Birney said.

"Look, Senator, do what you have to do. You're wrong about this. All you have is a woman who changed hotel rooms a lot. She did real work for the committee. She did not work in the committee offices, that's true. The reason she did not will soon become clear to you when we begin the hearings tomorrow. There are things we worked on we did not want others to know. It's true that I visited her in those hotel rooms, but that was for work. Nothing more."

Birney looked surprised. Joe felt as he sometimes did in a television debate when he could sense that he was starting to pull away from his opponent. Birney had nothing, he told himself. It looked bad, but it was really nothing. His gun was empty.

"What about the trip to Virginia?" Birney asked. "Business? Just business?"

"Nothing personal," Joe said quickly. "I paid for it or she paid for it—it doesn't matter. The government did not pay for it. We worked over things while we were there. She is sort of a business associate." He stood up.

"You're jumping to the wrong conclusions, Senator. You're wrong about this. You're wrong and filthy-minded and underhanded. This is no way to play. Do what you want, Senator, but I'm leaving."

He turned and walked to the door. He reached for the doorknob, opened the door, and slammed it shut, leaving the room in a staged huff.

In the hallway of the Senate Office Building, Joseph Tynan inventoried his closest friends and associates, trying to find someone to turn to. He could come up with no one. His colleagues were out of the question and Francis was also no good. He needed someone who he knew would never come to him and hold this against him—never. The person he trusted the most, whose judgment he truly valued, was Ellie, but this was no problem for her to tackle. The same was true of Karen, although Joe had no idea whether Karen had good judgment and good political instincts. In truth he wondered if she wasn't something of a groupie—a groupie with class.

He walked slowly, heading toward the subway and then to the Capitol building and then to his hideaway office. He let himself in and went to the desk. He sat down with a sigh and did something he almost never did: he poured himself a drink—Scotch. He tentatively tasted some of it, found he still liked it, and downed what was left in the glass.

Joe searched in his mind for someone whom he could talk to about this. It was important to talk to someone. He knew that. That's the way you thought things out. That's the way you learned how to respond to questions. You had to say them—talk them, live them. He poured himself another drink. He was feeling the booze, liking it, liking what it was doing for him. He thought of Pie-Face. "Shay," he said, mimicking the old family friend. "Shay, id dis da end?" He laughed. Then it hit him. His father! He wished he could talk to his father. He reached for the phone and put it down. He couldn't do that. It would have broken his father's heart to know that his son was having an affair. His father, he was sure, had never done that. His father did not believe in that sort of thing. His father never thought highly of his fellow entertainers who neglected their families and ran around with women. He poured himself another drink. He got up and walked around the room. He came back to his desk and pushed the hold button on the phone. He could do it. He dialed his father.

"Dad, I'm in trouble, Dad," he said into the dead phone. "First I have to tell you that I'm troubled because I'm in trouble and I have no one to talk to. No one. Isn't that just terrific. I'm sitting here in the capitol of the United States and I have a staff and seven zillion and four point two billion people voted for me and two women love me and I have no one to talk to. Even you, Dad. I can't really talk to you." He cupped the receiver with his palm as if someone was really on the line. "This is silly," he said to himself. He went on anyway.

"See, I've been having this affair, Dad. I'm sorry, Dad. I know you don't approve, but it's different now. It's really wonderful, I hate to say it, Dad, but it feels different. It's hard to explain. You know what I mean, Dad. Gee, maybe you don't. Anyway, it's all right. I have it under control. Ellie doesn't know a thing. It's no threat to the marriage." He laughed and poured himself another drink.

"You know what I've been thinking Dad? I've been thinking about how little time I spend with her and how tough it all must be for her and how you think that an affair won't matter, but it does. I mean, she's willing to give up so much for me and I won't give up anything for her. Make any sense to you, Dad? I mean, isn't that how you measure love—by how much you give up? I've been thinking of that. It's easy to say 'I love you' but the only way to really prove it is by what you're willing to give up or sacrifice. Do you follow me, Dad? Jeez, I'm drunk.

"Look, Dad, it's like this. This other senator knows about the affair. He can't prove anything but he's got lots of circumstantial evidence. Looks bad. The papers will print that sort of stuff nowadays. Anyway, he can make a formal charge to the Ethics Committee. What a joke. I voted to strengthen it. I hope they name the committee after me—the Joseph Tynan Memorial Ethics Committee.

"Look, Dad, if he goes public with that stuff, it'll kill Ellie. It'll kill the kids and it'll kill me. I think I could maybe tough it out. After all, lots of guys have been found with their pants down. But it will mean that this Anderson creep will get through. I won't have much credibility left when it comes to him.

"You know something, Dad? I'm not sure anymore that Anderson wants the job. Something Birney said. I'm not even sure anymore what the White House wants, or whether maybe the President wants something and the staff wants something else. That sometimes happens to me.

"No matter what, Dad, that guy Birney will always have this on me. If I do what he wants, it means I'm guilty; it's an admission and he'll always have me in his pocket. Maybe he's told some others—Kittner maybe. And the more I think of Anderson, the more I don't like him. He's no great jurist, I'll tell you that, and I'll tell you something else. All things considered, if I wasn't such a big shot and didn't have a shot at the White House and all that, if you just asked me, Dad, if the guy was going to be a good judge or a bad judge, whether he was going to give a damn about blacks and women and hunchbacks and all the ugly people of the world, I would say no. I could vote against him. Drop dead! Isn't that what you'd say, Dad? Do the right thing. Right? Huh? Dad, I'm crying. Dad, I'm drunk. Dad, I got to get off now. Thanks, Dad. I love you. I miss you. Christ, I'm in bad shape."

He hung up the phone, tears streaming down his face, and dialed a number.

"Mary Anne, get me Francis," he said. There was a momentary pause. "Francis. Don't put out any press release. Just confirm the CBS story. That's all. Just tell them it's the truth. I'm going home tonight, Francis. I'll be back in the morning. I want to see my wife."

Joe looked at the phone as if it had made him say what he just said. How could he go home tonight of all nights? Never mind that he was drunk. The Anderson hearing was in the morning. He picked up the phone and dialed his home. It rang six or seven times before it was answered.

"Hi, it's me. Where were you?"

"Talking to Paulie," Ellie said. "His rabbit's got some sort of ear infection and he's afraid the poor thing might die. You know how he is about death."

"Can you put him on? Where are you now?"

"Our bedroom."

"Good, go get him. Okay?"

"Just a second." She went down the hall and summoned the boy from his room. "Daddy's on the phone," she said. The child, dressed in pajamas with large Hershey bars for a design pattern, came down the hall, following his mother, walking from the light of his room to the half-light of the hallway to the light of his parents' bedroom. He picked up the phone.

"Daddy, hi."

"Hi, Paul. How—"

"Daddy, can you come home and look at my rabbit? I think it's gonna die."

"No, it's not gonna die, Paul. Mommy says it's just got an ear infection. You had plenty of those when you were a baby. Nothing to worry about."

"But a rabbit has big ears, Daddy."

"Just the outside of the ear is big, Paul," Joe said, wondering if he was right about that. His other line rang. "Hold on, Paul. I have to get the other phone." He pushed hold and pressed the button for the other line.

"Yes?"

It was Francis. "Francis, give me your number and I'll call you back." There was a pause. "Okay, make it quick."

He punched hold and then the line that Paul was on. "Hold on, Paul. I'll be right back." He did his punching routine again.

"Francis? Just a second." He reached for a long yellow pad, took a pen out of his pocket, and pulled the top off with his teeth. "Okay, now what about Anderson?" He made quick, sure notes, filling first one page and then another with scribbling from the black felt-tip pen. "How do you know that?" he asked at one point. He continued to write, turning three more pages. Finally, he put down the pen. "Is that it?" he asked. "Thanks. Of course I'm still here. No. Please, I have to get off." He hit the other line.

"Paulie?"

"It's me," Ellie said. "Paul fell asleep. I'm sorry, darling, but it's very late for him and he was up very early to take care of that rabbit."

"It's okay. It's my fault. How are you?"

"I'm all right. Tired, but all right."

"I love you."

"Yes. That's nice. Is tomorrow the hearing?"

"Yes."

"There have been some phone calls here for you. Do you want them?"

"No. I'll have the office call in the morning."

"Good luck tomorrow."

"It'll be all right. I love you."

"Yes. I know. I love you, too. I wish you were here. You sound so nice."

"I wish I were with you, too. Ellie?"

"What? Oh, Paul is calling me. I guess he woke up. What is it, Joe?"

"Nothing. Go see about the rabbit or whatever. Good night."

"Good night."

He hung up the phone, his eyes red and watery. He called the weather and listened to the forecast and then he called time and checked it with his watch and then, after a moment's hesitation, he called another number.

"Karen? It's me. Can I come over?"

CHAPTER 9

Very early, about dawn, the hard-core of Joseph Tynan's staff began the day. They awoke in homes and apartments all over the Washington area and they began, some of them, by reading first *The Washington Post* and then *The New York Times* to see if there had been any late-breaking developments. In New York a professor at Columbia University's Law School named Alexander Kreghoof was prepared to come to Washington to advise Joe informally. He was already up, ready to catch the 7 A.M. shuttle from LaGuardia.

At eight thirty they all assembled in Joe's office. Francis was there and Alex Heller and Eric Barnston and Kreghoof from Columbia. Arthur Briggs came in shortly after and then Joe and Karen walked in, having met, they said, in the hallway. They trooped into Joe's office, where he forsook his place behind the desk and instead drew up a chair and straddled it, facing front. Francis gave Joe a memo on suggestion questions. From Kreghoof he received a similar memo, and also a copy of another one he had received in the mail and already read. That one summarized all the important decisions involving Anderson when he was state attorney general and what higher courts had to say about them.

Kreghoof then stood. He was a short, stout man with an enormous stomach that was contained by what someone said must be an iron vest. He always wore tweeds and always had a pocket-watch chain woven through the vest and always seemed in need of a haircut. He was a foremost legal scholar, a rising star on the intellectual circuit. He and Joe had attached themselves to each other because they both felt something in common—they were both men on the way up. Over the years a relationship had developed, a measure of respect had crept in as Kreghoof had learned that there was more to politics, as he once said, than lying.

"What we have here is a man with two weaknesses, one of them a flesh wound, the other quite fatal," Kreghoof said. "There are times when our friend Mr. Anderson seems not to know the law and there are times when he seems simply to disregard it. The first is forgivable and may result from sloppy staff work, bad clerking, in other words, and maybe a deficient education. He did not, after all, attend a really first-class law school and I presume his scholarship is not of the first rank.

"His second weakness, though, is unforgivable. He has on at least six occasions attempted to use the law to buttress his own reactionary and mindless views, attempted, moreover, to have the law do what previous courts had already said it could not. In other words, we have here a man whose only innovative acts are to march backward, whose only triumphs of imagination are in the cause of reaction, who can only think originally when he is attempting to thwart human rights."

Joe rose. "Alex, that was terrific. I'm going to steal all of it." He laughed and so did Kreghoof and then, as if taking a cue, the rest of the staff. "As long as I'm standing, let me go through my strategy with you," Joe went on. "Alex, I think you're right. I think those seven cases are gems and I'm going to use them. I lead with *Laycock* vs. *Louisiana* and then go to Ownes and then to Parish of Pascaqualemes. Karen thinks the transit case is a pip, so I'll put that one in next. That's Rapid Rail . . . no, no. That's *Southern Rapid Rail* vs. *Louisiana* and then we go to the other three— Henderson, Water Authority, and . . . let's see, Laycock. No, I've counted that one. Morrison! Yeah, Morrison." He looked around the room, smiling like a kid who has just finished reciting a poem. He meant to impress, and the fact was that everyone was impressed. He had, as usual, done his homework. Karen wondered when he had had the time.

"I think first you ought to ask him about his statement and then go to the law cases," Karen said, looking up at Joe from the couch.

"Right," said Francis. "We'll have all the networks there at the beginning and they'll have the lights on you right at the beginning and we might as well make use of it."

"No," Joe said. "First I cite the cases. I will be as detailed as I can be without being boring and silly. I will show I know these cases."

"How will you phrase the questions?" asked Kreghoof. "It's important here to get across the notion that you are not talking about fine points of the law, but broad principles. Therefore, you should begin by outlining the cases—summarizing them. Then tell what is at stake in each. What issue of law."

"What issue of social justice," Joe put in.

"Right. And then say what he did and then what the appellate court found. Now you will find that some of them overlap. Laycock and Morrison, for instance, which is probably why you got them confused earlier. They both involve schools, but more important they involve a deliberate attempt by the state to persist in the segregation of public-school students. You have to be careful here. You are not talking about busing or anything like it. You are talking about what amounts to a scheme by the state to lie in the federal court. A lie. An out-and-out lie."

"Right," Joe said. "Our problem is going to be Birney. He's the chairman and the lead-off questioner. Normally he'd go first. That will give me time to size up Anderson. I think I'll probably come up with some questions as they serve him their underhands. Okay," he said, slapping his hands, "this is going to be fine. We've done a good job and I just want to thank all you people. It's important to understand that nothing can happen in committee. Anderson'll make it out. Then we have to fight on the floor and before that we have to fight in the newspapers and on television and in lots of speeches. None of us is going to get any sleep from here on out."

"Okay, coach," Francis cracked.

"Ah, a sense of humor," Joe said. "Remind me to

have you fired when this is over and I no longer need you."

Francis looked a touch shocked, knowing it was a joke, yet not absolutely sure. Everyone else, though, laughed and Francis thought it must be safe to do so. He laughed.

The night before, at exactly five o'clock, Monique Schwartz, dark-haired and turned-up nose, had sat down at the phone in her little office in the CBS bureau on L Street, N.W. and called her competitors at NBC and ABC. This was the month for CBS to arrange the pools, arrange for the lighting of various places where Washington news events were scheduled for the next day. None of the networks saw any reason to send three lighting crews to the same events and so they had worked out this arrangement. Monique Schwartz had discovered that everyone was prepared to cover the Anderson hearings. ABC would provide the lights. Good, Schwartz thought, that would allow CBS to set up in the hallway for interviews with people going in and out of the hearing room.

Over on 15th Street, N.W. at about the same time, the national editor of *The Washington Post* was also making plans. He would send one reporter to the hearings and he would have another one, a specialist in legal affairs, monitor the hearings on public television. Also tentatively planned was a side bar on the political implications of the nomination fight, if there was to be one. The whole thing had become rather murky—rumors that Senator Joseph Tynan was going to come out against the nomination being balanced by rumors that he was not. It was, as usual for Washington, confusing.

At the *Washington Star* similar plans were being made. They, too, would devote at least two reporters to the story. Rumors were going around town that something might happen—that this rather routine nomination to the Supreme Court might turn into a first-class story. At *The New York Times* Washington bureau the bureau chief and his news editors had already made their plans. They had, at the last minute, killed a story predicting easy nomination for Anderson when the tom-toms of rumor started beating through the Capitol, and they had switched instead to an attempt to find out if the Anderson nomination was truly in trouble. Like everyone else, they, too, were getting contradictory signals. Even within the White House, you were likely to find someone who would tell you one thing and someone who would tell you something else.

For all the news organizations, word of what was about to unfold had seeped out too late. Until late in the day the nomination of Edward Anderson had been considered a foregone conclusion. He was not the best of appointments, not the worst. He merely was. He was a given, and he had been accepted as such. It was thought that some of the civil rights organizations would oppose him, but that was hardly newsworthy and the organizations themselves no longer had either the political or moral clout they had enjoyed in the heyday of the civil rights era. Liberal senators, too, might oppose Anderson, especially the northern ones, and it was thought that labor might be able to swing one or two votes against him. But in Anderson's corner stood the President of the United States, the bulk of the Senate's moderates, nearly all the Republicans, and, of course, the chairman of the Judiciary Committee, the Hon. Samuel Birney, who had not lost a fight in something like twenty-five years.

A blast of heat greeted anyone who walked into the hearing room of the Senate Judiciary Committee. Already the television lights were cooking the place. The ABC crew was there and so was one from Public Television, which was telecasting the hearings live, and there was also one from Metromedia Television, covering for the local affiliate and for stations subscribing to the syndicate. Outside in the hallways a long line of people stretched along the wall, waiting to be seated. By nine thirty, a half hour before the start of the hearings, all the seats had been filled and now the guards were only allowing someone in if someone else left.

Down at the front of the room both press tables were full. Large stacks of unlined yellow paper, provided free by the Congress, sat in the middle of the table, there for the note-taking reporters. It was now nearly ten, and the reporters joked among themselves, passing rumors back and forth, knowing now that the Anderson nomination was in trouble, knowing also that they would be covering the best story of the day. This, they knew, would be one hell of a show.

The hearing room itself was one of the larger ones in the Russell Senate Office Building. The front of the room was convex in shape, a bulging outward of the wall that added depth to the room and a touch of grandeur to the senators who sat before it. The dais, too, was curved and behind it the walls were painted a plaster white. Half columns rose up the walls to the ceiling, and up at the top the columns flared, topped with the great seal of the United States. The ceiling was painted sky blue, white stars twinkling among the blue. It was the Senate of the United States as the senators of the United States would like to see it.

Facing front, Republicans sat on the left and Democrats on the right. Birney would sit in the middle, Kittner to the right, and then Joe, who was third in seniority; each senator could have two aides behind him. Joe had chosen Karen.

From the dais Joe looked into a bank of popping lights from the cameras of news photographers. Anderson, who sat at a table facing the dais, was the attention of still more photographers, and over at the chairman's spot Birney had his own little claque. Suddenly, as if responding to some unheard signal, the photographers backed off. Birney sat down and reached for the gavel. He hit it twice and immediately the room was stilled. The guards closed the door and then scanned the room to find the talkers. There were none.

"Ladies and gentlemen, we are here today to begin the process by which a member of the Supreme Court of the United States is nominated," Birney began. He was reading from a statement.

"It is an awesome process, as old as the Republic, and as hallowed. The man before us today, Mr. Edward Anderson of the State of Louisiana, will be entitled to serve for the rest of his natural life if he should be confirmed by the Senate. No one else in our system gets that sort of mandate, although there are some who act as if they do." There was a small amount of laughter, most of it coming from people who thought they were expected to laugh, and then some coughing by people who thought they could take this opportunity to clear their throats. Birney himself smiled at his remarks and then hit the gavel to restore order.

"We intend to hold these hearings in a judicious and fair manner," he went on. "We intend to insure that the man we endorse as fit for this high office is indeed fit, and we intend to conduct ourselves as a committee in such a manner that no one will have cause for criticism. We will, like Caesar's wife, be above suspicion and beyond reproach."

He looked around the room to see if his point had been understood. He smiled as he did so, as if he did not mean to be saying what he was saying. It was a peculiar performance. Every so often a photographer would scramble out on his knees and squeeze off a shot. Joe, two seats down, looked straight ahead, glancing only occasionally over at Birney. He thought the chairman was acting a touch strange but he attributed it to tension.

"This committee, like many committees of the Congress, has for years followed a procedure in the questioning of witnesses. In the case of a confirmation hearing, we usually entertain a statement by the nominee and then begin the questioning with the chairman, proceeding by seniority to the ranking member, my good friend of the other party, and from there to other committee members, alternating by party and seniority. I would like to change that procedure today. The man before us comes from my home state. I have known him for something like twenty years, during which time he has been both a colleague and a friend. He is a man I deeply admire, a man of courage and conviction and character—the three *c*'s that I hold to be paramount in a public man. I have to admit that I cannot think of a question to ask him." He smiled weakly again, scanning the room as if he thought his point would not be understood.

"I stayed up very late last night, trying to come up with questions that I could ask of the nominee. I could find none. I referred to the transcripts of earlier nomination hearings to see what questions were asked then, but none of them seemed appropriate here. Should I ask him his age or his name or maybe something about his wife, the darling and beautiful Carol, who, I think, is sitting right over there." Birney squinted into the lights and pointed off to the left.

"Should I ask about his legal career, which I know so well and which has been so brilliant? Shall I ask about his career as a public man, which has been distinguished and which the voters of my state have reaffirmed time and time and time again? You see my predicament. So I have resolved to pass during the first round of questioning, hoping that my colleagues will come up with something that will then generate further questions from me. I now ask Mr. Anderson if he has a statement."

Joe was thunderstruck. The old man had pulled off a tactical coup, something they had not expected. He would wait for Joe to show his colors before he made his own move. He would wait to see how Joe questioned Anderson before he himself said anything—maybe something about Karen. Joe felt himself grow suddenly afraid. He could do that—Birney could! He could maintain it was germane! He could ask Anderson about the film and how they got it and who was this Karen Traynor. He could create enough confusion and supply enough headlines to confuse the issue and ruin Joe. Anderson might or might not go down, but Joe surely would.

"Thank you, Mr. Chairman," Anderson said, looking up at Birney from his position at the witness table. At that moment a committee aide rose, his arm cradling lots of paper, and went over to the press tables where he distributed copies of Anderson's statement.

"I cannot thank the chairman enough for the warm endorsement he has given me," Anderson said. "As he said, we have been friends and colleagues for a very long time now, and I myself would be hard put to ask him a question if our roles were reversed." Anderson smiled at Birney and Birney nodded to him.

Birney stood. He walked behind the row of Democratic senators, heading for the side door. When he reached Joe, he leaned over and in pretended friendliness for the television cameras and the spectators, patted him on the shoulder a couple of times. "It's up to you now, sonny," he whispered. Then he patted him twice more on the shoulder and walked off.

Anderson continued with his statement. His voice was deep and warm. He sounded like a judge. The statement was the usual, nothing much in it except how he considered appointment to the Supreme Court to be the highest honor for a lawyer—"short of president, Mr. Chairman." The chairman now was Hugh Kittner, the number two ranking Democrat.

Joe reviewed his notes. He mentally rehearsed his strategy. He remembered Karen telling him to keep away from voter registration and stick to schooling. Over and over in his mind he rehearsed and then thought about what Birney might say. He imagined that first Birney would attempt to counter the substantive arguments against Anderson—a more or less standard rebuttal. Then he would get into the personal stuff. He might ask Anderson what he knew of this Karen Traynor—"This Karen Traynor," Joe could hear him saying it. He would ask him if the Traynors and the Andersons were political enemies and did he know, as he himself had just discovered, that this Mrs. Traynor was the daughter of the Democratic Party Chairman of Louisiana, a true political enemy. What did he make of the fact that this Mrs. Traynor was on the staff of the committee and that she was being paid on a per diem basis at the request of Senator Tynan? And what could he make of the fact that she stayed in a different Washington hotel every time she came to town and always the committee paid for it and always she had a room-service meal for two?

Joe saw himself on the dais as those questions were being asked. He heard himself demand to be recognized and then saying something about it all not being germane and Birney gaveling him to shut up. "Shut up, shut up," the old man yelled. Joe did just that. He sat still as the questioning went on, Birney asking questions of Anderson that needed no answers, the photographers rushing forward in their Groucho Marx walk, hitting the floor with their knees, taking dozens of pictures with their electric cameras—ka-ching, ka-ching—the strobes lighting him and then . . . the newspaper reporters at the press table would be taking notes and later they would be contacting everyone in the hotel—the bellhops and the busboys and the countermen and the waiters from room service.

They would go to the hotel in Virginia and maybe, just maybe, that old idiot Senator Aikers would say something to someone—something about Joe and the blonde.

"Senator Tynan," yelled Kittner. "Senator Tynan, do you or do you not have any questions for the nominee?"

"Yes," said Joe, flustered. They were up to him already and he had no idea what the others had asked. "Mr. Chairman, I'm sorry. I was deep in thought."

"That's behavior unbecoming to a senator and I'm obliged to report you to the Ethics Committee," cracked Kittner.

Joe laughed, and the rest of the room rocked with laughter. The old bird was irrepressible.

"I'll try not to have that happen again, sir," Joe said. Kittner beamed. "Mr. Anderson, you have some friends on this committee, the chairman, being, of course, one of them. I will leave it to them to ask you questions that would bring out some of the things you have done that are good and noble. I myself know of some of these things, and I am sure there are matters about which I know nothing. But our time here is limited and rather than go through some sort of back-slapping dialogue with you, I would rather turn my attention to some matters which, frankly, disturb me. They are matters that have to do with civil rights and civil liberties—especially the rights of black Americans.

"Now I want to say something here right at the start. There is a tendency in this country to hold a different standard for the South, to say almost that it cannot be judged by the same standards that apply to the rest of the country. If a northerner, for instance, espoused the racial segregation of the schools he would never be considered for the Supreme Court of the United States. He would not, I think, be considered for dogcatcher. Such is not the case for a southerner. It is almost a given that southerners of your age have at one time or another espoused the racial segregation of the schools or fought against the integration of them. This, for some reason, is excused. I, however, do not excuse it. I, for one, know of plenty of southerners who did not go along with the program, who were willing to speak out. From our perusal of the record, sir, you were not one of them. If I am wrong, I would like you or one of my colleagues to correct me . . . but I would like them to do it on their own time." That brought some laughter.

"I would like to begin with your opinion in *Laycock v. Louisiana*." He turned behind him. Karen handed him the decision. "I would like to read from it: 'Nothing can compel a community to open its doors to any group which it fears for its very survival.'"

The hearing room went silent. Television lights snapped on. Reporters quickly hunched over their notebooks, concentrating intensely on their note-taking. The air was a familiar one to Washington— the feeling that news was about to happen, that what was happening here would be a front-page headline the next day. Joe looked up at Anderson and then back down at the paper. "'This is the very principle of self-defense which precedes all others.' Did you say that, sir?"

"Yes," Anderson said, "but you don't understand the context."

"I think I do," Joe said. "It had to do with school integration and it had to do with an attempt by you to keep the schools segregated. Isn't that what you did?"

"No, sir."

"You didn't?"

"No, sir. I was attempting to keep them from integrating."

Laughter erupted in the room. Kittner hit the gavel. Joe mugged a puzzled look for the benefit of the photographers. In fact, he understood Anderson's meaning.

"Let me explain, Senator, if I may."

"Go ahead," Joe said.

"The schools were already segregated. They had been since 1890 or so. You can't pin that one on me. We had all gone to segregated schools. I did and my father did and probably my grandfather did. But that is not the point. The point is that I was trying to stall a school integration plan that would have resulted, I thought, in violence and the closing of the schools. There would have been a widespread flight of white children to private schools. It would have been the end of the public school system in my state as we have come to know it. What you would have had, I think, is yet another segregated school system, only this one would be state-supported—public. There would have been no white kids in it."

"Nevertheless," Joe said, "you wrote what I just said."

"I did."

"And nevertheless, your appeal was rejected by the appellate court in a matter of hours. Something of a record, I was given to understand."

"True. But it's also true that just hours after that I personally issued an order directing the state to comply."

"In just hours," Joe repeated, sarcastically. "How about the fact that it's been *twenty years* since the Supreme Court ordered the schools integrated with *all deliberate speed?*"

"You can't change the old ways overnight," Anderson said, aware that the lights had been on the whole time he and Tynan were debating. He felt his back grow wet with sweat. "We have to learn to crawl before we can walk."

"*Twenty years*, Mr. Anderson," Joe said, hitting the words like a hammer. "Mr. Anderson, we have people going to the moon and you can't walk yet?" A ripple of mocking laughter went through the room and then a burst of applause. Kittner hit the gavel hard.

"We will have quiet in the room," he barked. "There will be no more outbursts in here or we will clear the room." He scanned the room and noticed a commotion over by the side door behind the dais. Birney had reentered, his face contorted in rage. He moved slowly toward his place on the dais, stopping at Joe and patting him twice on the shoulder. Then he continued to the chairman's place.

"In as much as Senator Birney has returned, I will yield the gavel to the chairman of the committee," Kittner said. He rose, whispered something to Birney, and went to take his chair. Birney sat down heavily, spread some papers out before him, and studied them. He said nothing for what seemed like minutes and then he suddenly looked up. Joe prepared to resume his questioning, but Birney had something else in mind.

"Mr. Anderson, when you were attorney general of the State of Louisiana, you worked to tone down a desegregation plan, didn't you?"

"Yes, sir, I did," Anderson answered crisply.

"Would you tell us why, Mr. Anderson?"

"Because the schools would have closed, Senator. Forced integration of the kind required by the court order works smoothly in almost no community. This order would have required massive busing and we feared it would have resulted in widespread school closings. This is not what either side wanted. We effected what we thought was a compromise."

"Mr. Anderson, did you get any help in drawing up your compromise?"

"Yes, sir, I did. I worked the compromise out with members of the black community. We met in my office and we had people there from all over the state. We did not have them all, sir. I cannot say that. But we had a substantial number of what I would call the responsible, moderate black leadership. These were the people, sir, who were more interested in getting a quality education for their children than in scoring political points or fomenting trouble. You would not find their pictures on the cover of *Time* or *Newsweek*."

Joe had heard enough. "Mr. Chairman," he broke in, "I'd like to point out that under the rules I still have time remaining to me. I would appreciate it if I could use the remainder of my time and I would appreciate it even more if the time you used so well just now would not be counted against me."

"The senator from New York is right," Birney said. "I'm sorry for intruding on his time and he should not worry. It will not be counted against him. We'll call it house time." The spectators laughed.

Joe waited for the laughter to die down, his own smile vanishing from his face. He leaned back to Karen and whispered something and then sort of set himself like a football player before the hike of the ball. He tensed, suddenly looking very serious.

"Mr. Anderson," he began, "I've felt from the beginning that you were a decent man. I'm not impugning your basic motives, but my problem is that I'm not sure what they are. I don't get the sense that you understand or feel anything at all for the plight of the underprivileged. I get the feeling that you have to be kicked pretty hard to challenge the accepted ways of doing things and I get the feeling also that you have been slow to get the basic drift of the law. It seems to me, Mr. Anderson, that you sometimes use subterfuge to delay implementation of certain court decisions, that you are somewhat sly and less than candid about where you stand. My question, I guess, is this: do you feel in your public life you have devoted yourself to carrying out the spirit, if not the letter of the law?"

Anderson stiffened. "To the very best of my ability," he said in an offended tone of voice.

Joe glanced at some papers. He looked up. "When you said, 'If the Supreme Court wants to take crime off the streets and out into our schools, let them, but we don't have to send our children there!'—was that the best of your ability?" Joe picked up a sheet of paper and put it aside. He could hear murmuring in the room.

"Was it to the best of your ability to raise funds for segregated private schools in your state?

"When you said, 'In my heart I have never accepted integration and I never will,' was *that* to the best of your ability?"

Anderson reddened. "Now that is untrue. It is an old lie. An old lie. It is not true. You should know it is not true. It's an old lie. Used before. A lie."

"Would you like to see the film I have of your saying that?" Joe demanded. "Would you like to see that film played right here? We can do it, you know."

Anderson looked over at Birney as if he was seeking help. Joe waited a moment and then moved in for the kill.

"What about the law of the land, Mr. Anderson?" he bellowed. "What about simple human justice?" The stirring in the hearing room erupted into applause. A few people whistled and the policeman on the floor moved down the aisle to look for the guilty. Birney banged away with his gavel.

"All right now, come to order," he yelled. He looked down the dais at Joe.

"No further questions, Mr. Chairman," Joe said. He stood, scooped up his papers and walked down the length of the dais and out the door. He paused there to see what Birney would do. His heart was beating wildly in his chest.

"Now I want order," Birney said. "These proceedings will be conducted with dignity," he yelled. "I'll remind our guests that this is a Senate hearing . . . *et pas un cirque. En tout cas ce n'est pas un cirque romain.*"

Some of the senators looked over at the chairman,

unsure of what to do or what he was doing. Joe started back into the hearing room to force Birney to come out of his French trance. He walked two steps and then stopped. He turned and walked the other way.

"En quelle façon ferons-nous nos conseils, mes amis?" Birney continued. *"Permettez-moi de vous rappeler que ce n'est pas l'opéra comique, là."*

He sat back in his chair and put down his gavel, seemingly satisfied and pleased with what he had said.

"Mr. Chairman," Kittner called out.

Birney sat forward again and leaned into his microphone. *"Rappelons-nous les mots de Monsieur Stendhal avec lesquels il commence* Le Rouge et le noir. *"La petite ville de Verrières peut passer pour l'une des plus jolies de la. Franche-Comté." Ça, c'est le sens de quiétude que je cherche ici."*

The other senators on the dais looked at each other quizzically, trying to figure out what to do. Their confused expressions were picked up on the television cameras. On live television the narrator told the audience that Birney had said something about the book, *The Red and the Black,* but he was not sure what. He apologized for his French, which he said was poor, but he added that he did not think he would be using it when covering a hearing of the Senate Judiciary Committee. He chuckled in an understated way and then said he did not have the foggiest notion of what was going on—"and from the looks on the faces of the senators here, neither do they." It was the truth.

Senator Hammer made the first move: "Mr. Chairman, if I may . . ."

Birney waved his hand and cut him off. " *'Ses maisons blanches avec leurs toits pointus . . .'* " The cameras tightened on Birney's face. His eyes were unfocused.

"Mr. Chairman," Hammer insisted.

"'. . . dont des touffes de vigoureux châtaigniers marquent les moindres sinuosités.' "

"Monsieur le Chairman," Hammer yelled. The audience broke up and several of the senators laughed, too. Birney, confused by the laughter, managed a weak smile himself. A touch of saliva formed in the corner of his mouth. Joe stood at the door tight-lipped. He turned at last and left the room.

In the den of the Cedarhurst home later that day the television was on. It was the only light in the room. The house made the sounds of children being put to bed—the last-minute requests for water, some question that had to be answered right then and there, a cold insecurity that demanded yet another hug. Ellie moved about her errands, going from bedroom to bedroom, watching the clocks in the rooms she passed.

Finally Ellie came into the den. The television was already set to the CBS station, channel two, which for some reason Ellie trusted above the others. She sat down on a hassock which she had pulled up close to the set. She had talked to Joe and she knew what had happened. She wanted very much to be with him. He had asked her down and she had given it some thought, but there was just too much to do at the last moment—too many arrangements to make, the children, the house, the plane, her work. Too much.

The news of what Joe had done came on. The voice from the television set talked about the committee hearing while the film showed it. Ellie saw a shot of the committee room and then a close-up of Birney and then one of Joe and then a shot of Joe and a blonde woman. She leaned over and handed him a paper. The blonde woman whispered something to Joe, he said something to her. She smiled and he smiled, and it would have meant nothing had it not been for that smile. It took maybe a fraction of a second, but it was enough for Ellie. Very quickly the announcer said, "Later in the day, the President withdrew the nomination of Anderson and instead submitted the name of Richard Emerson, a New York University law professor. Confirmation is expected within days. Whatever else may come out of this, observers are saying this much for sure: this was a clear victory for Senator Joseph Tynan, who now, whether he wants it or not, has been admitted to that select circle of politicians from which, in all likelihood, our next president will be chosen."

Ellie heard little of that. She was still leaning over, trying to get closer to the set and a better look at the blonde woman behind her husband.

Earlier that day that same blonde woman had been walking down a hallway of the Dirksen Senate Office Building when she passed Senator Birney. She took in the old man with unbelieving eyes. The politician whom she had known since infancy was suddenly a very old man. He walked slowly and unsteadily. His left leg seemed out of control, as if it wanted to go its own way. He leaned on the arm of an aide and his eyes, the eyes that once twinkled and hinted at the wonderful stories that could dazzle even a jaded lobbyist, were dull. Karen started to walk over to say something, thought better of it, and continued instead to Joe's office.

From the hallway she could hear something was going on inside, but when she turned into the office itself she was unprepared for what greeted her. A blast of heat from both bodies and television lights greeted her. In the outer reception area paper cups filled with champagne were held high. Staff people had come from all over the Hill when word of the party spread. Many of them, of course, were from Joe's various committees, but some of them had merely drifted in when they heard of the party. Karen thought they would have gone to Birney's office if the vote had gone the other way, but that was not true. They were mostly people who worked for liberal senators and felt they had genuine reasons for celebrating. Karen smiled at everyone and pushed through to an inner office. She opened the door and again got a surprise.

She saw a cluster of people, packed very tightly. A camera crew lit up the small room. In the middle of what looked like a football huddle, stood Joe, answering questions at an impromptu news conference. Karen walked up to the huddle to listen.

"Senator, you said you have no ambitions beyond your present office," a reporter said.

"Did I say that?" Joe said, smiling.

"Yes, you did."

"Then I did," Joe said. "Next question." Everyone laughed.

"No, seriously, folks, I never said that. I said that I am not actively pursuing another office, that I do not now seek another office, but I never said anything about ambition. I think I have the same ambitions as any normal American boy, only I can't remember if that has anything to do with being president or something about a movie star." Again the reporters laughed. "I hope that does not answer your question." They laughed again.

Karen circled to see who was asking the questions. The next question came from a black woman with something of a theatrical manner. Karen put her down as a lapsed drama major.

"But the governor of New York has said that the Anderson matter could be your launching pad into presidential orbit," the reporter said, checking the quote against a slip of paper she held in her hand.

Joe smiled. "Well, I'm glad the governor has this much confidence in me, but I think that's premature. I mean, it's only been a couple of hours. I think it's too early to have me in orbit yet, but I can understand that the governor would want me out of this world." The small audience laughed again. Joe was clearly enjoying himself.

The same reporter came back at him. "Isn't it true that Professor Woodruff of Harvard has been coming down here to advise you on foreign policy matters?" she asked.

"Yes, that's true," said Joe, giving it the old kiss-off.

"Next question," he said, pointing to a well-known Washington columnist. The minute he did so, he knew he had made a mistake. "Jules," Joe said tentatively.

"If you're not running for higher office, why this sudden need for a foreign policy adviser?" Jules Witcover asked.

"Well, Jules, I thought I could use some help. After all, I have to deal with foreign policy matter even though I'm not on the Foreign Relations Committee. I have to vote and I represent a state where foreign policy, especially the Middle East, not to mention Greece, Turkey, and that sort of thing, are of the utmost importance." Joe hoped that had worked, but he doubted it.

"But you've never felt any need to have an adviser until now, Senator."

Jeez, Joe thought, will someone cut this off. He smiled. "Yes, that's right. But I've decided that it would be useful to have one now. I'm not the only senator with one. Senator Kennedy has one, for instance." He knew before the sentence was out of his mouth that he had made a mistake. Kennedy, of course, was always seen as a potential candidate.

"Senator," yelled another reporter, "someone has said that you've engaged a speech coach of some kind. Is that true?"

Joe forced a smile onto his face. "You think I need a speech coach, Frank?" The reporters laughed once again, but not Witcover, who noted that once again Joe had not answered the question. Francis, who had been standing behind Joe, noticed the evasion also, and thinking the time had come to cut things off, threw his hands into the air and shouted, "That's it everybody. Thank you."

He started to push forward, leaning into Joe who got the hint and started to move out of the office himself. With a quick pace he got in front of the group and nudged by Francis took a hard right into a small conference room. Francis, Eric, Angela, and Karen followed him and the door closed.

"First of all," Joe said, "let's kill the speech coach." They all laughed.

"We have things we have to do," he continued. "All this has happened a lot faster than I thought. We have to make plans. We are unprepared. We should be able to capitalize on this."

He stopped and looked around and broke out into a broad grin. "Gee, I feel terrific," he said. "Francis, call in the staff." Joe stood in the middle of the room as Francis went to the door and out into the outer office. One by one the staff trudged in, those on the personal staff, and those from the committee staff who had been hanging around for the victory celebration. Francis stood at the doorway, stopping those who were not staff from entering. Soon they were all in the room.

"I should have something really eloquent to say right now," Joe began. "I guess I could use that speech coach I'm supposed to have. But all I really want to do is thank you. This thing happened so quickly and so fast and . . . and I just didn't expect it." He threw his hands up into the air. "You all helped. You all made it possible. You all are the sort of staff that makes other senators green with envy. I want you to know that. I want you to know that even when you think I don't know what you're doing and how you're doing it, I do and I am always grateful.

"Now look, some of you may have heard the questions outside about my future and what this means and that sort of thing. I don't know what it means myself, but it sure as hell means that things have changed. I won't lie to you. I won't say we're not going to be shifting into something a little bit different now and that I'm not pleased as punch to be where I am today. For some of you the hours will be longer and the pressure a little greater, but the rewards can be bigger, too. I intend to use whatever clout this thing has given me to push the programs we all believe in. Out there they may interpret this thing as a victory for Joe Tynan or a defeat for Birney or a setback for the President, although I'm not sure he didn't want this to come out this way all along. But you and I can look at it differently. For us it's a victory for national health insurance, which we will be pushing much harder, and for sound and safe energy programs and for comprehensive programs to help our larger, older cities. Could be one of them is New York.

"So all I want to tell you is that we will be at the same old store, pushing the same old programs, introducing the same old bills, serving the same old constituents, only doing it better and with more power from here on out. I want to thank you all for what you've done and tell you once again what should be obvious to everyone here: it couldn't have happened without you."

For a second there was silence and then a small young woman down in the front clapped tentatively. The others took it up and soon everyone clapped. Some of the staff cried, including Karen. Joe just stood, a bit awkwardly, acknowledging the applause with small bows of the head. Finally, Francis opened the door and one by one the staff filed out. When they were gone and the group was down to Joe's inner circle, Francis once again closed the door.

"Now," Joe said, "we have some work to do. I think

the first thing to do is to set up some interviews with major newspapers—maybe the editorial boards. Eric, let's try the usual and maybe *Time* and *Newsweek* as well. I'm going to be in Chicago, so let's try the *Tribune*, too. Let's go over the schedule and see what large cities we're going to be in and whether it would be worth it to sit down with the editorial boards or something. Let's also hit the people we've got cards on."

"A money letter?" asked Francis.

Joe shook his head no. "Too early. Too brash. What I have in mind is something else. I want to push national health insurance. I want it to be our next priority. Now we have the wherewithal to do it. I can command lots of attention now. Those editorial boards, for instance, will be happy to hear from me now, and when we get there we'll talk insurance. We can discuss other things as well and I want you all to draw up a list of priorities for me—what you think I ought to be doing next. Have the committee people do the same, Francis, and I'll get in touch with others like our friends at Columbia and Harvard." He paused for a second and smiled. "We ought to get someone at someplace like SMU or something. Look into that Francis, huh.

"The letter should say something like, 'Dear Clyde, I've been giving a lot of thought to the state of the nation lately and I've become particularly concerned about etc., etc., etc. and so on and so on.'" He rolled his hands as he talked. "We remind them of the Anderson thing and then we tell them where we are going from here and then throw in our continuing concern with whatever it is that we have on the cards. Air pollution or nuclear energy or whatever we have them coded for."

He went on talking, rolling his hands when he couldn't come up with the words, not noticing Karen and how her eyes feasted on him. She loved him like this, totally in charge, on the move, marshaling the resources of a savvy politician to advance both his own career and the common good. She liked him even more because he was taking advantage of his own break. He was not waiting for events. The Anderson thing had come fast and easy and it had been unexpected, but it had not thrown him for a loop. He had, instead, taken it almost in stride; he had, though, worked hard for this moment.

The cards he referred to, for instance, had been collected over the last ten years. Whenever he spoke anywhere an aide afterward circulated through the crowd, collecting the names of persons who showed some interest in Joe—maybe even a desire to see him run for president. The card contained the person's name, their address, where they had come forward, what their past political experience had been, if any, and the issues they thought were most important.

From time to time these people received letters from Joe. The letters usually did nothing more than keep the people up-to-date with what he was doing and what he thought the major issues were. They were designed to keep the people on the string, to make sure that they knew they had not been forgotten, and even though many of the more sophisticated of Joe's admirers knew that their letter had been written by computer, they nevertheless appreciated receiving them.

Periodically Joe and Francis would go over the

list. After a while they had at least one person in all of the country's major counties—in some counties more than enough to form the nucleus of a campaign organization. In some places, however, they were pretty bare and so they tried to schedule speeches for those areas. On slow days Joe would sometimes telephone people on his list, chatting with maybe six or seven of them. Joe considered this to be not only good politics, but a valuable way of learning what people were thinking. He made sure that half his calls went to New York State residents and he made sure, also, that at least one third of his speeches were given in the state. He knew that the surest way to defeat was to have your constituents think you'd gone "national"—no longer cared about them. It had doomed more than one senator.

Joe looked around at his staff. He rocked back on his heels, wondering what to say next, wondering if he should somehow hint that there might be trouble coming. He doubted that Birney was in any condition to mount the sort of smear campaign he had once threatened, but there was no telling whom he had told and no predicting what could happen next. He decided to say nothing.

"One thing I want to ask you," he said. "There's going to be a lot of talk about me and the presidency—that sort of thing. It's all premature, of course. You know that. I know that. Let's not do anything to add fuel to the fire. I don't want to encourage speculation. What will be, will be. But we don't have to goose it. Right?"

A chorus of "rights" came back at him. He smiled. "Okay, that's it. Let's go back to work." He looked at

Karen. "There's something I want to discuss with you," he said. She stayed behind when the others left and when the door closed, they moved toward each other. They kissed and held each other, and when they separated they simply looked at each other, Joe shaking his head as if in disbelief, she just smiling, running her hands up and down the sides of his arms and then up his back and then across his back and up his neck. She caressed his neck then pulled him closer and said, "Later?" He said yes and later, after he had called Ellie, he went to the Sheraton-Carlton Hotel with Karen and they were making love when Senator Birney went to his home, took his gun, and returned to his office.

CHAPTER 10

It was the wrong gun. It was not a gun for committing suicide, not something nice and neat, light enough to do the job but not heavy enough to make a mess. This one made a mess. This one was a Magnum and when it fired, it literally blew off the back of Birney's head.

He had gone into the little bathroom of his office and there he had put the barrel of the gun in his mouth and pulled the trigger. The force of the explosion had taken off the back of his head, leaving deposits of bone and brain all over the wall. The sound of the explosion had summoned his receptionist, a woman named Kate McAndrews, who had come running from the outer office where she had stayed late catching up on some mail. She ran to the office, threw open the bathroom door, and fainted on the spot, pitching over onto Birney. For a while it looked like a double murder or a double suicide. It was a mess.

Angela was in the hallway when it happened. She

had been walking by Birney's office on the way to Joe's when she heard the explosion. It sounded like a backfire in the halls of the Dirksen Office Building. Angie spun around to see what had happened. She spotted Kate McAndrews. She saw her leap from her desk and run into the back office. She heard a weak yell and then nothing more. Angela stopped at the doorway, waited for Kate to come back, and tiptoed into the office herself. The phone on the reception desk rang. No one inside made a move to pick it up.

Angela paced the outer office, waiting for Kate to come back. Another telephone line lit up. The first one went dead. Angela was nervous, not knowing what to do. She knew Kate a bit, a colleague from down the hallway and one time co-chairperson along with her for the United Way campaign for their building. They knew each other, but the two of them were not friendly people, not used to talking about their bosses with persons from another office, and their bosses, after all, were the only thing of interest they had to talk about.

Angela walked past the desks in the reception area and knocked lightly on the door leading to the back. She heard no response. She knocked a bit harder and then opened the door slowly, cautiously. "Kate?" she called. "Kate?"

She turned to the right and headed for Birney's personal office, walking softly as if not to disturb someone, calling "Kate, Kate" from time to time. She got down to the end of the narrow inner corridor and went to push the bathroom door shut. It was sticking out into the passageway, blocking her path. It wouldn't move. She pushed harder and then looked

270

down and saw a woman's leg. She gasped, brought her hand to her mouth, and pulled the door open. It was Kate, her dress up around her thighs, her mouth wide open, gaping, her hand stuck into a sort of mess that once was the head of Senator Birney. Angela threw up.

She pitched backward hitting the desk with the small of her back and collapsed in a chair. She kept looking into the bathroom, taking deep, frantic breaths, but it was no use. The vomit rose again within her and came spilling out. She frantically ducked under the desk and put her head in a waste-paper basket. She retched, her eyes growing watery, the terrible acid taste getting stronger in her mouth. She thought of the senator—Joe. She gasped at the thought, forced herself to rise, and took another look into the bathroom. She took careful mental notes this time, noticing that the back of Birney's head was missing, that the brains and pieces of skull were stuck to the wall, noticing, too, that there was no mark on Kate and that her chest was heaving up and down. She was breathing.

Angela stepped over Kate and looked down at Birney. She had to make sure it was Birney. It was hard to tell. She recognized the suit, a black one with light, red stripes that she had often seen him wear, and the shoes, black loafers, were the ones he wore, and the face looked like it could be Birney, but it was distended and out of shape and the eyes, though his color, were lifeless. The sockets were black and the lip for some reason was pushed out and swollen.

Angie, satisfied that it was Birney, and guessing correctly that Kate had only fainted, planted her hand over her mouth and ran down the narrow corridor, out into the reception area and then down the hallway to her own office. She rushed into the reception area and into the little cubbyhole where Eric Barnston worked. She ran her finger down a list of telephone numbers pinned to the wall until she found the one for NBC Television's Washington bureau on Nebraska Avenue. She had no trouble reaching Francis. He took the call and told Angie to call the police.

Francis ran off to find Joe who had been taken to makeup. The makeup trailer was located in a wide passageway between two studios. It had three chairs, like barber chairs, along a wall of mirrors. The lights were bright and hot. Joe sat in the middle of the three chairs, feeling a bit uncomfortable as a woman painted his face with what looked like a fat paintbrush. He was being briefed by John Woodruff, a professor at Harvard University and one of Joe's academic advisers. Joe was about to be interviewed by David Brinkley for the nightly news and he wanted to be ready.

"Foreign entanglements, that sort of thing," Woodruff said waving his hands in the air. He was a very serious man whom Joe did not like one bit. He considered him ambitious and a touch ruthless, the sort of academic who latched on to someone like Joe in the hopes he could hitch a ride to the White House. Woodruff was determined to be another Henry Kissinger, the president's foreign policy adviser, although he would be willing to settle for secretary of state. "It depends on whether I get to pick the under secretaries," he once said at a cocktail party. It had been a bravura performance in gall and the story had quickly gotten back to Joe.

In the trailer he was giving Joe another foreign policy briefing. Joe had figured that he would be asked something about foreign policy, if only because domestic policy—especially the Anderson matter—was so obvious a choice. Woodruff, tall and nearly bald, though not yet forty years old, was pacing before the chair, talking to Joe by talking to his image in the mirror. Every time Woodruff turned around, the makeup lady would lean over Joe and dig her shoulder into him. Joe didn't notice at first and when he did he became momentarily annoyed, but then he realized that her actions were keyed to Woodruff, and he settled back to enjoy it. Woodruff turned and faced him.

"SALT," he said sternly. "SALT is an obvious question. Very easy to handle. There is not a single journalist in this city who is prepared to ask a follow-up question about SALT. The subject is beyond them. It is almost beyond members of Congress, too. If I were you, I would use the 'throw-weight' answer we worked up for *Meet the Press*. Do you remember it?"

Joe nodded. "Uh huh. The important thing is not parity in numbers of missiles, but parity in throw-weight. That it?"

"That's it," Woodruff said, turning around to pace the other way. Joe braced himself. The lady leaned over and pushed into him once more. He pushed back slightly with his chest. The lady walked around in front of him and studied his face carefully. She looked down at him and smiled and then took the brush and gave his nose two light whacks. "It keeps makeup interesting," she said with a smile.

"I'll bet it does," Joe said.

"What's that?" Woodruff asked, turning around.

"Nothing," said Joe. "I was just saying something to

273

this lady here." Just then Francis burst into the room. He was pale and upset.

"Senator, can I see you alone for a moment? It's important." Francis glanced at Woodruff and the makeup lady, signaling them to leave. Joe started to rise from the chair throwing off the apron that had been covering him.

"Stay," said the makeup lady. "It's time for a smoke anyway." She threw Francis a drop-dead look and walked out of the trailer. Woodruff, obviously upset at having been lumped into a category with the makeup woman, simply stared back at Francis and then at Joe for permission to stay. Joe was impressed by the look on Francis's face.

"Give us a minute, John. Okay?"

Woodruff nodded and moved slowly out of the trailer, purposely leaving the door open as he left. Francis shut it hard and then turned the lock for good measure. He turned to Joe.

"What's up?" Joe asked.

"Senator Birney's killed himself."

"Jesus."

"In his office," Francis said. "He shot himself."

"Oh, Christ."

"Angela said he blew part of his head off. There's blood and brains all over the walls of the office . . ." Francis suddenly raced for the sink in the back of the trailer. He leaned over and gagged, but nothing came. He turned around to face Joe.

"Sorry," he said. He went on with his report. "This is bad, very bad." He felt it coming again and turned back to the sink. Joe said nothing. He gripped the armrests of the chair really hard, watching his knuckles turn white. He tried to think of something to say to Francis—maybe something he could do. There was something he should do, wasn't there? He felt sad.

Someone knocked at the trailer door. Francis shrugged his shoulders, walked over to the door, peered through the glass at the top of the door, and said, "It's Alex." He turned the lock and opened the door. Alex Heller burst in, a look of panic on his face.

"You've heard?" he asked excitedly.

Joe nodded. "I just spoke to Angela," Alex said. "This is terrible. Jeez, what are we going to do? This is a terrible thing. A terrible thing."

Joe nodded agreement. He understood why they were giving him their condolence. Birney had taken him with him—two senators with one bullet, one physically, the other politically. He could hear the question being asked at the press conference: "Tell me, Senator, do you feel yourself responsible for the death of Senator Birney?" He shook his head as if to reject the idea, but the truth of the matter was that he did feel himself somewhat responsible—how responsible only he would ever know.

A head ducked into the trailer. "We're ready to go on, Senator," the head said.

"C'mon, Francis," Joe said. "Get your head out of the sink and let's go. We don't have much time." He got up from the chair and walked over to the door. He gripped the doorway to lean out of the trailer. "Be right out," he said to Woodruff. "Sorry about this."

"It's all right," Woodruff said. "Alex told me."

Joe looked startled. "Have you told anyone, John?" Woodruff shook his head no. "Good, we are not sure of some of the facts," Joe lied. "Be right with you."

He pushed against the doorway and brought himself back into the trailer. He closed the door and locked it, turning to Francis and Alex who were standing together.

"Angie say anything about a note?" Joe asked.

They both shook their heads no.

"She say anything about telling anyone but the police?"

"No," said Francis.

"You hear any commotion out there, Alex?" Joe asked, craning his head in the direction of the newsroom.

"Nothing."

"Okay, let's go," Joe said. He walked over to the door and stepped outside and down the two steps. He walked over to Woodruff and thanked him and then went over to the makeup lady and thanked her. A black man in running shoes was waiting for him and led him down a long corridor to an office near the newsroom. It was book-lined and had a typewriter prominently displayed. Joe was shown to a large leather wing chair and asked to sit. He did. The black man took a mike that had been snapped to the chair and clasped it to Joe's tie. He picked up a headset that had been lying on the desk and talked into it for a moment, and then he turned to Joe and asked him to say something.

"I am Senator Joseph Tynan, Democrat of New York," Joe said, knowing he was being asked to do a voice-level test.

"Fine," said the black man. He walked up to Joe and grabbed his lapels, straightening out the suit.

"Gotta look presidential, Senator," he cracked.

Another man with a headset walked into the office. He looked around, moved a pile of folders on the desk, and then turned his attention to Joe. He did not introduce himself either by name or title. He simply walked over to where Joe was sitting, yanked on the little mike to see that it was firmly attached, and then walked out. The black man smiled at Joe and then got some message on his headphone. He reached down to a switch on his belt, moved it forward, and said, "I'll tell him."

"We're all fouled up today, Senator," the man said. "Mr. Brinkley is still in makeup. Something's slowed us up. Don't know what. He'll be in soon and usually he does this and they asked me to do it. The first item on the show will be the Anderson thing and then they are going to cut right to you and Mr. Brinkley. You'll have either a minute thirty seconds or two minutes, depending. Mr. Brinkley will know and when he says, 'Thank you,' that's it. We are going to have to move. Remember, this is live."

Just then Brinkley walked quickly into the office. "Sorry to be so late," he said, sounding just as he did on television.

Joe started to rise but Brinkley motioned for him to keep his chair. "Good to be here, David," Joe said.

Brinkley nodded and checked his watch. "Did Fred fill you in?" he asked.

Joe nodded. He was becoming nervous.

Three men walked into the office. One of them got behind a television camera while another turned on the lights and started arranging them. The room became hot. The other man wore a headset with a switch on his belt.

"Thirty seconds, David," he said.

Brinkley shifted in his chair and looked directly into the camera. Joe, who was sitting off a bit to the side, tried looking into the camera also, but then noticed he would not have to do so. Another camera had been rolled into the doorway of the office.

"Twenty seconds," the man with the headphone said.

"We're either going to have a minute thirty or two minutes," Brinkley said. "Depending."

"Ten seconds."

Joe rubbed the palms of his hands on his lap to dry them. He licked around his lips and said, "Testing," and then looked at Brinkley.

"Five, four, three, two, one. You're on."

Brinkley looked up and into the camera.

"In the presidential sweepstakes, which seem to start earlier and earlier each year, the name of Joe Tynan has all of a sudden taken some sort of lead. In this town they say that if the President drops a bit more in the polls, he's going to be in trouble with his own party. And this man here is the one they say who could give the President a very hard time. Senator, what do you say to that?"

"David, I'll be glad to get into that, but if I may I'd like to get into something else first." He saw a look of surprise on the director's face and heard bells ringing in the newsroom. The bulletin of Birney's death was coming in on the wire-service machines.

"I just got word that the Senate has lost one of the

finest men it has ever known," Joe said. "Senator Birney is dead."

In the control room the director yelled, "Come in close." At the same time the producer, scanning the bulletins, decided to stay on Joe for the time being. While Joe talked, the anchorman, the new and very young Tom Jennings, wrote out his copy.

"You know a man is elected by his state and serves that state," Joe was saying. "But Senator Birney also served this whole country. In fact, he served humanity. Some people complained of his conservatism, but he had a workingman's understanding of the value of the dollar and a banker's knowledge of the economy."

Joe's voice cracked and his eyes welled. This pleased him. He had been worried that he would not be able to show emotion for Birney. He was showing it now. He was crying.

"Close in tighter," the director yelled. "Let me see his eyes."

"He was a man who gave life," Joe said, talking more slowly now. "He fed the hungry and he gave work to the jobless and he helped the sick. He and I differed many times, most recently over the Anderson appointment, but he was my mentor, my friend and now it is the nation's loss. We are all going to miss him." An image of Birney flashed into Joe's head. Joe hung his head.

In the control booth, the director yelled, "Hold it and fade on three. One . . . two . . . three . . ." The face of a crying Joseph Tynan dissolved from the screen and into a commercial for a laxative. In the office Brinkley stood and walked over to Joe. He extended his hand. "I'm sorry," he said. "I liked him, too." He turned and walked out. The man with the headset stepped forward. He nodded toward Joe in what amounted to a small bow and then the makeup lady came in. She walked up to Joe and stopped right before him.

"I'm sorry," she said, a tear running down her cheek. "I'm sorry."

One by one members of the crew came into the little office to shake hands with Joe. "A real eulogy," one of them said, and "very moving," another said and, then Francis came bounding into the room, his eyes wide with awe.

"That was the damnedest thing I ever saw," he said. He whistled, shaking his head from side to side, nearly beside himself with professional admiration. Only when he looked closely at Joe did he see that this was no act.

"I'm sorry," he said softly. "I'm really sorry. Sometimes I can't tell."

Joe looked at him. "It's all right, Francis. Sometimes I can't either." He rose. "Get the staff in early in the morning. We have lots to do."

"Senator," the young black man said, "it's your wife. The phone."

Joe looked around. He saw a phone on the desk, decided against it, and turned back to the young black man. "Is there another one?"

"This way," the black man said. Joe followed him out of the office and down a hallway and then into a little room with large audio equipment on three sides of the walls. "Take it there," the man said, pointing to a phone on the wall. One of the five buttons was blinking. Joe waited for the black man to leave the room, but he would not. Joe smiled at him and the man smiled back, apparently waiting for Joe to take his call so he could lead him back to the studio. Joe did nothing. The phone blinked.

"I'd like to be alone," Joe finally said.

The black man smiled broadly as if he had finally gotten the message. "Right," he said and walked out the door, closing it behind him. Joe reached for the phone.

"Ellie?" he said, punching the button. "Ellie? Did you see it?"

"I'm sorry, I couldn't," she said. She was speaking from the kitchen of their home. "We've got a problem here."

"Paulie's rabbit?"

"The rabbit died, Joe," she said, irritated. "It's Janet. She woke up with a fever of a hundred and four. She has the shakes and I'm worried about her."

"Did you call Sam?"

"He just left," she said. "He thinks she has viral hepatitis."

"What makes him so sure it's hepatitis?"

"Her skin is yellow," Ellie said, pausing before the bad news. "It seems she's had herself tatooed."

"What?"

"I didn't know about it either," Ellie said.

"What do you mean tatooed? I never saw a tatoo on her."

"It's on her behind."

Joe stopped, unsure of what to say next. The anger welled up within him. "Put her on the phone," he ordered.

"I can't," Ellie said. "She's sleeping."

"I want to talk to her," Joe insisted. "Put her on the phone."

"Joe, she's sleeping."

"What the hell is she doing with a tatoo on her behind?" he yelled.

"Relax," Ellie said.

"*Relax?*" he exclaimed. "What's she got it there for? Who's going to see it there?"

"That's what I've been wondering."

"I mean, for God's sake, what is it?" he asked. "Does it say something?" He had a sudden image of a cupid holding a clutch of arrows. It made him shudder.

"It's a flower," Ellie reported.

"Jesus, a flower. On her behind."

"Well, I just wanted you to know," Ellie said, in the manner of one who was just doing her duty.

"Birney's killed himself," Joe said.

Ellie gasped. "Joe, no."

"Yes."

"Oh, Joe. The poor man. What can we do?"

"Nothing, I guess. I don't know."

"The funeral?" Ellie said. "When's the funeral?"

"Ellie, he just died. He just died about a half hour ago. It may not even be on the news yet."

"I'll come down," Ellie said.

"No, you've got to take care of Janet. Look, I'll fly home tonight. I'll come home for the night and then come back here in the morning."

"No, stay there," Ellie said. "You have work to do."

Joe cast his eyes to the ceiling. "Christ," he muttered.

"Joe?" Ellie asked when she heard nothing.

282

"Everything's happening at once," he said. "Jeez, I don't know what to do. I'll have to see. I'll call you later, Ellie, okay?"

"Let me know and I'll have something for you to eat."

"Okay."

"Bye," Ellie said. She waited, but the other end of the phone simply went dead.

Joe walked out of the little room and tried to orient himself. He followed the corridor back to the office where everyone was waiting.

"Everything all right at home?" Francis asked.

Joe hesitated, not wanting to go into any explanations. He decided to lie. "Fine," he said. "A little family problem. My son's rabbit died."

"Well, that's better than if your daughter's rabbit died," Francis cracked. Everyone laughed and after a moment Joe did, too.

Francis was ebullient. He was feeling terrific, feeling that he, and of course his boss, was on the verge of great things. He was feeling so good he had not noticed that his boss, Joseph Tynan, was feeling absolutely miserable, depressed, and lost in thought. They were sitting together in a cocktail lounge of the Mayflower Hotel where they had stopped for a drink after leaving the NBC studios. Joe had downed a double Scotch right off the bat and was nursing another one. He was two Scotches over his self-imposed limit.

"It's been incredible," Francis chirped. "I mean, it's just been incredible." He knocked on the table. "Knock on wood. Incredible. We weren't off the air twenty minutes when we got that call from the White House. Not very suave of them. Bush. Very bush. Shows they're anxious, right?"

"Yeah," said Joe, showing minimal interest.

Francis was puzzled. He studied his boss in the shadowy darkness of the cocktail lounge, moving the little light in the middle of the table so he could see Joe's face better. Joe grimaced and Francis returned the light to the middle of the table.

"They want your help," he went on. "You're hot." He waited for a reaction. Nothing. Joe looked at him as if he had said absolutely nothing. "They need you," he continued. "You had the country in the palm of your hands tonight. That was the most fantastic performance I've ever seen. I mean, the guys in the studio could not believe it. You heard what they said." He waited. Joe didn't react. Francis leaned in to get a closer look at Joe.

"Senator," he said deliberately and slowly, "we're on the eve of a great moment in your life . . ."

Joe looked up. "Jesus, Francis, the guy is dead."

Francis gulped. "I'm sorry," he said. "I know you had a very good relationship." He hoped it was the right thing to say. There was not much he was sure of anymore.

"He humiliated himself and I just stayed there and watched him," Joe said.

"Well, what could you have done, really?"

Joe fixed him with his eyes. "I could have stopped him. I'd done it before and I could have done it then."

"I know how you feel, Senator, he was a very fine man."

"Francis, you're just saying that, but he was. He

284

was. He was like . . . He was like a father to me. He really was."

"I know," Francis said. "He was a wonderful man. I'll draft a statement. Something about how close you two were. We'll put something on tape, also. Maybe we should close the office for a day. We'll have to come up with something special."

"Francis, shut up, will you," Joe said. He stood and reached into his pocket for some money. Francis felt as if he had been kicked in the stomach by a mule.

"I'll pick you up in the morning," Francis offered.

"No. *Home*," Joe insisted. "I'm going home. Where my house is and my wife and my children. *Home*."

"Oh. All right. I'll have someone pick you up at the airport," Francis said. "I'll call you if something comes up. Can I drive you to the airport? Are you going now?"

Joe nodded. He threw some money on the table. "Good night, Francis," he said.

He grabbed a cab at the door. On the way to the airport they passed a tatoo parlor on 14th Street, N.W. Joe saw it and slunk down low in the seat. For the first time in a very long time he felt that events were out of control.

The cab took the scenic route. It went first down Connecticut Avenue to K Street and then over K to 14th Street where the porno parlors and strip joints are located and where the hookers patrol in the night. Washington is maybe the most open town in America, a city of brazen prostitution, and when the car stopped for a light, Joe watched with growing amazement as the girls strutted on the sidewalk, sometimes dancing over to the curb to have some words with a face in a stopped car. His cab, he noticed, was not moving in the late-night traffic of Washington's red light district.

"Can ya believe it?" the cabdriver said without turning around. "It's nighttime and the traffic isn't moving. The whores are taking over this city. I'll tell you, I wouldn't live here anymore. Moved to Maryland years ago. This place isn't worth a damn anymore. Nothing but whores and niggers."

"Shut up, will you," Joe said softly.

"What was that, mister?" the driver asked.

"Shut the hell up!" Joe yelled.

"Very touchy tonight, aren't we?" the driver said.

Joe looked out the window to the street. He saw two theaters and maybe half a dozen arcades showing nothing but pornographic films. He had never been to one—never. He thought of the time when *Deep Throat* was first released and it was the rage of dinner party conversations, but Joe had never seen it. He wanted to see it—he was curious. But he could not risk it. He could not risk being caught watching a porno film. He envisioned sitting down in some theater and having the guy next to him turn to him and say, "Hi, Senator, I didn't know you liked porno films."

He had a dream about it once. He dreamed he went to a porno film, although in his dream he never saw the movie. He was in the theater, a not very dark place, lit with lots of little red light bulbs, the people turning around from time to time, staring at him. In the dream he got up and left, and when he came outside, he walked right into the glare of television lights, reporters on the street waiting for him, their pads and pencils at the ready. He heard the whirl of the cameras as he approached the sidewalk.

"Tell me, Senator," one of the reporters asked, "was it a good film?"

"I don't know," he said. "I never looked at the screen."

"You never looked at the screen?"

"No, I wouldn't do something like that. Look at the screen."

He could remember no more of the dream and when he told it to Ellie, told it sort of as a joke one night when they were undressing for bed, she said she would think about it and bounce it off the Great Asher. She said nothing about it after that, but one night Joe brought it up and asked her what the Great Asher had said.

"He said you want to have an affair but are afraid to," she said.

"He said that?"

"That's what he said."

"That's ridiculous," Joe said.

"If that's what you say," she said.

"That Asher," Joe said. "The Great Asher. What else did he say?"

"He told me not to bring up the subject unless you did, and he told me that when I did you would say it was ridiculous."

"Well, it is ridiculous."

She reached her hand across the table and touched his. "Of course, it is," she said. "Of course it is."

The cab took off with a lurch. They crossed Pennsylvania Avenue. To the left the dome of the Capitol shone at them with reflected light. They drove down to the Mall area, where they could see the Jefferson Memorial and the Washington Monument, and then they crossed the river, turning right at the end of the bridge for the George Washington Memorial Parkway and the short, quick run to National Airport. Joe sprinted for the New York shuttle, getting the eight o'clock—the last one. He was at LaGuardia by nine and home by nine forty-five and knocking on Janet's bedroom door not too long after that. She was on the phone, curled up in bed, a rock record playing on a nearby phonograph.

"Hi, got a minute?" Joe asked.

Janet looked at her father. He was sort of hanging in the doorway, a growth of beard on his face. He looked awful. She turned her face into the phone and said, "One second."

"Hi," she said, turning back to Joe. "What's up?"

"I just came up to see how you're doing," he said. "Can you talk for a minute?"

She turned back into the phone. "I'll call you back." She paused for the response. "A few minutes." She hung up the phone. Joe sat on the edge of the bed. He touched the back of his hand to her forehead.

"Your fever's down."

"I'm bored to death lying here." She let a book that had been on her lap slip to the floor.

"If you want to get well, you have to rest." It was a line he once vowed he would never use on his children.

Janet rolled her eyes. "No kidding," she said.

He let it pass. "Can I ask you something?" he said. "Why did you get a tattoo?"

"No, you can't ask me."

288

"Oh."

She noticed the flowers. "What's that?" she asked.

Joe looked down at the flowers in his hand as if he couldn't figure out how they had gotten there. "I brought you some daisies from the garden," he said.

"Oh yeah?" she said, brightening.

Joe walked over to the bed table and plunked the flowers in a water glass.

"Thanks," she said. "They're nice."

Joe returned to the bed. "You know, I think we should know more about what's going on in each other's lives."

"Like what?"

"Well, you're seeing a boy and I don't really know him."

"You don't know him at all." The voice had shifted into smart-ass.

"So I'd like to meet him sometime," Joe said, determined not to lose his cool.

"Why?"

"Because you're my daughter."

"Look, will you just leave me alone?"

"No, I'm not going to leave you alone. Goddamnit, I love you." His voice was rising.

"Don't you think I'm old enough to make my own friends?"

"Of course you are," Joe said. "I just want to meet them."

"Why?"

"So I can know what you're going through."

"What for?"

"Because I love you," he shouted.

"Dad, I'm sick," Janet said, plaintively.

"All right, I'm sorry I raised my voice."

"And every time you tell me you love me you say goddamnit."

"I don't understand what went through your head," he said, lowering his voice. "You must have known that a tattoo doesn't come off."

"I don't want it to come off."

"How're you going to explain that later—in the future?"

"I don't have to explain my goddamn ass to anybody," she said. He winced. She had said goddamned with his exact inflection.

"All right, calm down," he said.

"It's my ass, isn't it?"

That blew it. "No, goddamnit, as long as your ass is in this house, your mother and I have to watch out for it," he yelled.

She recoiled from the force of his voice. "Will you leave me alone?" she pleaded. "Will you just leave me alone?"

"I'm not going to leave you until I get a response from you," Joe said sternly.

She reached for the water glass with the flowers and hurled it against the door. It hit hard, the water and the flowers spilling out onto the rug. The glass did not break, but the back of the door was streaked with water. A yellow petal clung to the door.

"That wasn't exactly what I had in mind," Joe said.

"Get out!" she yelled.

Joe left the room, closing the door behind him. He started to walk down the hall, but instead just sat down in the hallway right outside Janet's door. A minute or two went by.

"Janet?" Joe called after a while.

"What?" she answered.

"Don't you understand that I love you, that I just want to be closer to you?" He waited for an answer. There was none.

"Don't you understand that?" he asked, trying again.

"No," she said.

"Why?"

"Well, you're not here that much, are you?" The words tumbled out quickly. She was immediately sorry for them. It was the ultimate cheap shot. She knew that. She also knew she meant it. It was true and not true—true that he was not around much, but also true that the parents who were around a lot were not much closer to their daughters. She waited for Joe to say something, but he remained silent. She slipped out of her bed and went and sat on her side of the door.

"Janet, open the door," he asked.

"No."

"I just want to put my arms around you and then I'll go."

"Some other time, okay?" She found it hard to drop her pose.

"Just for a second, please." He sounded wounded.

Janet reached up to the knob and opened the door. Joe saw it open and started to get up, but then he saw that his daughter, like him, had been sitting on the floor. He reached over to her and held her tight, and for a moment she responded, hugging back as she used to. Suddenly, she stiffened self-protectively and pulled away. Joe knew the moment had passed.

Joe padded down the hallway and into his own bedroom. Ellie was in bed, reading a book. She put it on the night table. Joe staggered over to the bed and collapsed on it, face down.

"What happened?" Ellie asked him.

"How did I lose her?" he mumbled into the sheets.

"You didn't. She adores you."

"She says I'm never here," he said, rolling over on his back and facing Ellie.

"Look, it's not as if you worked nine to five in an office. You're pulled in ten directions at once. Think of the good you're doing." They had had this conversation before. Ellie had said her lines just perfectly. Joe reached for her hand. She gave it to him.

"What good is it if my own kid doesn't know I love her?"

"Why don't you take her away the weekend after next? Just the two of you. Take her up to the barn."

Joe let out a deep breath. "I have to do a fund raiser at the Waldorf."

"Suppose you were sick?"

Joe looked at her as if she had just said something terribly original—the notion that he could skip something important for something even more important. The phone rang, saving him from an immediate answer. He answered it.

"Hello? Yeah, Francis," he said. "No, everything's fine. I'll be back tomorrow. That's right." There was a pause. "That can wait. Listen, let's cancel me out of the fund raiser." Another pause. He looked at Ellie in triumph. She smiled.

His face dropped. "Well, why not?" he said. "Francis, who do I represent, the White House or the people of the State of New York?" Another pause. "Why?"

Joe asked. He was sounding very annoyed. "What's he offering? Yeah?" Joe sounded interested. "Is that definite? I'll call you back." He hung up the phone and bounded from the bed.

"What *are* they offering you?" Ellie asked.

Joe stopped his pacing. "Well, there's a lot of bullshit going back and forth, but it boils down to this: if I do a selling job on the New York committee next week, I can give the nominating speech at the convention."

"What about Janet?"

Joe spun around, his face suddenly red. "Jesus, Ellie, come on," he yelled. He said, "What do you want me to do?"

"Nothing, Joe," she said. "I want you to do what you want."

He lay down on the bed again, staring up at the ceiling.

"Pardew is quitting the Senate," he said. "Did you know that?"

"No. Why is he quitting?"

"I don't know. To save his soul, I guess."

"You think you're losing yours?"

He continued to look at the ceiling.

"Just a little." He said it softly, as if he wanted no one to hear him.

She wore her hair up that night, fluffy in the back, and little ringlets came down like sideburns. She wore a new dress, too, high around the neck so it would not offend. Around her neck she wore a gold necklace. She looked, as he moved along the dais to the lectern, beautiful yet fragile. Joe watched her admiringly. It was a tradition at these things, he had told her, for the wife to say a few words about her husband. She had done it before, he reminded her, and eventually she had relented. Now she was looking out at about fifteen hundred people gathered for the cause of the New York State Democratic Committee in the main ballroom of the Waldorf-Astoria. The men were in dinner jackets and the women were in chiffon and silk and Ellie, poor Ellie, was in a terrible fright.

"I guess," she said with a weak voice and she stopped, waiting for the audience to quiet down. She waited. After a while the audience noticed that she was waiting. "Shut up, for crying out loud," someone yelled. In a moment there was silence.

"I guess what makes my husband special is how much he cares," she began. "Not just about the people who can afford a hundred-dollar plate but about the ones who can't afford to eat. I'm very proud of being Mrs. Joe Tynan. Thank you for honoring us tonight." She smiled and acknowledged the applause, waved, and moved back across the dais on somewhat wobbly knees to rejoin Joe.

"Ellie, thank you," he said. "You were terrific."

A man neither one of them knew came over. "Ellie, you're just wonderful." He looked at Joe. "Now I know how you got elected." The man turned and left, and Joe and Ellie shrugged their shoulders at each other and laughed.

The band struck up the usual Democratic party melody of "East-Side, West-Side" and then "Happy Days Are Here Again." It brought even more applause. Joe felt a tap on his shoulder. A man in his sixties, his head bald back to the middle of his skull, stood behind him. He seemed friendly.

"Senator, I just wanted to pay my respects," the man said, extending his hand. Joe took it. "Dick Harman. I'm chairman of the Louisiana committee." He turned to Ellie and shook her hand, too. "That was a delightful speech, Mrs. Tynan."

"Well, this is a pleasure," Joe said, coming to his feet. "You've been a tremendous help."

"I think you know my daughter," he said looking at someone over Joe's shoulder.

Joe spun around. It was Karen. "Oh, yes, hello," he said, stunned. He knew immediately that he had not handled himself well. Karen smiled. Joe turned to Ellie. She had noticed.

"Ellie, this is Karen Traynor. She gave us enormous help on the Anderson nomination." He turned back to Karen. "It was wonderful. It was really very helpful." Joe looked for Harman to bail him out, but he had moved off and was now talking with someone else. He was caught, as Hugh Kittner always said, between a rock and a hard place.

"It was really a wonderful job you did," Joe said to Karen. He turned back to Ellie. "She . . . uh . . . Miss Traynor is a lawyer. Is it *Miss* Traynor or *Mrs.* Traynor?" he asked. Jesus, he thought, this is amateur night.

"Mrs.," Karen said flatly, not helping him in the least way.

"Right. And she gave us this very strong stuff about Anderson that really . . . well, turned the whole thing around."

Ellie nodded. She did not seem at all impressed. For a moment no one said anything. The silence was ugly.

"May I have your attention," a voice boomed out over the public address system. It was Ken Arjunian, the chairman of the New York committee, an Italian-looking man actually of Armenian descent who resembled an aging movie actor with his black dinner jacket, dark hair, and snowy white sideburns.

"We better get back to our table," Karen said at last. "Very nice to meet you, Mrs. Tynan, Senator . . ."

"Good to see you, Senator," Harman said in a hearty fashion. He gave Joe a small, friendly push from behind. "Keep punching."

"Right," Joe said, throwing a small right cross.

"Please?" Arjunian said, pleading for quiet. "Ladies and gentlemen, I now have the honor that comes too seldom in politics. A chance to introduce a man who deserves all the good words you can find for him." He turned to Joe and smiled his best headwaiter smile. Joe gave it back in spades and turned to Ellie.

"Remember six years ago when this guy tried to have me thrown out of the Senate?"

Ellie said nothing.

"A man who has fought hard to preserve our democratic institutions because he's a man who puts people first. Senator Joe Tynan."

The audience sprung to its feet. The band struck "Happy Days Are Here Again" and Arjunian pointed to Joe with a wave. Joe sat, looking out at the audience with unfocused eyes. He couldn't believe that business with Karen and Ellie. It was like a movie. He focused his eyes and looked at Ellie. She snapped her head away. She knows, Joe thought. Jesus Christ, *she knows.* He rose and walked to the microphone, pulling index cards out of his jacket pocket. He got to the lectern and smiled. He waved. He looked out at the audience. She knows, he thought. He waved some more. She'll leave me. Another wave and a big smile. Maybe she won't leave me. A flashbulb popped off in his face; little white circles appeared before his eyes, rotating counterclockwise. She knows.

They said it was a good speech. They came up to him afterward and they told him he had been terrific. First-rate. Stupendous. "The best speech since Kennedy," one of them said. "John?" Joe had asked. "Teddy," they had said. "Teddy, is the one who makes the best speeches." Joe thought maybe the guy was right.

They came at him in little knots. They shook hands and they had names and Francis took down some of the names. Francis stood to his side, somewhere behind his right ear, and whispered names to him and occupations and sometimes something about the last time they had met. Francis did not know them all, but he knew most of them—remembered them because they were important to Joe and that was important to Francis. In his notebook he took down their complaints and their requests—a job, a congratulatory letter to the Bar Mitzvah boy ("Dear Robby, . . ." the form was in the office).

Ellie waited off to the side, the toe of one foot pointed in the air, the foot resting on the sharp, high heel. Joe signaled her from behind his back: one minute. It meant nothing, Ellie knew. Joe whispered something to Francis and Francis joined Ellie. He held Joe's coat. Nearby the musicians were packing up.

"He'll be just another minute," Francis said.

"We started leaving twenty-five minutes ago."

"It's great, though, isn't it?" Francis said.

"Holding his coat?" Ellie said, nastily. It went right by Francis.

"How things are moving. He can go all the way now."

"All the way where?"

"Well, we're giving him a more national image," Francis confided. "We have a new press aide, an adviser on international affairs. We're really moving."

Ellie raised her eyebrows as if impressed. "Is that so?"

Francis attempted a laugh. "Listen, we have to have a little talk." He sat at an empty table, pushing away the empty coffee cups and the dirty dishes. Ellie took a seat.

"We're starting to play for really big stakes now, and we have to watch what kind of face we present to the media," he said. "I got hold of that *McCall's* interview you gave. I was really floored. I mean, she had you in *analysis*." He said the word as if it was "syphilis."

"What's wrong with that?" Ellie asked, annoyed.

"Well, analysis is usually a code word—it means you've got a drinking problem. Or worse. Now that was our fault, really. From now on you won't do an interview unless there's someone from our office sitting right there with you. I mean, we can't just throw you to the wolves like that."

Ellie stood and took Joe's coat from Francis. She

draped it over the back of the chair. It was a meaningless gesture, but she was stalling for time, waiting until her anger subsided. Francis went on, oblivious to the effect his words were having.

"Look, don't worry. I fixed it. All the article says now is that you have an interest in psychology. That's ambiguous. I told them they misunderstood what you had said. Interest in psychology? It could mean anything. We would have been lost if she used a tape recorder."

Ellie started to march to the door. Francis could see that she was steamed. He ran after her, grabbing Joe's coat as he passed the chair.

"Look, I know you're not crazy about this," he said, walking beside her. She accelerated her pace. "Don't you think we should discuss it?" She stopped in her tracks.

"Francis," she said, spitting his name out, "there's only one thing I have to say to you and I'm afraid it's not ambiguous enough." She turned and marched away. Francis watched her go. He was holding Joe's coat.

In the night, a New York City cab felt its way across the strange terrain of Cedarhurst. A man inside pointed and the cab stopped in front of a certain house and Joseph Tynan, senator of the Empire State, got out, paid the driver, and marched up the walk to his house. He was pissed.

He put his key into the lock and shoved the door open, letting it bang against the wall. He made no move to close it. He tossed his coat on the banister and bounded up the stairs, taking them two at a time. His face was set in anger. He went directly to his bedroom and threw on the light. Ellie turned over and looked at him, not knowing what to expect. He did not notice that her eyes were red.

"What the hell is the idea of leaving me thirty miles from home without a car?" he yelled.

"Drop dead!" she yelled back.

Joe was startled. After all, *he* was the injured party. He dropped his voice. "Do you want to explain that behavior?" he asked.

"How about your behavior? You want to explain that?"

"What behavior?" he asked, fearing the worst.

"How do you do it? How does a man who's decent and loves humanity, the champion of the oppressed, who speaks out for the underdog, how do you manage to act like such a total shit?"

"I don't recall ever leaving you in the street at one o'clock in the morning."

"No, you never kept me waiting," she said, her voice dripping sarcasm. "When were you planning to tell me you were running for president? At the inaugural ball?"

Francis! Joe thought immediately. "Jesus Christ, grow up," he yelled, relieved it wasn't what he feared. "You hear one—"

"No, I'm not going to grow up," Ellie yelled back, throwing the covers off and climbing out of bed.

"Listen to me," Joe said. "You heard one sentence from an administrative assistant who's got stars in his eyes and you walk out and leave me in the—"

"Don't you understand?" Ellie cut in. "I never wanted to get in the way of your career."

300

"Not much, you didn't . . ."

"No, I didn't. I just wanted you to tell me what's going on. To include me in your *life*. I wanted *you*, that's all."

"I've discussed everything with you."

"Did you tell her?" Ellie's eyes were blazing.

"Did I tell who?" Joe said. She *did* know. "Which her?"

"Her, goddamnit. Did you tell her?"

"What her? Who?"

"That lawyer you're screwing, you son of a bitch." She grabbed the clock radio from the night table and hurled it against the wall. It hit hard with the sound of breaking plastic, and when it hit the floor, what looked like a fatal crack appeared on the top. Joe was stunned.

"Jesus Christ, you broke it," he said, picking it up.

"You told her, but you wouldn't tell me." Ellie reached for the night table lamp. She hurled it at Joe. The lamp caught him on the shoulder. He said nothing. He was taking his punishment. He had been wrong and he would take his punishment. This was better than divorce, he reasoned. He looked down at the clock in his hands as if it was a wounded bird.

"How the hell am I gonna get up tomorrow?" he said. "I gotta be in Washington at nine o'clock."

"Why don't you go there and why don't you stay there!" She reached for his suitcase, taking it by the handle and bringing it back for a throw. Joe grabbed her by the wrist.

"Will you cut it out?" he said. "Stop it."

She struggled free of his grasp and moved quickly to the table near the door where some of Joe's papers and his briefcase were kept. She took the papers and the briefcase, gathered them up in her arms, and ran to the door.

"And take this crap with you," she yelled. "Get it out of my bedroom."

Joe went to stop her, but she brushed past him. Her eyes were red and her cheeks were puffed. She glared hatred at him and then tossed the briefcase and the papers down the stairs.

"Goddamnit, cut it out," Joe ordered.

The door to Paul's room opened and Paul stepped out into the hallway, rubbing sleep from his eyes. The boy looked frightened.

"What's the matter?" he asked timorously, in a voice full of sleep.

Joe lowered his voice. "Go back to bed, Paul. It's all right. Close your door."

The boy stepped back into his room, but kept his door open a bit. Joe bounded down the stairs. Ellie stood in the stairwell, grabbing at the papers she had thrown, ripping them into pieces. Joe, in his tuxedo, grabbed Ellie. She tried to scratch him, but he bundled her arms into him. She shook with rage and snapped her knee up. He arched away from her and then both of them went down on the steps, frozen for a panicky second in which they both seemed to realize what was going to happen next, and rolled down the stairs. They went one over the other, hitting the steps hard, his tuxedo over her nightgown and then her nightgown over his tuxedo. Joe pinned her to the bottom step. He gritted his teeth.

"I live by the skin of my teeth down there," he said.

"All I get from you is *venom* and *anger* and *contempt*."

Ellie took the last word and hurled it back at him. "Contempt!"

She pushed off him and got to her feet. "You don't have contempt for the nineteen years we put into this life together?"

Joe fastened her with his best television-interview sincerity. "I swear to you I am not having an affair with a woman from New Orleans or anybody else."

Ellie answered with an antique washbasin. She hurled it against the wall.

"You crazy lunatic!" he yelled.

Joe moved in on her in a menacing fashion. Frightened, she ran into the living room. "You want to wreck this whole house?" he yelled.

"Don't tell me you care a bit about this house or anybody in it," she screamed. "All you want is somebody sitting here, looking nice when the magazines come around." She grabbed the small early-American rocking chair, brought it up to her chest, and heaved it into the fireplace with a grunt.

"Don't give me that shit," Joe yelled. He ripped a shutter from the window. The screws stuck out of it.

"I put these shutters up with my own hands. I made this place with you. And you know it, goddamnit." He yanked another shutter and it gave way. He tossed it on the floor as if it were a statement of some sort. He looked at it with satisfaction and then his eyes fastened on the piano. "I fixed that piano myself," he screamed.

Ellie rushed over to the keyboard side of the piano and pushed hard against it, trying to roll it at him.

"Here, take it. It's yours," she yelled, but the thing wouldn't move. She gave a final furious push and the front leg buckled, collapsing inward, the piano settling on it, emitting a sound like a wounded harp. Ellie looked down in amazement. Then she started to throw the piano music at Joe. The Beethoven sonatas that Janet had been butchering for years went sailing by his ear. He went quickly for her but the music kept coming at him. He put his arm in front of his face and rushed her. Tackling her around the waist, she went down, he on top. He tried to pin her arms, but she freed one and swept a lower shelf with it. Porcelain objects fell to the floor, splattering like eggshells. Finally he had her. He held her tight until he felt her body relax and then slowly, testing, he relaxed his grip and he let her go. She got up and took in the destruction. The sound of a person startled them and they turned. Janet stood in the doorway. She was dressed in pajamas and bathrobe. Her hands rested on her hips.

"I just want you to know that Paulie is up there crying," she said.

"I'm sorry," Ellie said. "We were fighting."

"No kidding," Janet said. She started to leave but turned back for a second. "Why don't you act like adults?"

"I'll be right up," Ellie called after her.

Joe looked around the room and then at Ellie. "What happened?" he asked.

"That's a question I ask myself everyday."

Later they had coffee. They went into the kitchen and sat around the table. Ellie made the coffee. Joe, exhausted, sat silent in his tuxedo. They made no attempt to clean up the mess in the living room. There was no sense hiding it from the children now. While the coffee was working, Ellie went upstairs to soothe Paul and to say something to Janet and then she came down again. She had brushed her hair and straightened her face and she looked a bit better, but suddenly older.

"I feel like such a fool," she said to Joe as they sat at the table. "Making that speech about you while she watched. I was even talking the kids into moving. Why? So you and she could have more time together?"

Joe said nothing. This was not supposed to happen. This thing between he and Karen was never supposed to involve Ellie. It was supposed to have nothing to do with her, and even if she found out she would somehow understand. He would say it was just sex or something and she would understand. It had nothing to do with her. It had to do with Karen and Joe and maybe Washington, but not Ellie.

"I hated you tonight," she continued. Her voice was low and husky from crying and lack of sleep. "To think that you would let that woman into our life. It feels like someone has broken into my house and gone through all my private things, that this stranger knows everything about me—all my habits, my weaknesses, even what I am like in bed." Her eyes welled again and her voice cracked. Joe felt her pain. He wanted to hold her and tell her it would be all right, but he didn't know if she would allow herself to be held, and he didn't know anymore if everything would be all right.

"How much does she mean to you?" Ellie asked.

Joe looked down. "I really don't know."

Ellie looked away, biting down on her lip. She nodded her head, as if she understood.

"But I know how much *you* mean to me," he said, regretting he had tried to be cute in answering her question.

"Really?" Ellie asked, not believing him.

"Ellie, everything I care about in my life we've made together. You think anything could ever mean more to me than you?"

"Not until tonight."

"Look, I've been cruel to you, but it doesn't have to happen again. It won't."

"Okay," she said without conviction. "Good."

"Ellie, what can I say? What can I do?"

"Nothing, Joe. I don't expect anything of you."

Joe looked hurt. Ellie took in his pained expression. She shook her head. "I'm sorry. I don't."

"You really don't have any reason to, but please forgive me. Please give me a chance. Will you?"

She had no response.

"I wish I knew what to do," he said, looking to her for a hint.

"All I ever wanted was for you to love me," she said, starting to cry again. "That's all."

"Ellie, I do," he said. "I love you."

Joe had a worried expression on his face. It was the expression of a child about to pull a prank, a silly expression—half whimsy, half evil. He was dressed in khaki pants, plaid shirt, and hiking boots. He was standing in a phone booth.

"Karen? Can you talk? I can't get away. I'm in a meeting with the mayor. We're going to go over the city budget. Listen, I'll call Wednesday, okay?" A horn sounded as a car pulled into the gas station looking for service. Joe hurriedly covered the mouthpiece. They talked a few seconds more and then Joe hung up. He walked out to his car. It was parked on the side away from the gas pumps, on Sunrise Highway in Suffolk County. They were heading east. Joe, the children, and Ellie. The car was loaded with luggage and fishing gear and with the awful butterfly-catching kit that Paul had received as a gift from an uncle. Joe dreaded a catch. He would probably have to mount the butterfly.

"I called the office," Joe said to Ellie as he got back behind the wheel. "No problem. They're not expecting me until Wednesday."

"Good," she said. "Thanks."

Joe moved out into the line of traffic. He grabbed her hand and held it on the seat next to him. He squeezed it. It lay lifeless in his grip.

Francis O'Connor, dapper as usual in his three-piece suit, slapped the hotel key in his jacket pocket and walked into Joe's Senate office. Joe was standing at the window, his back to Francis, reading a memo and looking out absentmindedly at the view.

"Senator?" Francis said.

Joe turned around.

"Four oh two at the Hilton," Francis said, slipping Joe the key with an unsaid wink in his voice.

"Washington Hilton?"

"Capitol Hilton."

"Jesus Christ, Francis. That's right across the street from *The Washington Post*." Francis started to say something. "Never mind," Joe said. "It doesn't matter anyway," he said, waving Francis out of the room. Joe read the phone number off the key and dialed it.

"Four oh two, please," he said.

In the hotel room the phone rang. It was perched on top of a night table parked between two single beds. Karen had said something to the bellhop about the bed, saying she preferred a double—"I sleep better in a double"—but the bellhop had said the hotel was full and they couldn't give a double bed to a single person. Couples had to have priority, he said. He said Karen would understand. She said she did. She wondered if it would matter anyway.

The ringing phone summoned her from the bathroom where she had been setting her face in order and brushing her hair. She rushed out and picked it up.

"Hello?"

"Hi, it's me."

"Hi," she said, brightening. "Guess who can stay the whole weekend?" Her heart seemed to pause. She sensed something.

"God, I can't," Joe said. "I have to go home. My daughter's come down with hepatitis."

Joe waited for a response, but Karen said nothing— not even that she was sorry about Janet's sickness.

"Karen?" he said, his voice searching for her.

"Look, I think you ought to be with your wife," she said. "You don't have to make up stories."

"I'm not. My daughter's got hepatitis."

"She had hepatitis four weeks ago. How long does that last?"

"Well, she's not really over it. I'm not making up stories."

"How'd your meeting with the mayor go?"

"Good," said Joe, relieved that the subject had changed. "I like him."

"He does a good imitation of a car horn."

Joe made a face.

"Joe, I've seen this before. You're falling in love with your wife."

"Karen, listen, I need to talk to you. I'll be right over."

"Maybe you'd better not, Joe."

"Look, I have to see you. I'll be right there." He waited for her to say something.

"Hello?" he asked.

"Joe, I'm sorry," she said. "I have to go." She hung up the phone and gulped a deep breath. Then she went into the bathroom and cried.

Joe heard the phone click and bounded from the office. "Four oh two," he yelled to Francis and went out the door without waiting for a response. He grabbed a cab in front of the Dirksen Building and reached the Capitol Hilton in about ten minutes. He was out of the cab even before it came to a complete stop, throwing his fare on the front seat. He pushed through the revolving door and ran into the lobby, stopping to orient himself and look for the elevators.

In a moment he was on the fourth floor, reading the signs to find the way to 402. He bolted down the hall and knocked hard on the door. It was opened by a man in his forties, dressed only in pants and a T-shirt. Joe looked past him and saw a suitcase open on the bed, the man's shirt slung over the back of the chair. The man gave Joe a quizzical look and then his face brightened with recognition.

"Oh, hi," he said.

"Is this 402?" Joe asked.

"Sure is. Hey, I just saw you on Mike Douglas. Nice to see you."

Joe ignored the man and sprinted back down the hall to the elevators. He pushed the button and waited. The man from 402 followed.

"Senator, you look much better on television." He gave Joe a look up and down. "Slimmer."

Joe hit the button again.

"How is Mike? He a nice guy?"

The elevator arrived and Joe stepped inside, relieved. He pushed the lobby button, but the man from 402 held his finger on the elevator call button. The door stayed open. The man reached into his pocket and fished out a piece of paper and a small ball-point pen of the kind that come with fancy address books.

"I hate to bother you, but my kids would never forgive me," he said, handing the paper and the pen to Joe. The man smiled, but his finger held the button. Joe scribbled his name on the paper and handed everything back to the man. He shoved the pen and paper into his pocket. His finger still held the button.

"Tell me, Senator—Dinah Shore—does she wear a wig?"

"Listen, I hate to be rude, but if you don't take your finger off that button, I'm going to throw you right on your ass."

The guy withdrew his finger as if the button had suddenly turned hot. The doors started to close and from inside Joe could see the man, a horrified expression on his face.

"Jesus, pardon *me*," the guy said.

In the lobby Joe made for the desk and asked the clerk about Karen.

"Miss Traynor checked out a few minutes ago, Senator," the clerk said.

"Can I use your phone?"

The clerk nodded and reached under the counter for the phone. It was one of those models where the push buttons are built into the receiver. Joe pushed the numbers for his office.

"Francis? Have Delta hold the next flight for New Orleans." He handed the phone back to the clerk. "Airline guide?" The clerk found him one, handing the large book over the counter to him. Joe thumbed through it. "Damn," he muttered. "Dulles."

His cab made good time. It raced through the traffic of downtown Washington and then out the parkways and highways on the forty-five-minute run to the Virginia countryside where Dulles International Airport is located. Joe kept looking at his watch, anxious now about having the flight held, hoping that it would be no more than five minutes late, hoping that he would attract little attention by holding the flight or by seeing Karen in so public a place, yet knowing that this was what he wanted to do.

At Dulles Joe started to run again. He jogged down the ramp, at the gate and he realized as he ran that everyone was watching him. The word was out. A senator had held the flight. Karen moved toward him, slowly, tentatively, looking beautiful to Joe—her hair down, wearing a blue suit, that wonderful combination of sexpot and business woman that he found so attractive.

"I hear you got them to hold my plane," she said.

"You left without saying good-bye."

"I guess I thought I'd be the one to leave. While there was still time."

"I have to go home," he said very softly. "I have to."

"I know."

"I've been ditching them in little ways and I can't anymore. It's too . . ." He looked around at the people watching the two of them. "Look, I have a whole speech prepared for this, but I can't say it in an airport."

"That's okay," she said, her voice beginning to break. "I've heard it before."

"I wish I could touch you."

"Actually, I do, too."

"Why couldn't this have been back at the hotel?"

"So we couldn't touch."

"Listen," Joe said, but he said nothing. He started again. "Listen, I'm going to lie about this later even to myself, but I think I'll always love you."

Karen flushed. She looked at him and then she looked down, and when she looked up again, her eyes had brimmed. The two of them looked at each other for a long moment, both of them wanting to move in for a hug, for a last clinch, for the touch of each other once again. Joe tried to smile.

"Good-bye," he said.

"Good-bye."

Karen turned and headed for the gate. Joe returned to his waiting cab. He would see her again, he thought. He would see her at the convention. Already he was thinking of the convention.

In the time before the convention Ellie wrestled with

her decision. She would wake during the night and sit by the window, the moon lighting her face, saying nothing, just looking up. She shared the bed with Joe and they made love occasionally, but she was not sharing the experience with him. She was, in fact, sharing nothing with him, and the more he tried, the more flowers he brought her and the more attempts he made to reassure her of his love, the more estranged he felt from her. The hurt was deep—deeper than even she had first imagined. It lingered and it hardened and it threatened to drive them apart forever. In his bed, watching Ellie at the window, the moonlight bathing her, Joe found her more lovely than at any time before and he loved her more than any time before and he feared he would lose her. His heart thumped in his chest and he was afraid.

From the platform built high over the convention floor, the pool television camera for all the networks followed the movement of Ellie and Paul as they walked across the floor, through swarms of people knotted together here and there and then through areas of openness and then back into the knots of people. Ellie, dressed in a dignified charcoal gray suit—"I feel like Dean Acheson in drag," she had told Joe when she bought it—held Paul's hand. The young man was dressed in a blue suit, white shirt, and maroon tie and he felt awkward and under scrutiny as young men do when they wear suits. He felt for his tie and for the buttons of his jacket, unaware, of course, that his name had come up on millions of television screens, written on the bottom of the screens, and that his short biography was being read to the American public—including his unsuccessful run for school office.

The two of them worked their way to the rostrum where they took a side stair up to the speaker's level and then to a back door where they disappeared from the view of the television audience. Francis had been standing at the door, waiting for them since the start of their journey from the New York delegation had been reported to him by walkie-talkie. He led them down a short, dark corridor with walls made of freshly painted boards to a large room where speakers sweated out the moments until they were called to speak. Francis opened up the door with a theatrical gesture.

The room contained about twenty people. Some of them were people from Joe's staff whom Ellie recognized. Others were perfect strangers. Some were big contributors and some were new staff aides, some of them part-time and volunteer, and there was even one free-lance reporter who was betting that Joe would be the party's next presidential candidate four years hence and wanted an early start for a campaign book. Joe sat on a side table, one leg on the ground. He held his speech in his hand. This one had been written out.

"No, I'm cutting that paragraph," he said to someone. "I didn't want to antagonize the Southwest." He spotted Ellie and Paul.

"Ellie! Paul!" He waved to them and then he turned back to the person he had been talking with. "Make sure the TelePrompTer guy gets that change. We have about five minutes." A couple of people dashed out of the room, looks of great importance on their faces. Joe stood and walked to Ellie and Paul. He gathered them in his arms and hugged them with a grunt and then stepped back to give them a look of happiness mixed with pride. Suddenly he seemed concerned. "Where's Janet?"

"She couldn't come," Ellie said. "It's kind of complicated. I'll tell you later."

There was a minor commotion at the door and Hugh Kittner barged in. He walked right up to Joe, his hand extended. "Joe, good luck," he bellowed. "They got me saying a lot of lies about how great you are, so you can't fail to do great. Won't be a dry eye in the house." He turned to Ellie. "Say, how are *you*?" He pumped her hand. "You've got a great man there." He turned back to Joe, giving him a playful punch in the arm. "See ya on the hustings, fella." He turned to go and noticed Angela. His eyes seemed to twinkle. "Hi. How're yew?" Angela drew herself up in horror. She nodded politely. Kittner cast his eyes around the room looking for someone to explain Angela's behavior. He shrugged his shoulders when only one so much as even winked at him, and walked for the door, closing it behind him, leaving a massive sigh of relief and the faint aroma of bourbon. Joe turned his attention to Ellie.

"Is everything all right?"

"Yes, fine," she said.

Joe took Francis by the elbow. "Francis, why don't you take Paul to his seat for me?"

"Sure, Senator."

Joe sunk to one knee before Paul. "I just want to talk to Mom for a minute, okay?"

"Yeah."

Joe hugged the boy. He rose and accepted some papers from Francis, who humbled by his role as usher to

315

Paul was going to show everyone that he had important things to tend to also.

"Senator, here's our schedule," he said. "Right after you speak we're meeting with the national chairman and his staff, then we're meeting the press. Tomorrow we have interviews with *The Washington Post* and *The New York Times*."

"All right, fine, Francis," Joe said, patiently. He turned to Paul. "Go ahead. It's exciting out there." He watched Francis and Paul leave, and then he clapped his hands once like a camp counselor and asked everyone to leave the room.

"I'm sorry, I'm going to need this room for a few minutes, folks," he said. People reached for papers and loose-leaf books and coffee cups. They filed by Joe as he stood by the door. Some of them patted him on the back or playfully poked him in the arm and said their good lucks and their knock-em-deads. Finally, Joe and Ellie were alone.

"Where's Janet?"

"I couldn't get her to come. Joe, I'm sorry."

"I've really done a great job with her, haven't I?"

"She'll be all right."

"Are *you* all right?"

"Sure, I'm fine."

"Ellie, come on, what is it?"

"Let's talk later, okay?" She turned away and started to walk to the other side of the room.

"No, tell me now."

Ellie kept walking. "Joe, not right before you go out there. Later."

"No, not later," he said insistently. "Now. Go ahead. Say it."

316

Ellie stopped her pacing. She turned and faced him. "Joe, I love you, but I can't take it anymore."

"Ellie, don't do this," he said, launching into the speech he had been working on since those nights by the window first began. "You have to give me a chance. I can slow down. I can make time for the things I care about."

Ellie eyed him suspiciously. "You think so?" she said. "Two months ago you were in tears because you thought you had lost Janet. You were going to take her away. Did you?"

"No."

"So what is it you really care about?"

"Ellie, I love you," he said weakly. "Stay with me."

"I still never see you. Or touch you or tell you what I'm going through. We're not married anymore. Why *should* I stay with you?"

"Because you've put nineteen years into this marriage and you have a responsibility to it. And so do I. And *I'm* going to be there."

"Until Francis calls with another offer."

"No, I can take that same energy I put into my work and I can put it into our life."

"But will you?"

"I know how to get what I want, Ellie."

Francis and Angela entered without knocking. Ellie shot Francis a look that he ignored.

"You're on, Senator," he announced. Joe shook his head to show he understood.

"Ellie . . ."

"Do well out there," she said. She started to the door where Angie was waiting.

"I'll take you to your seat, Mrs. Tynan," Angie said.

They left. Joe was alone with Francis. Francis walked over to the chair where Joe's coat was draped and picked it up. He held it by the shoulders and walked it over to Joe. Joe bent at the knees and slid his arms into the jacket. Francis worked a crease out of it and then walked in front of Joe, taking him in as a painter does a model. Finally, he fixed him with his eyes.

"You're gonna be terrific."

Joe started for the door. Francis beat him to it and opened it. A rush of noise greeted them. Most of the staff were in the small hallway. Joe moved down the corridor, Francis a bit out in front of him feeling very big. Hands reached out. Joe took them and shook them and then they returned to their owners. He nodded and he said thank you and finally he reached the door to the rostrum. A sergeant at arms held him back. The door opened and he could hear Kittner finishing his speech introducing Joe.

"We have a new vision in this great land of ours. A new spirit. A new hope and a confidence that justice and decency will guide us in our public hours. There is a man who has come to symbolize that hope for justice and decency in government. A man who has brought humanity to the cold, gray halls of the law. It is my privilege to present to you, SENATOR JOE TYNAN."

Kittner swung his arms in the air and then turned, pointing to Joe. An arm came up from behind Joe and thrust him forward and he hit the rostrum on the run. The band struck up "East-Side, West-Side" and Kittner threw his arms around Joe, kissing him on the forehead. Joe could smell the sweat and the booze of the man mingled with the scent of old age, and sud-

318

denly he was filled with loathing for Kittner. What was this man doing here anyway? He had killed his colleague, his old friend, Birney. He, Joe, had done that. Was there no sin that is unforgivable in politics? Kittner grabbed Joe's hand at the wrist and yanked his arm into the air.

In the television booth the anchormen were reading the biography of Joseph Tynan. They recited his schools and the data about his parents and the places where he had camped as a boy. They had talked to his high school teachers and to his former football coach, and they were prepared to talk as long as the crowd kept applauding and the band kept playing. They had a loose-leaf book on Joseph Tynan and they had information that was not in the book—stuff about a certain lady from New Orleans that had come from a senatorial office. Some thought it could only have been Kittner.

But Kittner now was dancing up and down, holding Joe by the wrist and not letting go. He looked at the national chairman and signaled with his eyes to let the band play on and it did, reeling into "Happy Days Are Here Again." The crowd went even wilder. Joe scanned the auditorium, looking for the New York delegation. He found it and then his eyes traveled up the delegation until he came to the section reserved for alternates and VIP guests. He found Ellie. Paul was next to her.

Joe fastened his eyes on Ellie. She looked around at the crowd and then back at him. Her eyes brimmed and she nodded yes. Joe smiled and she nodded yes one more time and then a big tear slipped down her cheek. Joe's smile widened. His gaze left Ellie and he swept the room. He ripped his wrists from Kittner's grip and raised his arms to hush the crowd. The band ceased playing and the crowd stilled and Joe waited. The place quieted and still Joe said nothing. On television the cameras zoomed in on him in close-up. He said nothing. The seconds slipped by, the crowd stirred in anticipation. Finally, he spoke.

"Let me ask you something," he yelled into the microphone. "Let me ask you something." He waited. Finally someone yelled, "What?"

"Let me ask you something," Joe yelled.

"What?" the crowd roared back.

Joe smiled, pleased.

"What are we here for?" he yelled.

"To nominate a president," someone yelled.

"What are we here for?" Joe repeated.

"To nominate a president," the crowd roared back.

Joe smiled broadly.

It had been the answer all along.